MAR 1 1 2021

WATTERS • LEYH • NOWAK • LAIHO

LUMBERJANES™

ON A ROLL

BOOM! BOX™

BOOM! BOX™

LUMBERJANES Volume Nine, July 2018. Published by BOOM! Box, a division of Boom Entertainment, Inc. Lumberjanes is ™ & © 2018 Shannon Watters, Grace Ellis, Noelle Stevenson & Brooklyn Allen. Originally published in single magazine form as LUMBERJANES No. 33-36. ™ & © 2016-2017 Shannon Watters, Grace Ellis, Noelle Stevenson & Brooklyn Allen. All rights reserved. BOOM! Box™ and the BOOM! Box logo are trademarks of Boom Entertainment, Inc., registered in various countries and categories. All characters, events, and institutions depicted herein are fictional. Any similarity between any of the names, characters, persons, events, and/or institutions in this publication to actual names, characters, and persons, whether living or dead, events, and/or institutions is unintended and purely coincidental. BOOM! Box does not read or accept unsolicited submissions of ideas, stories, or artwork.

For information regarding the CPSIA on this printed material, call: (203) 595-3636 and provide reference #RICH – 782183.

BOOM! Studios, 5670 Wilshire Boulevard, Suite 400, Los Angeles, CA 90036-5679. Printed in China. First Printing.

ISBN: 978-1-60886-957-2, eISBN: 978-1-61398-628-8

THIS LUMBERJANES FIELD MANUAL BELONGS TO:

NAME:_____

TROOP:_____

DATE INVESTED:_____

FIELD MANUAL TABLE OF CONTENTS

LUMBERJANES
FIELD MANUAL

For the Intermediate Program

Tenth Edition • September 1984

Prepared for the

**Miss Qiunzella Thiskwin
Penniquiqul Thistle Crumpet's**
CAMP FOR  HARDCORE
LADY-TYPES

"Friendship to the Max!"

A MESSAGE FROM THE LUMBERJANES HIGH COUNCIL

miss Quinzella Thiskwin
Penniquiqul Thistle Crumpet's
Camp for
HARDCORE LADY TYPES
FRIENDSHIP to the MAX!

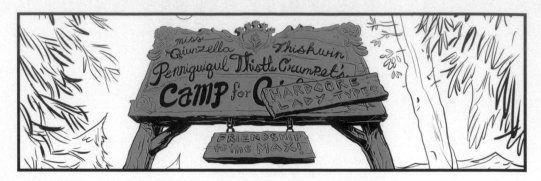

Throughout your life, but most especially when you are young and only just beginning to learn the tips and tricks and other ephemera of life, it can be far too easy to look around at your friends and peers and think, perhaps a bit worriedly, that everyone seems to know precisely what they are doing but you. Perhaps you are trying a new skill, and beginning at square one for the first time in a long time sits on you awkwardly, like a pair of shoes put on the wrong feet. Or perhaps you find yourself wondering time and again if the road you're heading down is the right one for you or if you are making swift enough progress. Perhaps you know exactly what it is that you want, but the path between you and your goals is unclear and muddled, and you find yourself tracing over the same steps of progress again and again, feeling frustrated and lost, while everyone else seems to be going along swimmingly.

It can be far too easy to become discouraged when you are trying something new, and it can be exceedingly difficult to avoid falling into the trap of comparing your insides to everyone else's outsides.

Remember this, scouts: everyone has had to begin at the beginning, whether it is a skill they began learning at the age of two, or twelve, or twenty-two. And whenever you start, everyone else has felt those same awkward and anxious wonderings about whether or not they were doing it right, and has heard the same needling voice of doubt, wondering if another road may have been the wiser option.

You have only just begun to scratch the surface of the skills you'll want to pursue, and the hobbies, games, and activities at which you will want to try your hand… all of the things which will bring you hours of joy and entertainment throughout your life. You may not get the hang of them right off the bat, but the more you keep at things, and push through those feelings of doubt when you really want to learn something, the more rewarding it will be when you finally accomplish your goal, or make your first baby steps toward it. Be patient with yourself, and forgiving, but keep going forward.

THE LUMBERJANES PLEDGE

I solemnly swear to do my best
Every day, and in all that I do,
To be brave and strong,
To be truthful and compassionate,
To be interesting and interested,
To pay attention and question
The world around me,
To think of others first,
To always help and protect my friends,
[redacted]
And to make the world a better place
For Lumberjane scouts
And for everyone else.

THEN THERE'S A LINE ABOUT GOD, OR WHATEVER

ON A ROLL

Written by
Shannon Watters
& Kat Leyh

Illustrated by
Carolyn Nowak

Colors by
Maarta Laiho

Letters by
Aubrey Aiese

Cover by
Brooklyn Allen

Badge Design
Kelsey Dieterich

Designer
Kara Leopard

Assistant Editor
Sophie Philips-Roberts

Editors
Dafna Pleban & Whitney Leopard

*Special thanks to **Kelsey Pate** for giving the Lumberjanes their name.*

Created by **Shannon Watters, Grace Ellis, Noelle Stevenson & Brooklyn Allen**

LUMBERJANES FIELD MANUAL

CHAPTER
THIRTY-THREE

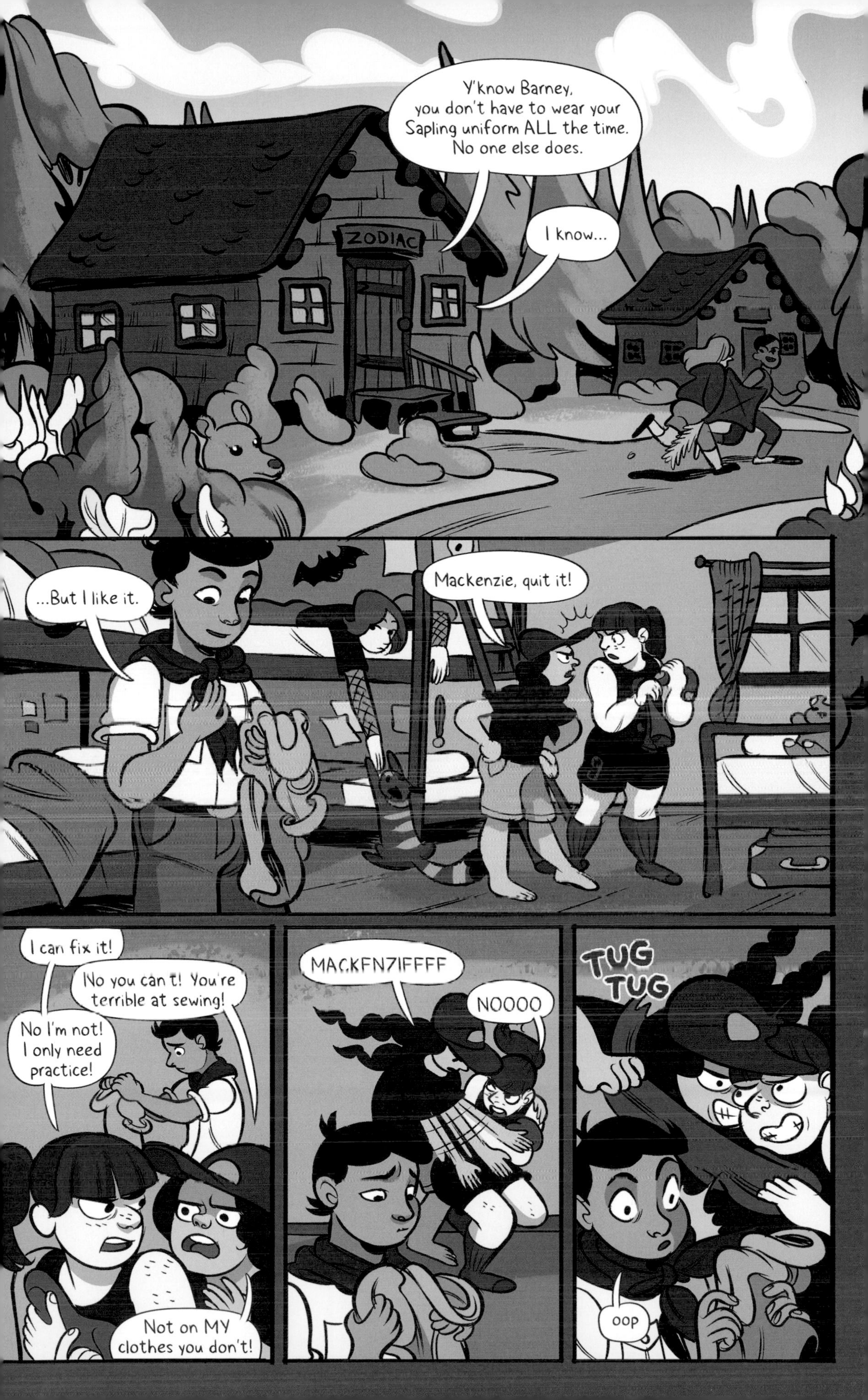
Y'know Barney, you don't have to wear your Sapling uniform ALL the time. No one else does.
I know...
ZODIAC
...But I like it.
Mackenzie, quit it!
I can fix it!
No you can't! You're terrible at sewing!
No I'm not! I only need practice!
Not on MY clothes you don't!
MACKENZIEEEE
NOOOO
TUG TUG
oop

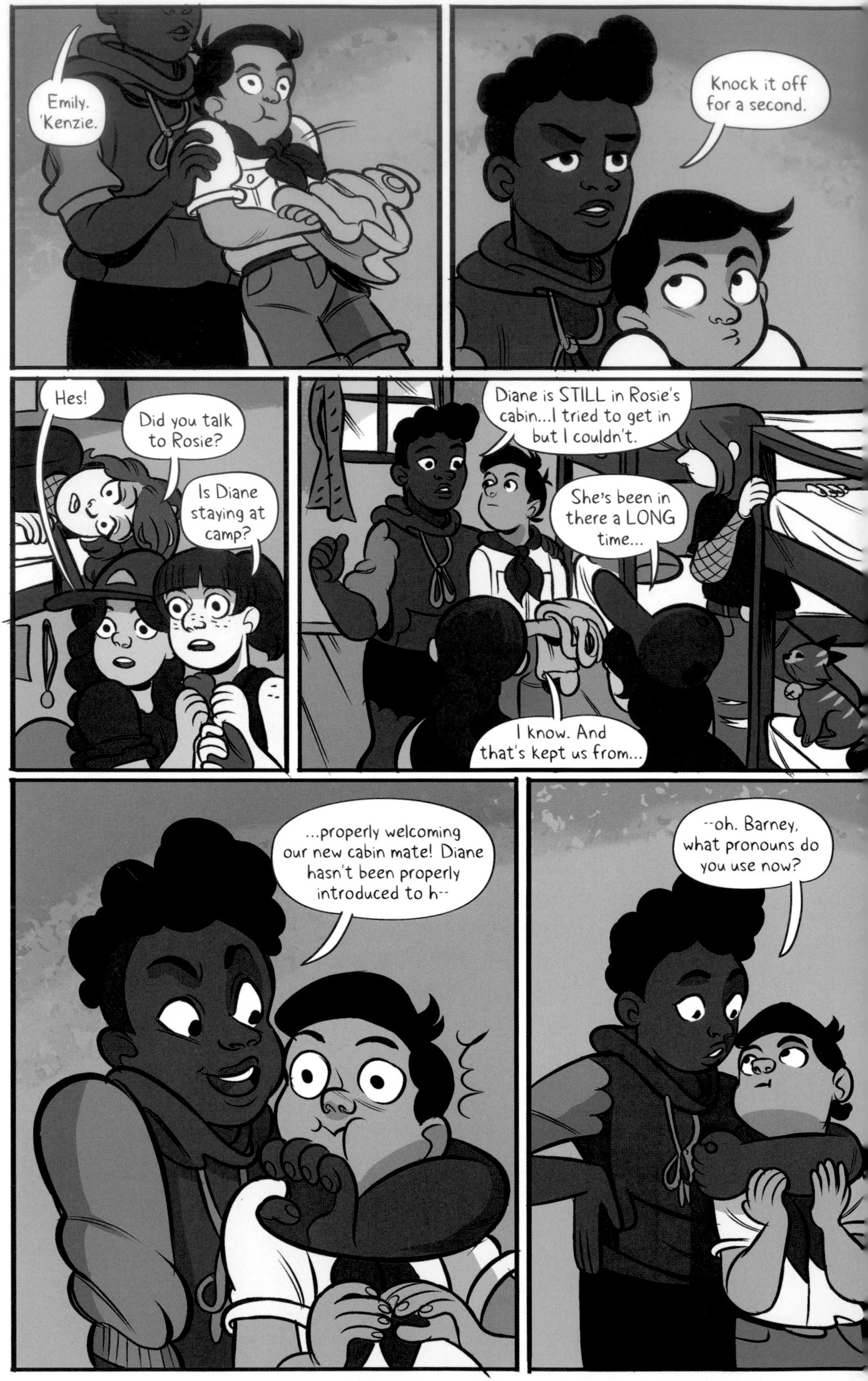

Emily.
'Kenzie.
Knock it off
for a second.
Hes!
Did you talk
to Rosie?
Is Diane
staying at
camp?
Diane is STILL in Rosie's
cabin...I tried to get in
but I couldn't.
She's been in
there a LONG
time...
I know. And
that's kept us from...
...properly welcoming
our new cabin mate! Diane
hasn't been properly
introduced to h--
--oh. Barney,
what pronouns do
you use now?

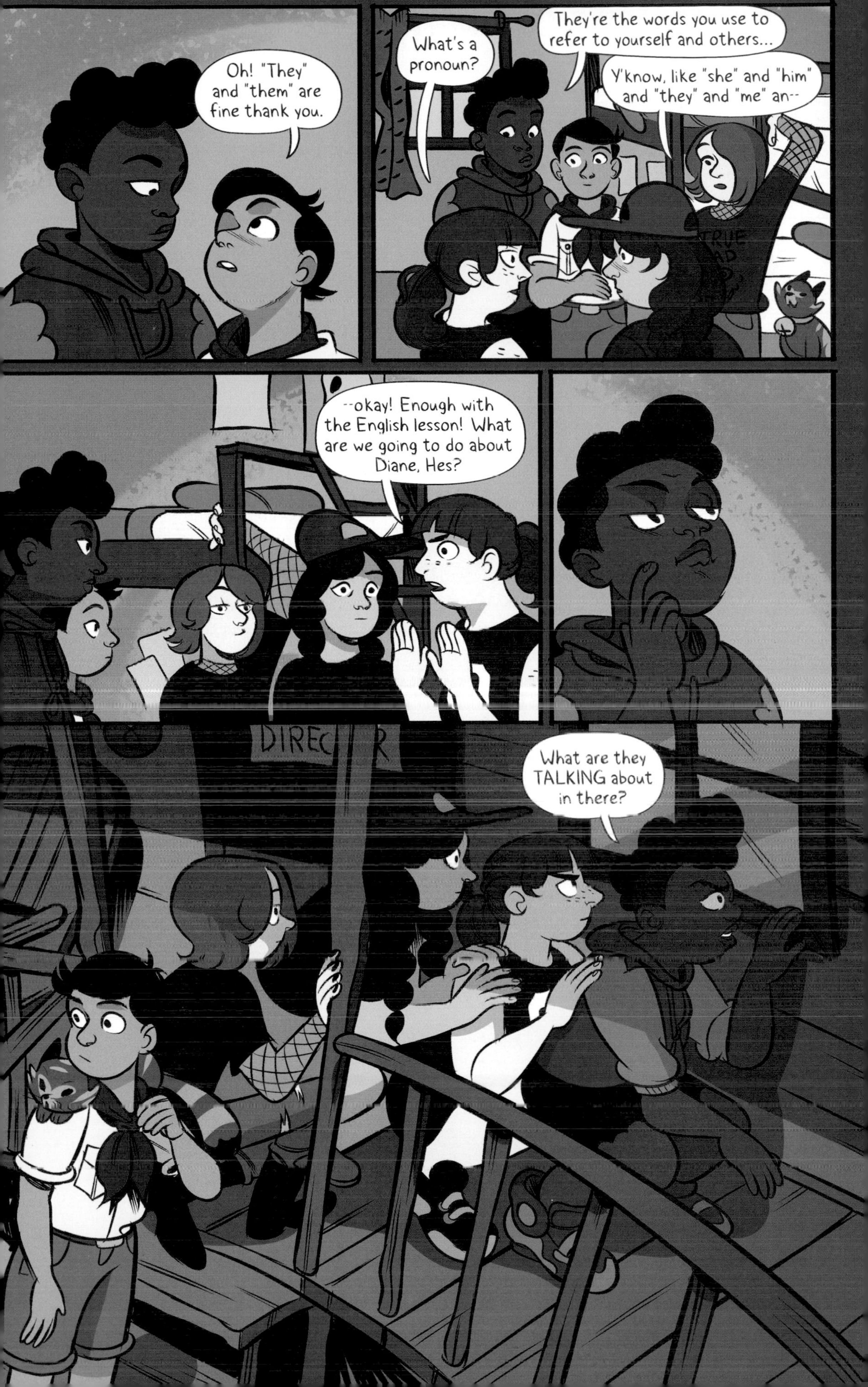
Oh! "They" and "them" are fine thank you.
What's a pronoun?
They're the words you use to refer to yourself and others...
Y'know, like "she" and "him" and "they" and "me" an--
--okay! Enough with the English lesson! What are we going to do about Diane, Hes?
DIREC R
What are they TALKING about in there?

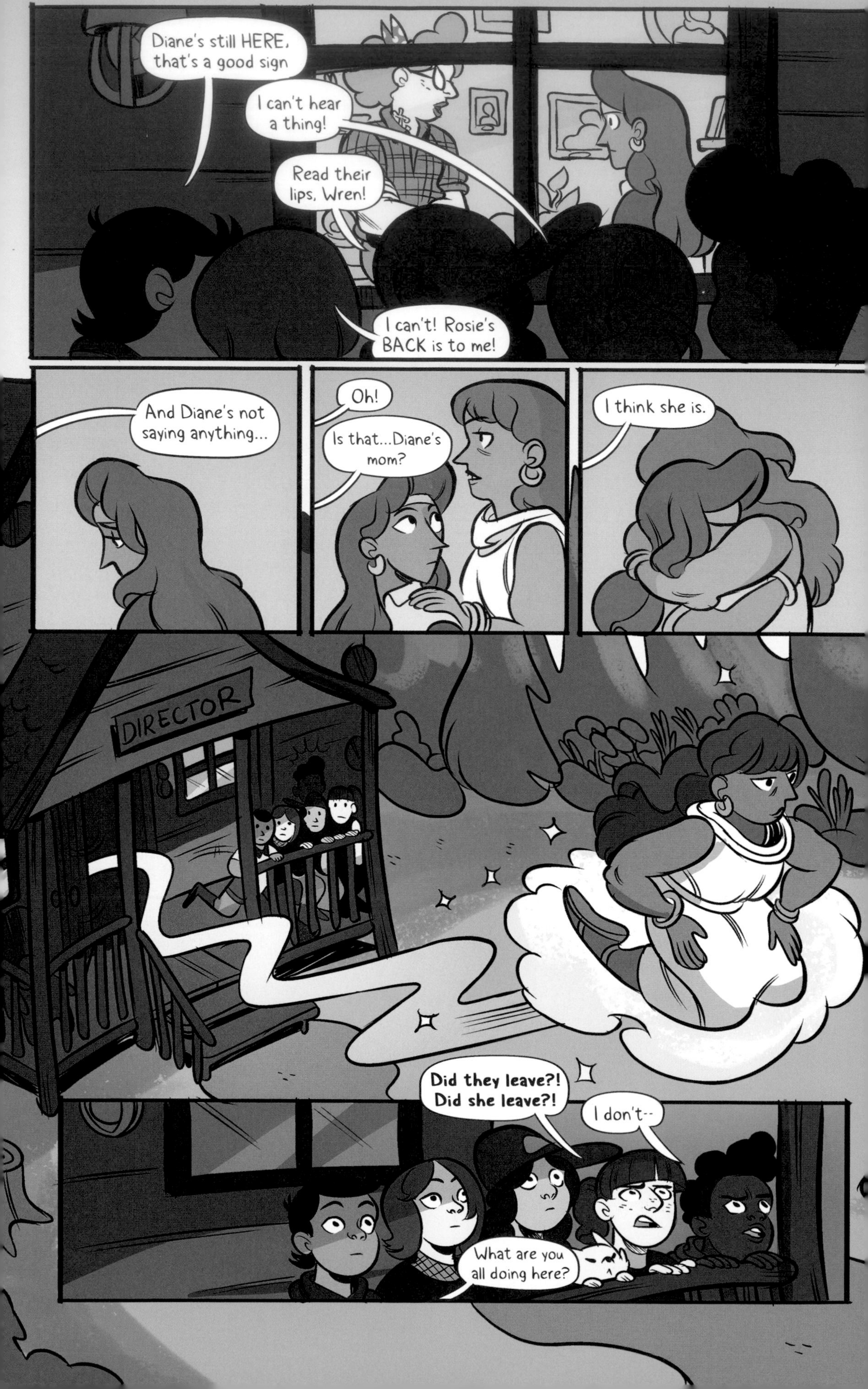
Diane's still HERE, that's a good sign
I can't hear a thing!
Read their lips, Wren!
I can't! Rosie's BACK is to me!
And Diane's not saying anything...
Oh!
Is that...Diane's mom?
I think she is.
DIRECTOR
Did they leave?! Did she leave?!
I don't--
What are you all doing here?

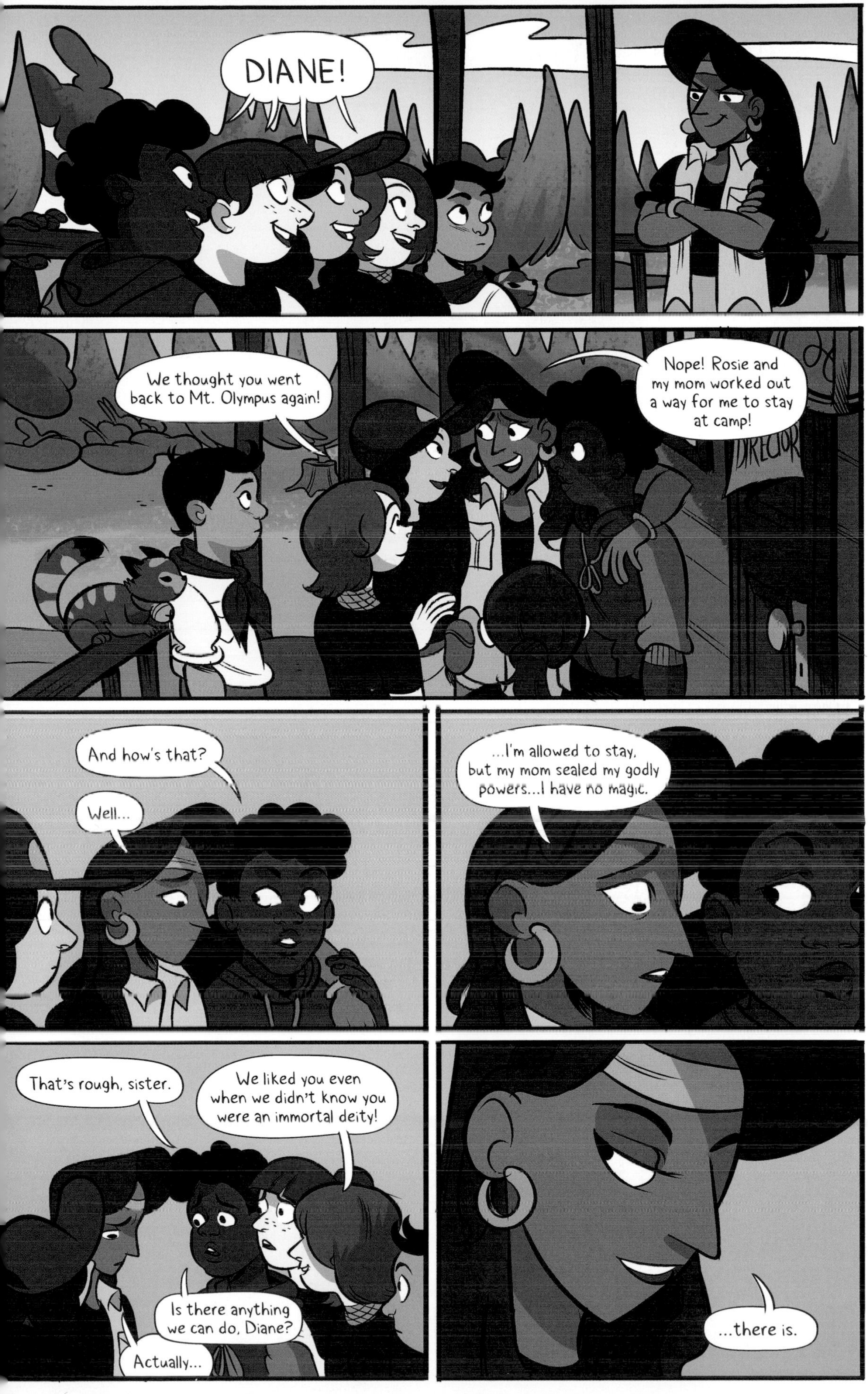
DIANE!
We thought you went back to Mt. Olympus again!
Nope! Rosie and my mom worked out a way for me to stay at camp!
DIRECTOR
And how's that?
Well...
...I'm allowed to stay, but my mom sealed my godly powers...I have no magic.
That's rough, sister.
We liked you even when we didn't know you were an immortal deity!
Is there anything we can do, Diane?
Actually...
...there is.

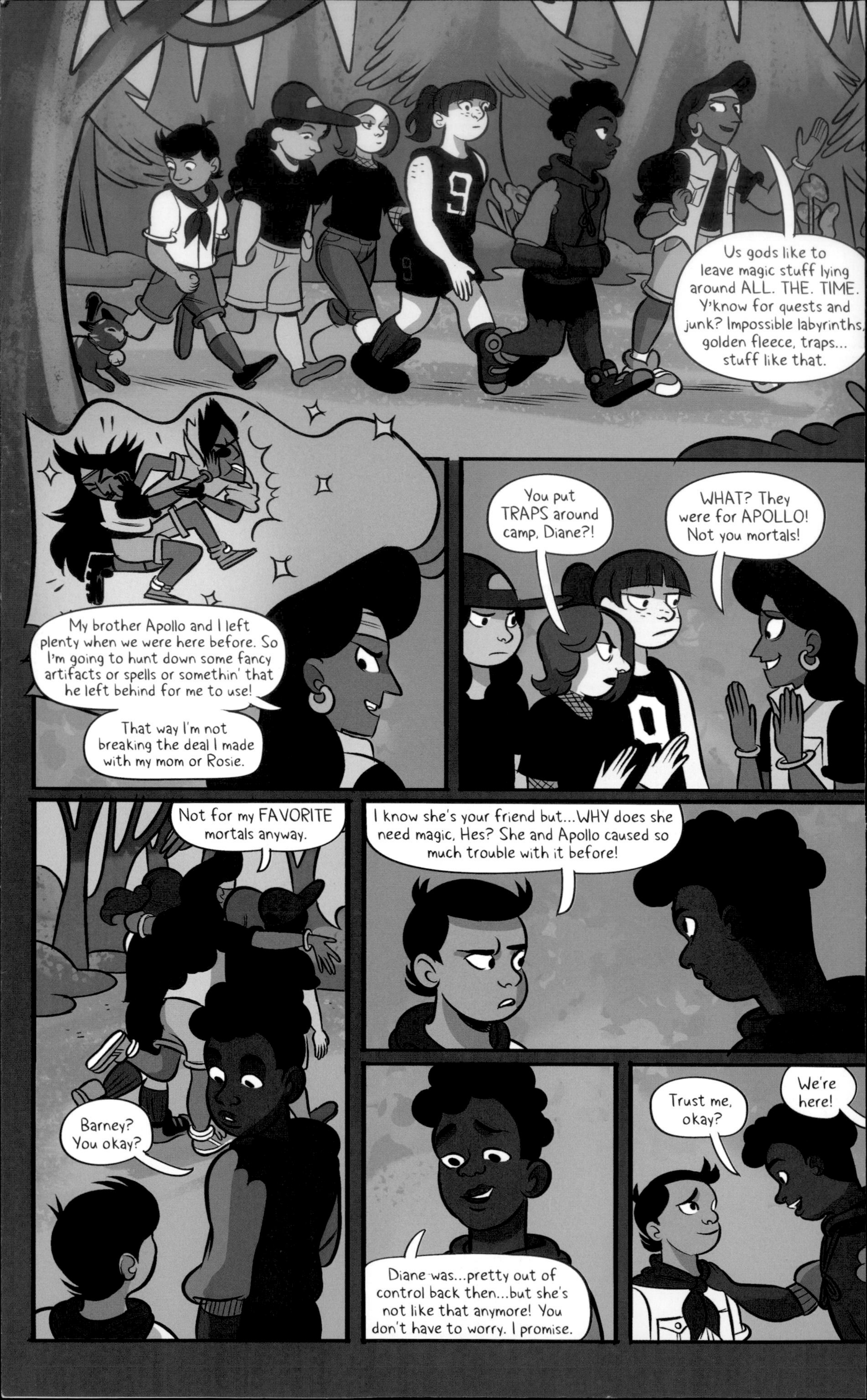

Us gods like to leave magic stuff lying around ALL. THE. TIME. Y'know for quests and junk? Impossible labyrinths, golden fleece, traps... stuff like that.
My brother Apollo and I left plenty when we were here before. So I'm going to hunt down some fancy artifacts or spells or somethin' that he left behind for me to use!
That way I'm not breaking the deal I made with my mom or Rosie.
You put TRAPS around camp, Diane?!
WHAT? They were for APOLLO! Not you mortals!
Not for my FAVORITE mortals anyway.
Barney? You okay?
I know she's your friend but...WHY does she need magic, Hes? She and Apollo caused so much trouble with it before!
Diane was...pretty out of control back then...but she's not like that anymore! You don't have to worry. I promise.
Trust me, okay?
We're here!

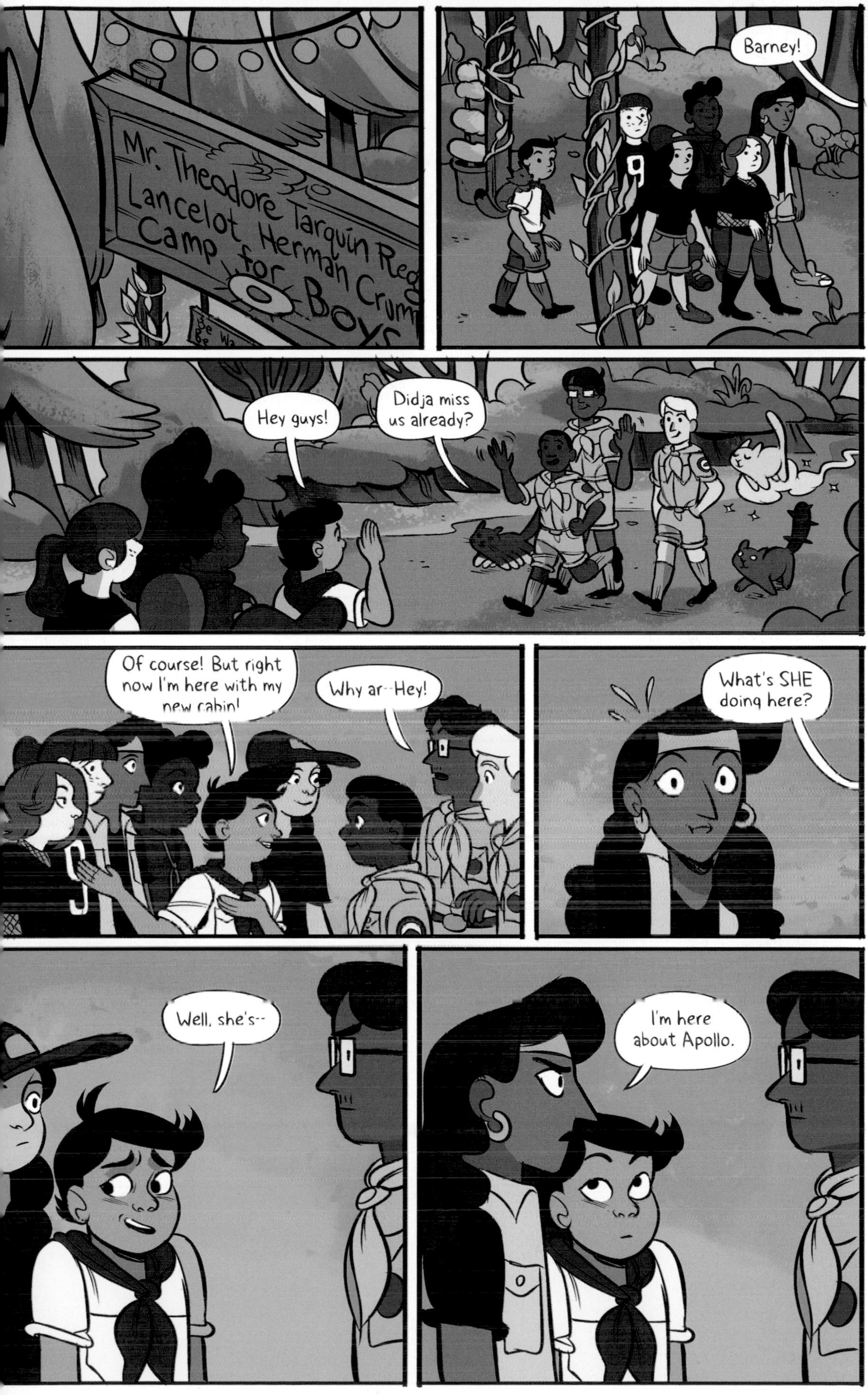
Mr. Theodore Tarquin Reg
Lancelot Herman Crum
Camp for Boys
Barney!
Hey guys!
Didja miss us already?
Of course! But right now I'm here with my new cabin!
Why ar--Hey!
What's SHE doing here?
Well, she's--
I'm here about Apollo.

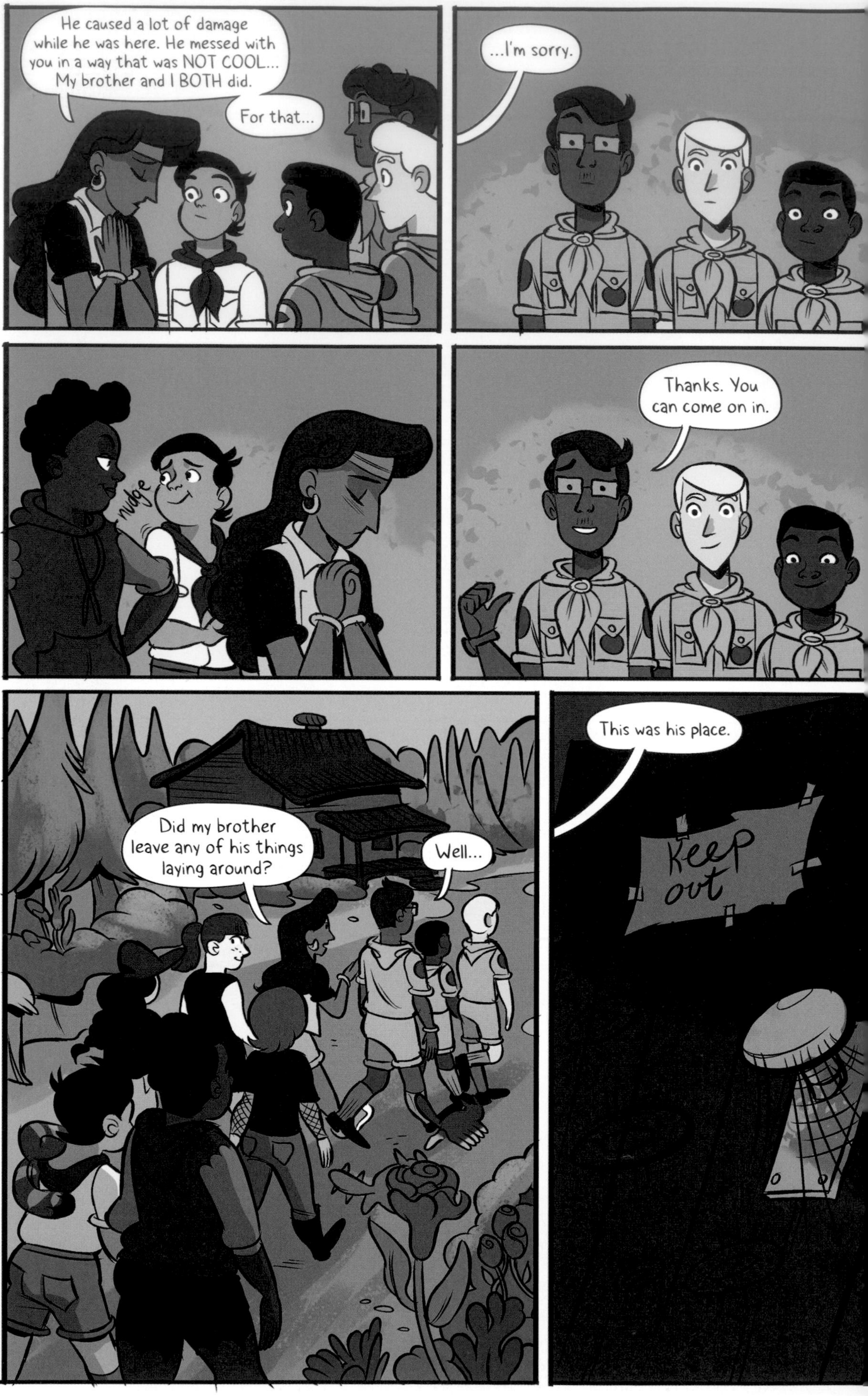
He caused a lot of damage while he was here. He messed with you in a way that was NOT COOL... My brother and I BOTH did.
For that...
...I'm sorry.
nudge
Thanks. You can come on in.
Did my brother leave any of his things laying around?
Well...
This was his place.
Keep out

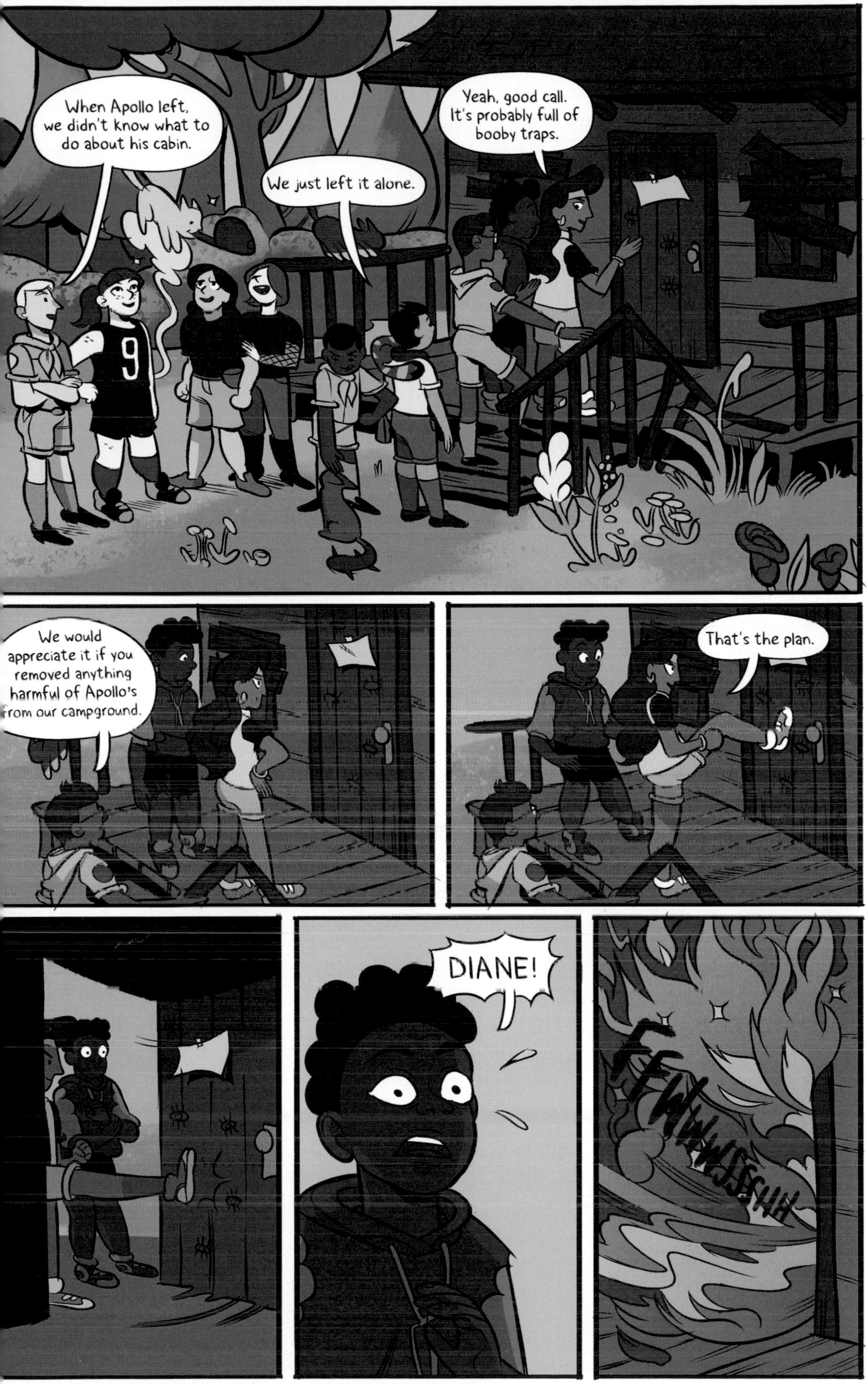
When Apollo left, we didn't know what to do about his cabin.
We just left it alone.
Yeah, good call. It's probably full of booby traps.
We would appreciate it if you removed anything harmful of Apollo's from our campground.
That's the plan.
DIANE!
FFWWWSSCHH

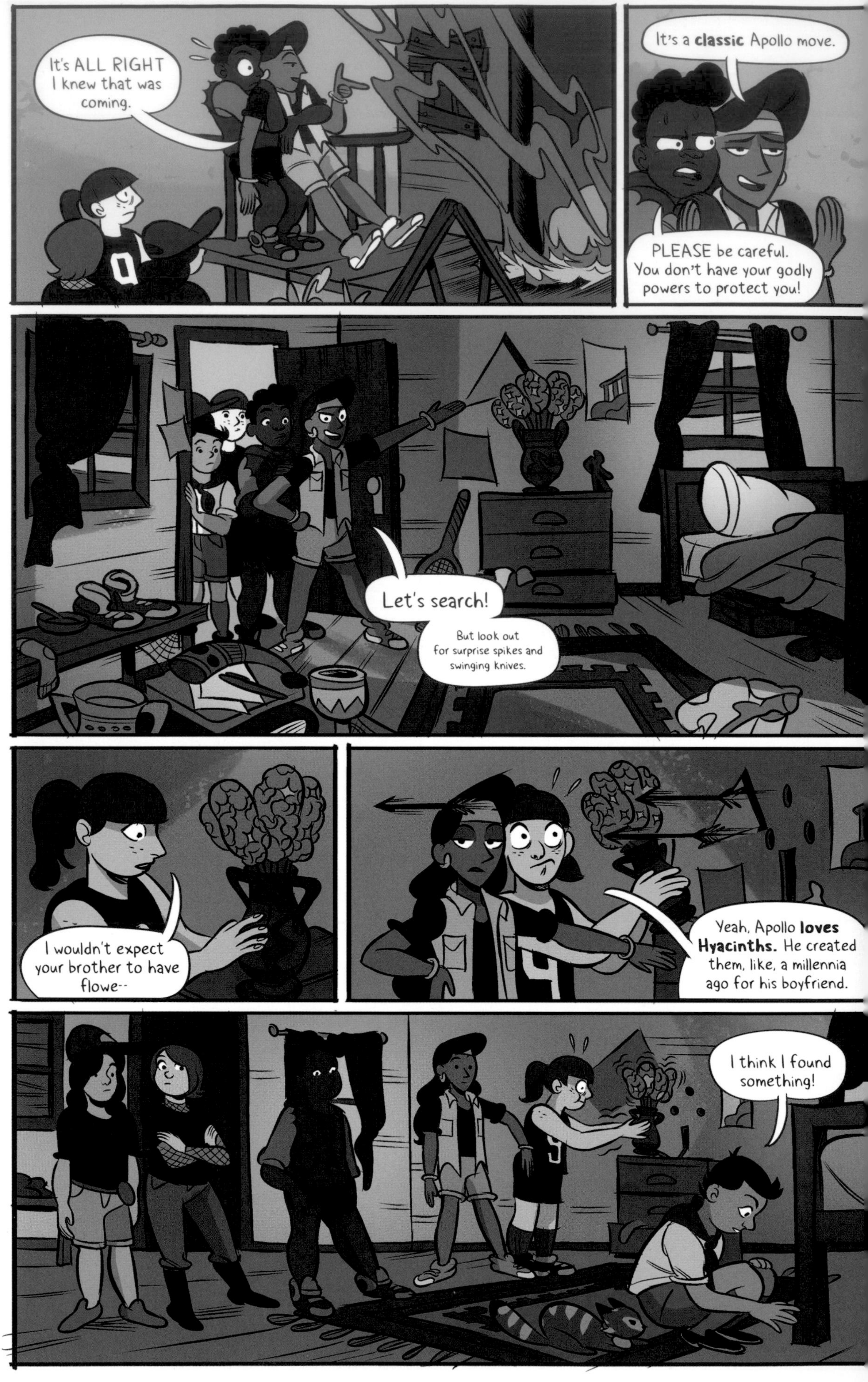

It's ALL RIGHT I knew that was coming.
It's a classic Apollo move.
PLEASE be careful. You don't have your godly powers to protect you!
Let's search!
But look out for surprise spikes and swinging knives.
I wouldn't expect your brother to have flowe--
Yeah, Apollo loves Hyacinths. He created them, like, a millennia ago for his boyfriend.
I think I found something!

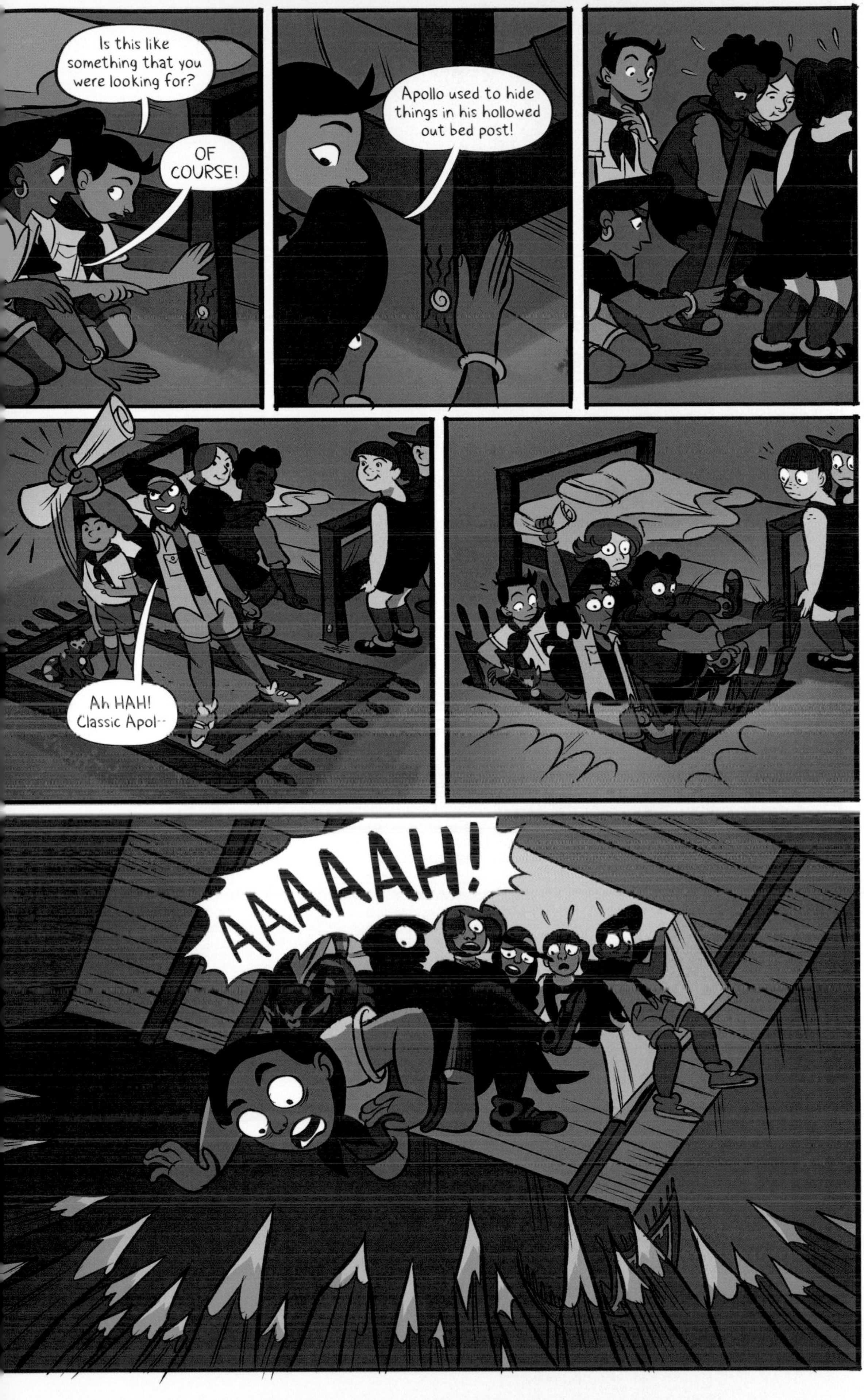
Is this like something that you were looking for?
OF COURSE!
Apollo used to hide things in his hollowed out bed post!
Ah HAH! Classic Apol--
AAAAAH!

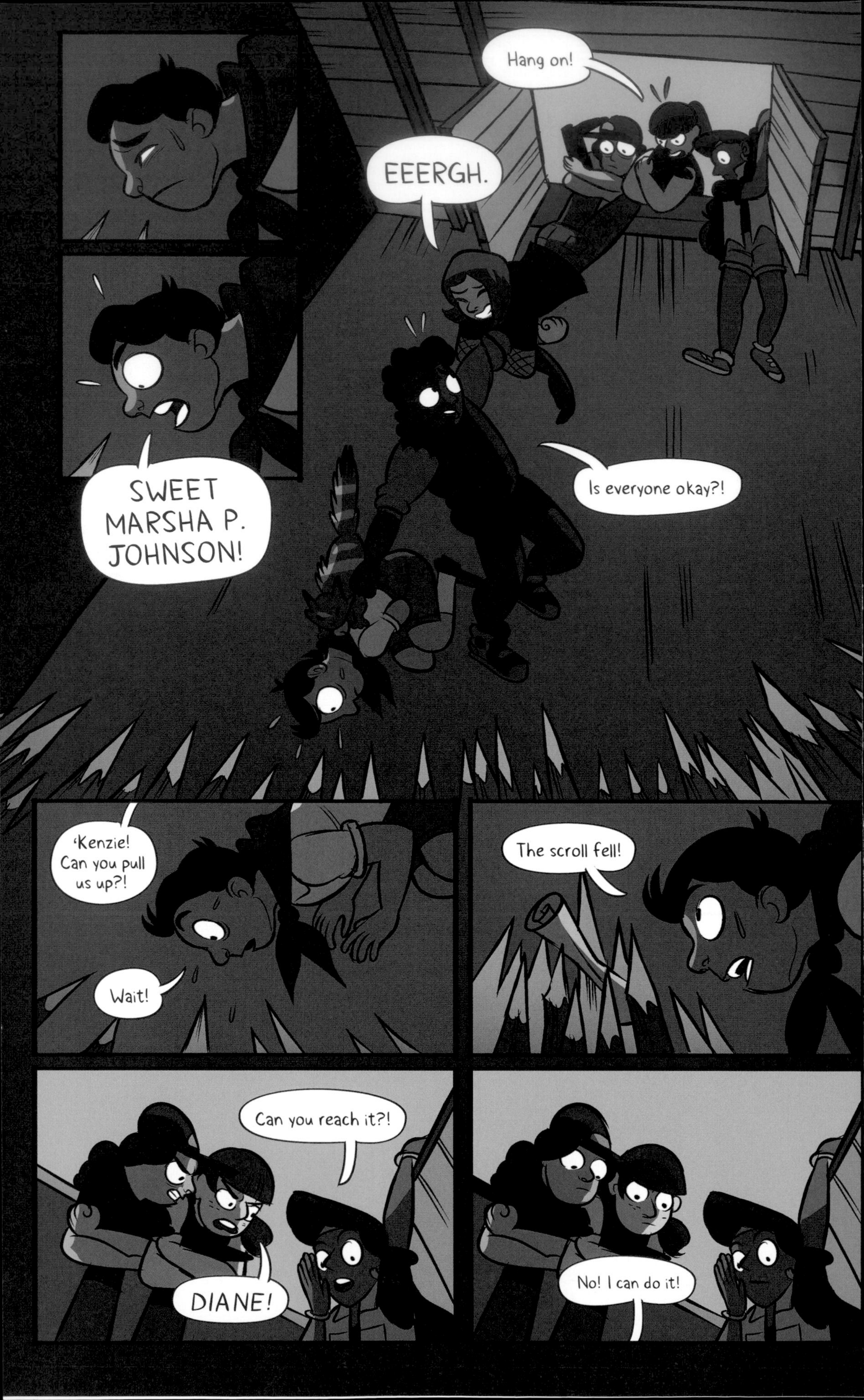
Hang on!
EEERGH.
SWEET MARSHA P. JOHNSON!
Is everyone okay?!
'Kenzie! Can you pull us up?!
Wait!
The scroll fell!
Can you reach it?!
DIANE!
No! I can do it!

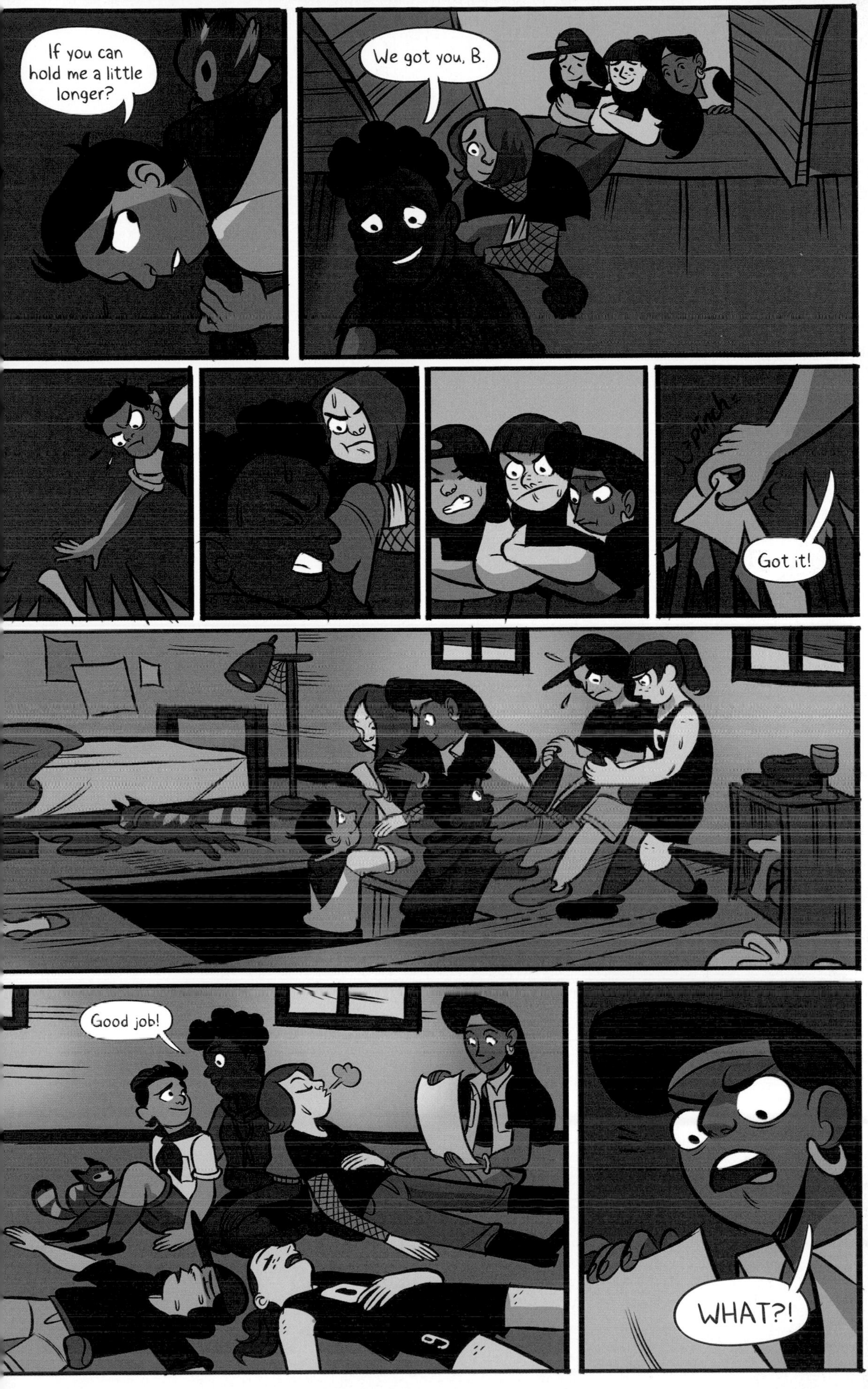
If you can hold me a little longer?
We got you, B.
pinch
Got it!
Good job!
WHAT?!

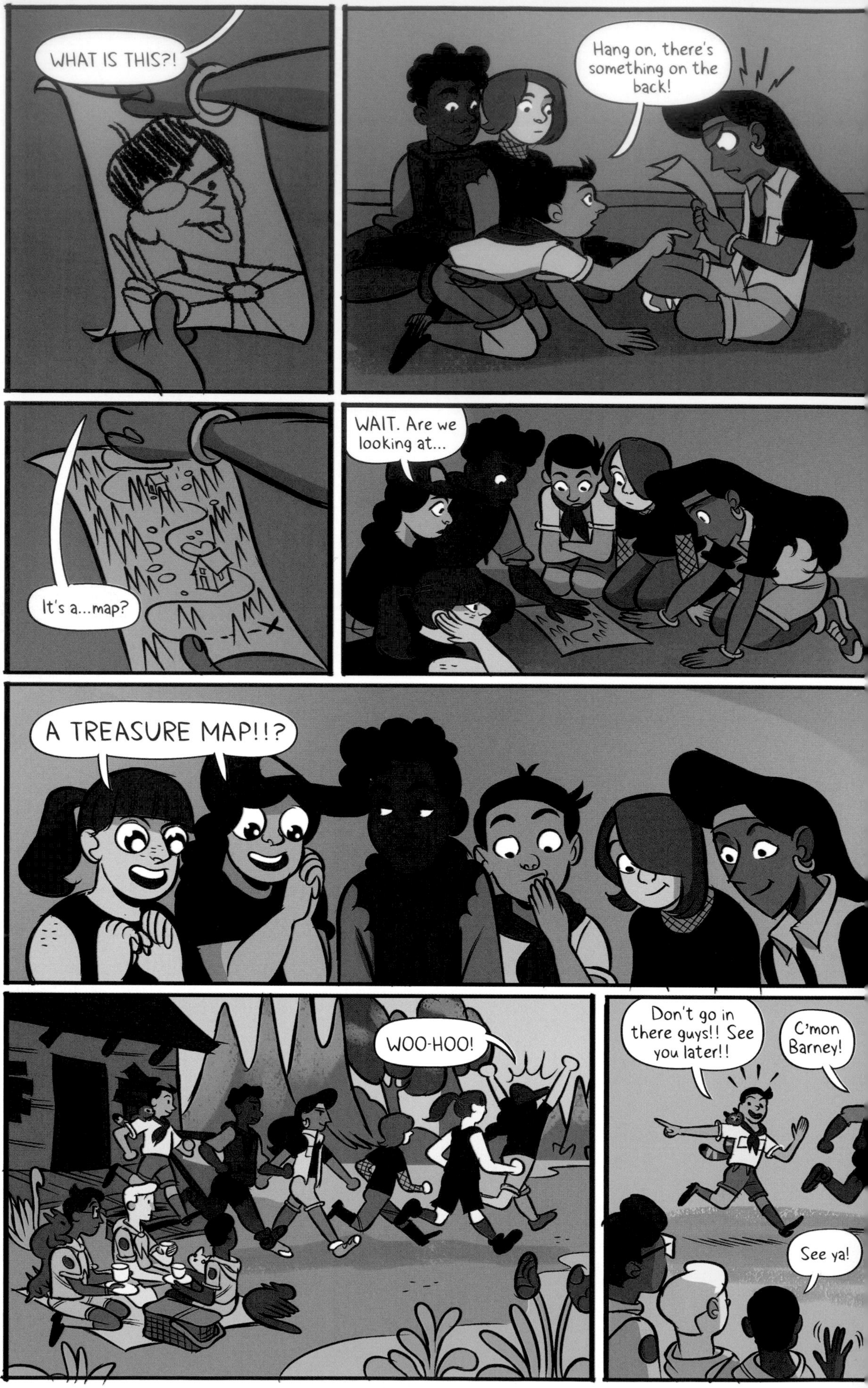
WHAT IS THIS?!
Hang on, there's something on the back!
It's a...map?
WAIT. Are we looking at...
A TREASURE MAP!!?
WOO-HOO!
Don't go in there guys!! See you later!!
C'mon Barney!
See ya!

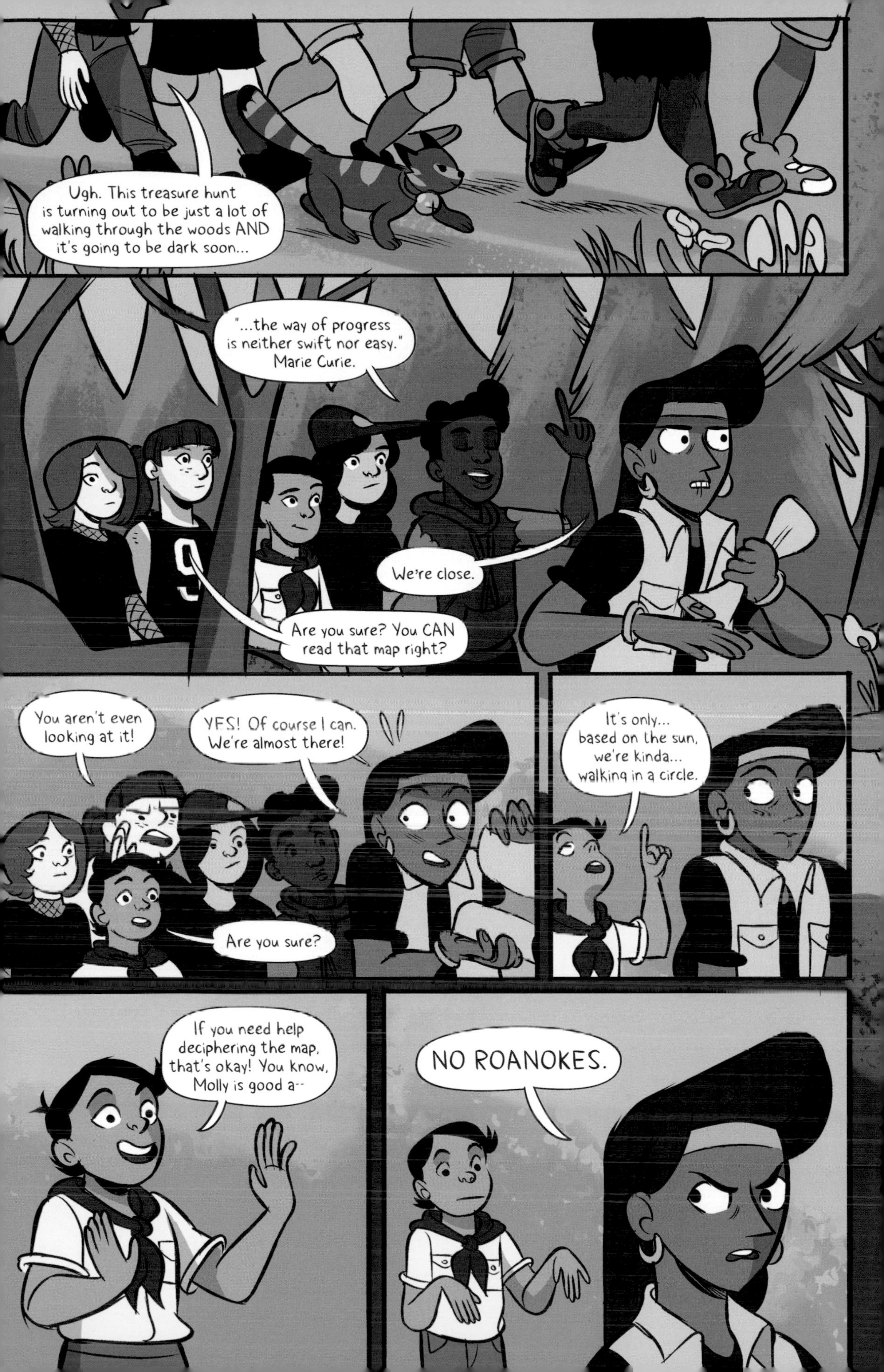
Ugh. This treasure hunt is turning out to be just a lot of walking through the woods AND it's going to be dark soon...
"...the way of progress is neither swift nor easy." Marie Curie.
We're close.
Are you sure? You CAN read that map right?
You aren't even looking at it!
YES! Of course I can. We're almost there!
Are you sure?
It's only... based on the sun, we're kinda... walking in a circle.
If you need help deciphering the map, that's okay! You know, Molly is good a--
NO ROANOKES.

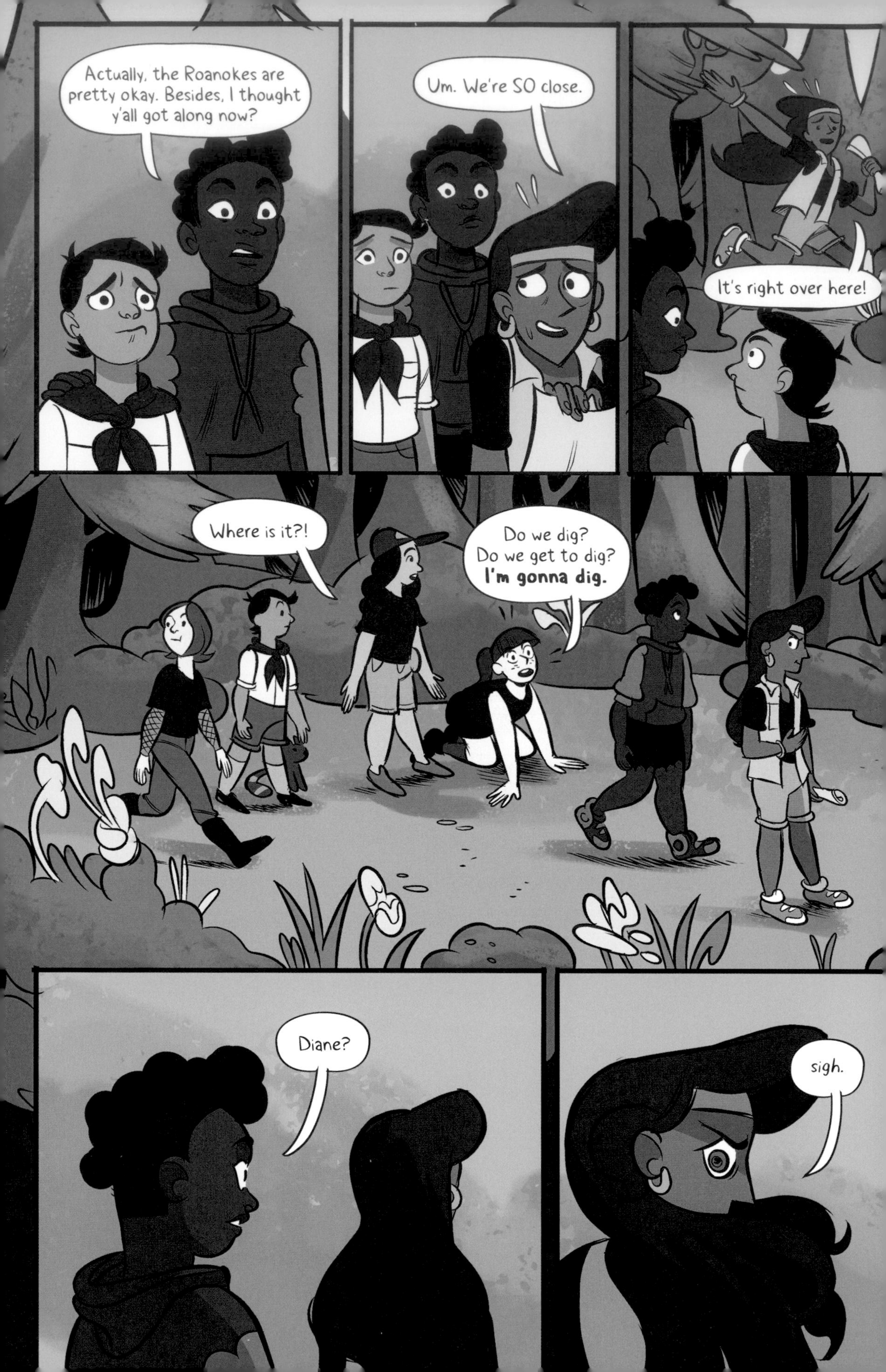
Actually, the Roanokes are pretty okay. Besides, I thought y'all got along now?
Um. We're SO close.
It's right over here!
Where is it?!
Do we dig? Do we get to dig? **I'm gonna dig.**
Diane?
sigh.

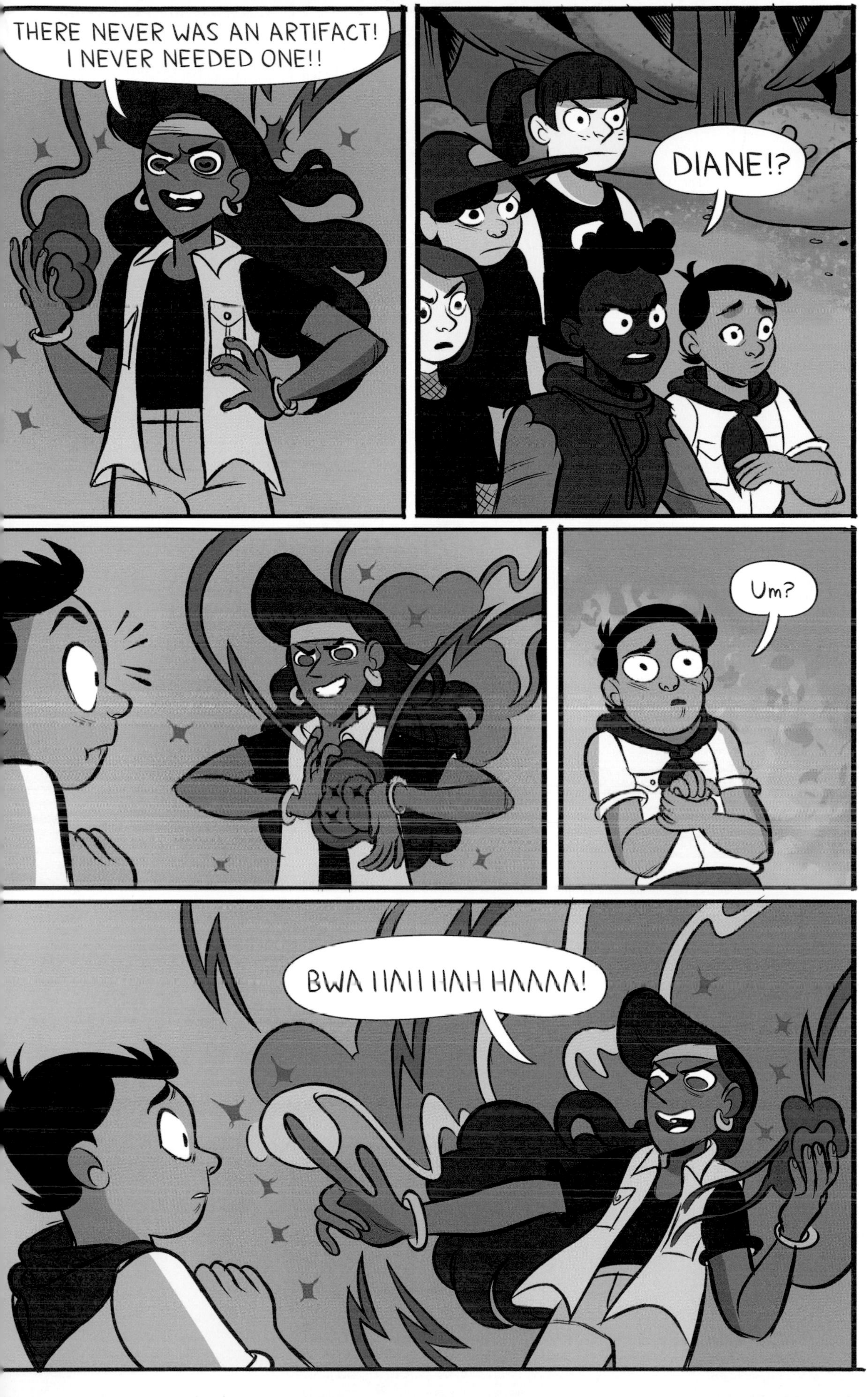
THERE NEVER WAS AN ARTIFACT! I NEVER NEEDED ONE!!
DIANE!?
Um?
BWA HAH HAH HAAAA!

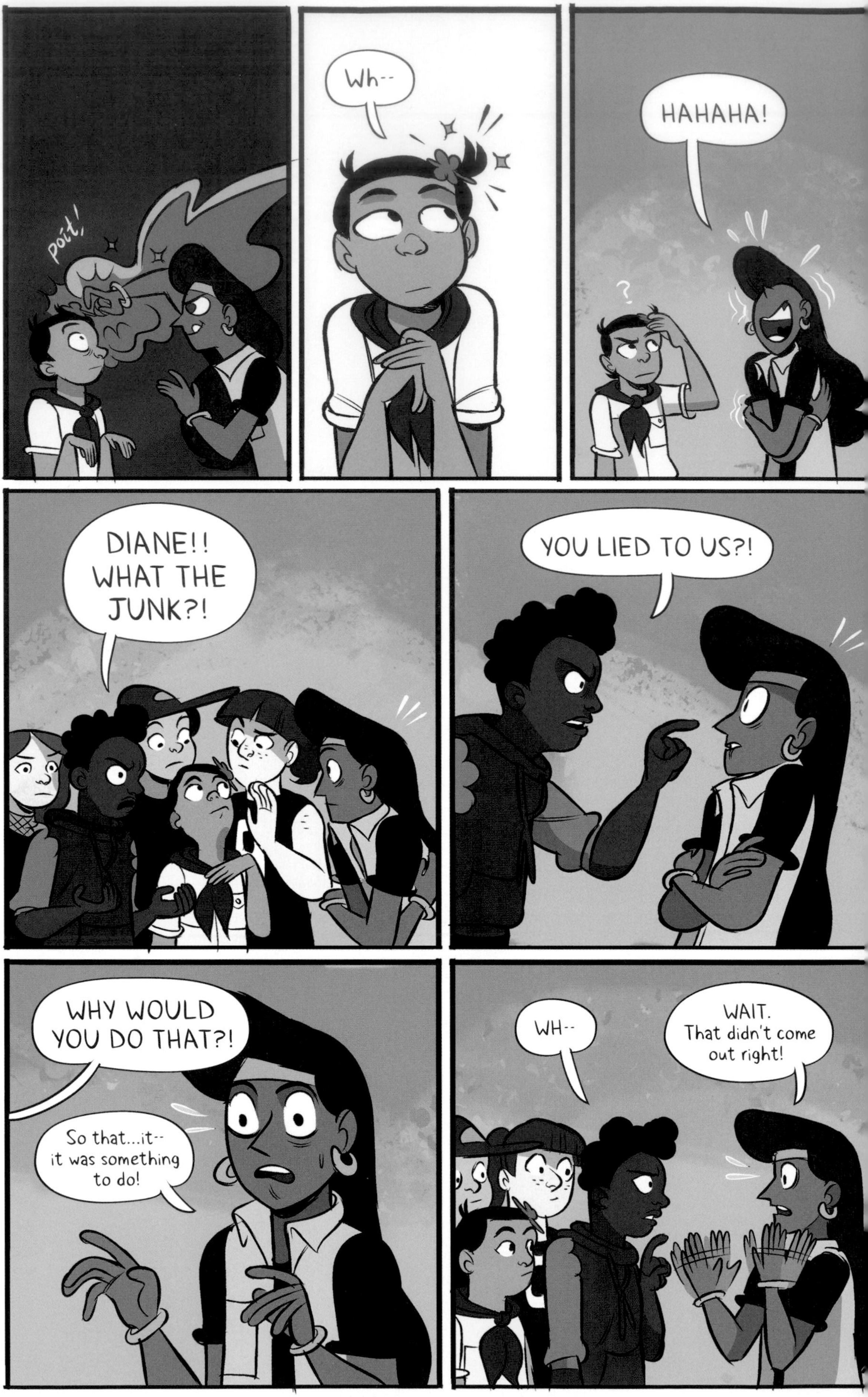
poit!
Wh--
HAHAHA!
?
DIANE!! WHAT THE JUNK?!
YOU LIED TO US?!
WHY WOULD YOU DO THAT?!
So that...it-- it was something to do!
WH--
WAIT. That didn't come out right!

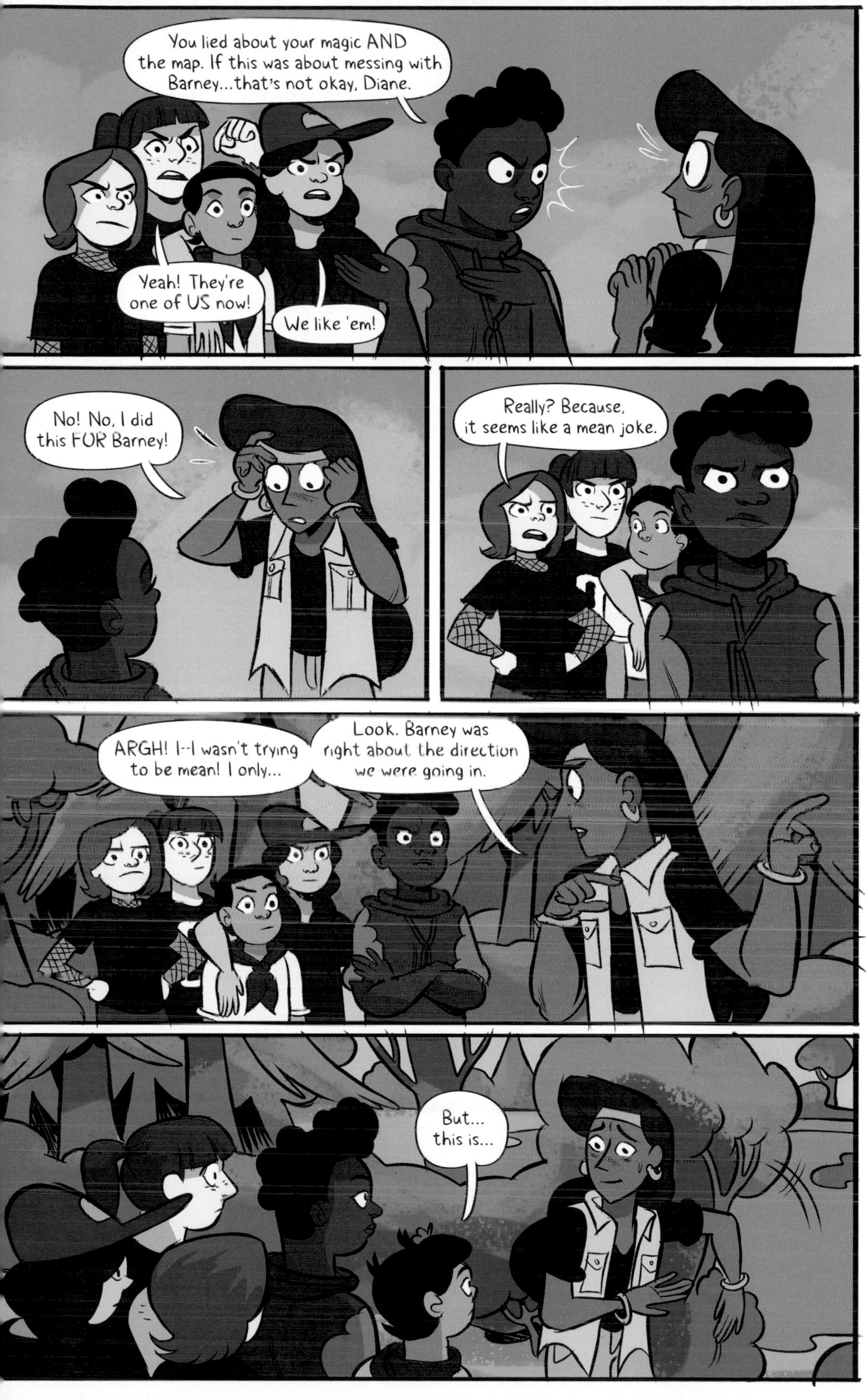
You lied about your magic AND the map. If this was about messing with Barney...that's not okay, Diane.
Yeah! They're one of US now!
We like 'em!
No! No, I did this FOR Barney!
Really? Because, it seems like a mean joke.
ARGH! I--I wasn't trying to be mean! I only...
Look. Barney was right about the direction we were going in.
But... this is...

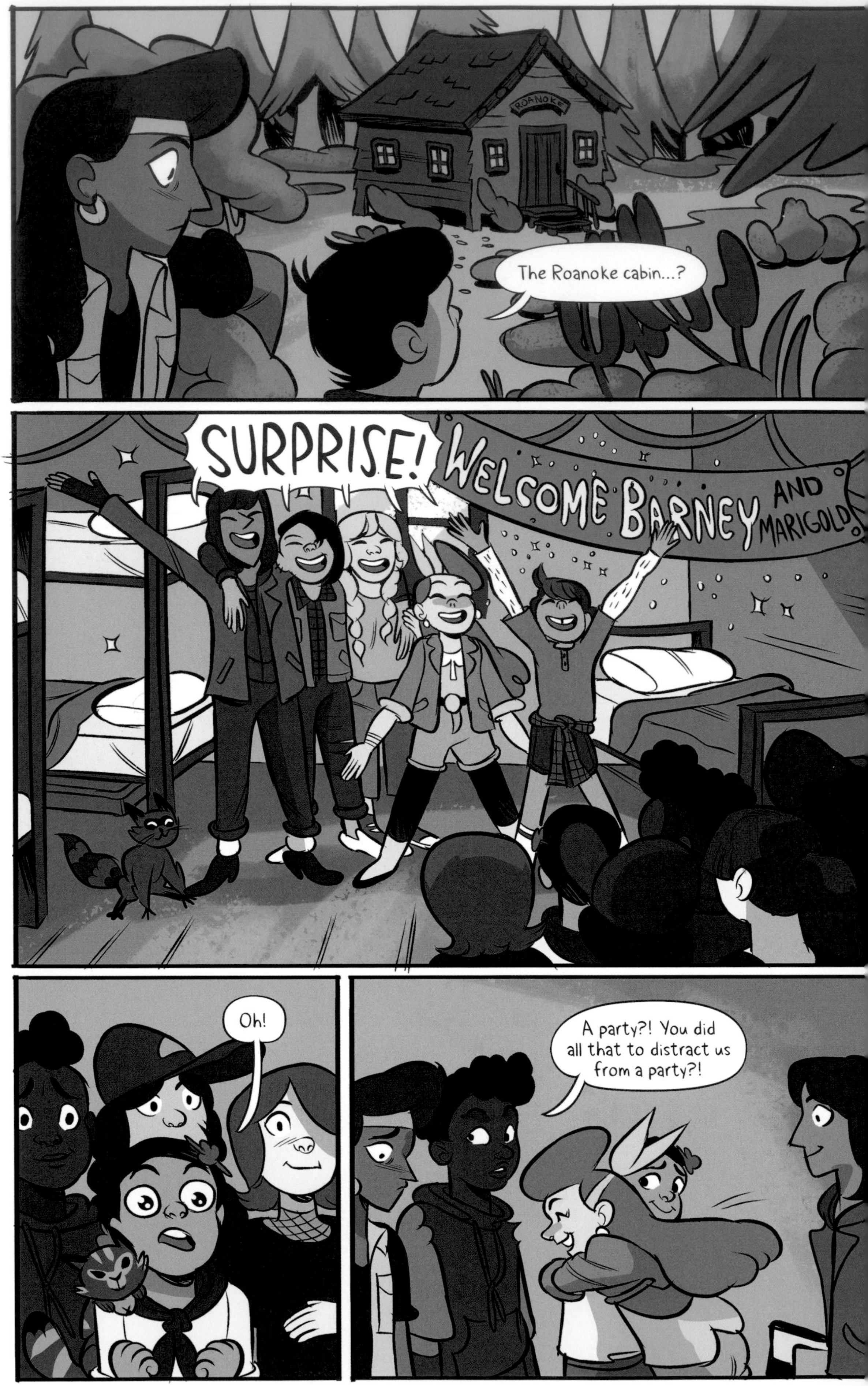
ROANOKE
The Roanoke cabin...?
SURPRISE!
WELCOME BARNEY AND MARIGOLD
Oh!
A party?! You did all that to distract us from a party?!

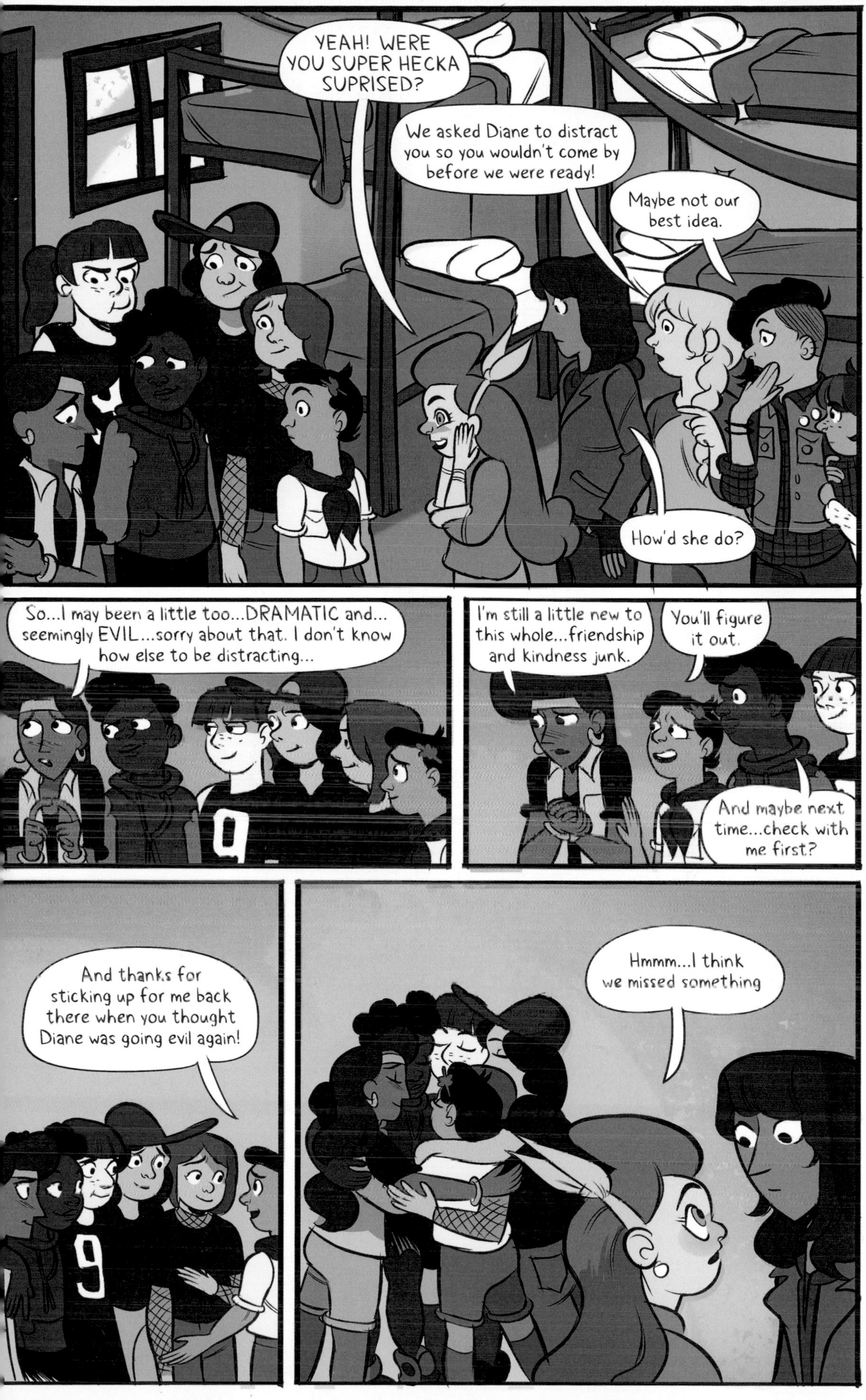
YEAH! WERE YOU SUPER HECKA SUPRISED?
We asked Diane to distract you so you wouldn't come by before we were ready!
Maybe not our best idea.
How'd she do?
So...I may been a little too...DRAMATIC and... seemingly EVIL...sorry about that. I don't know how else to be distracting...
I'm still a little new to this whole...friendship and kindness junk.
You'll figure it out.
And maybe next time...check with me first?
And thanks for sticking up for me back there when you thought Diane was going evil again!
Hmmm...I think we missed something

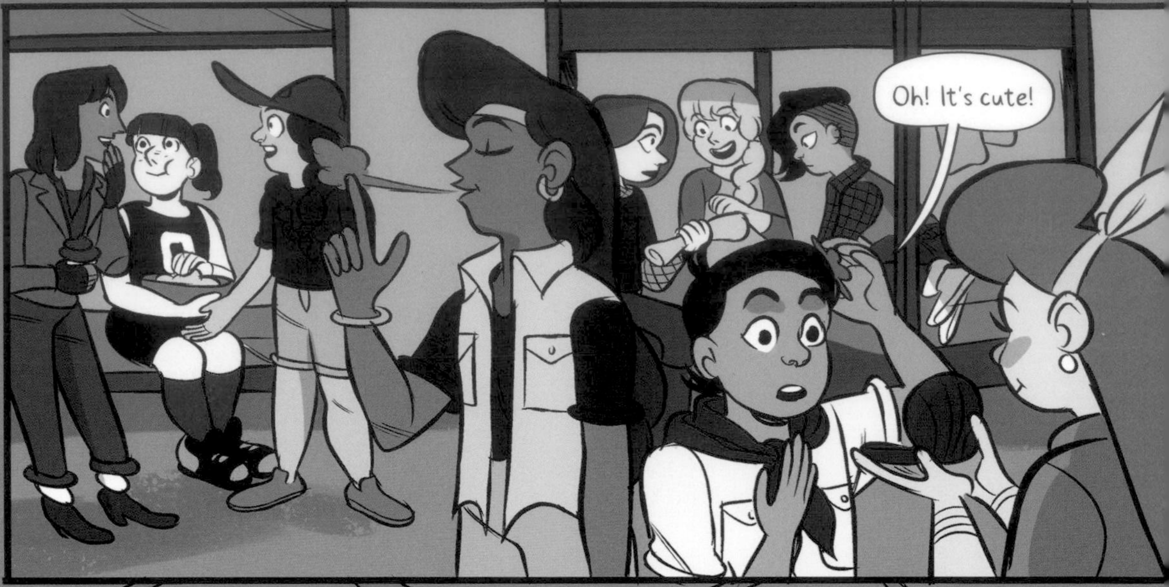

Oh! It's cute!

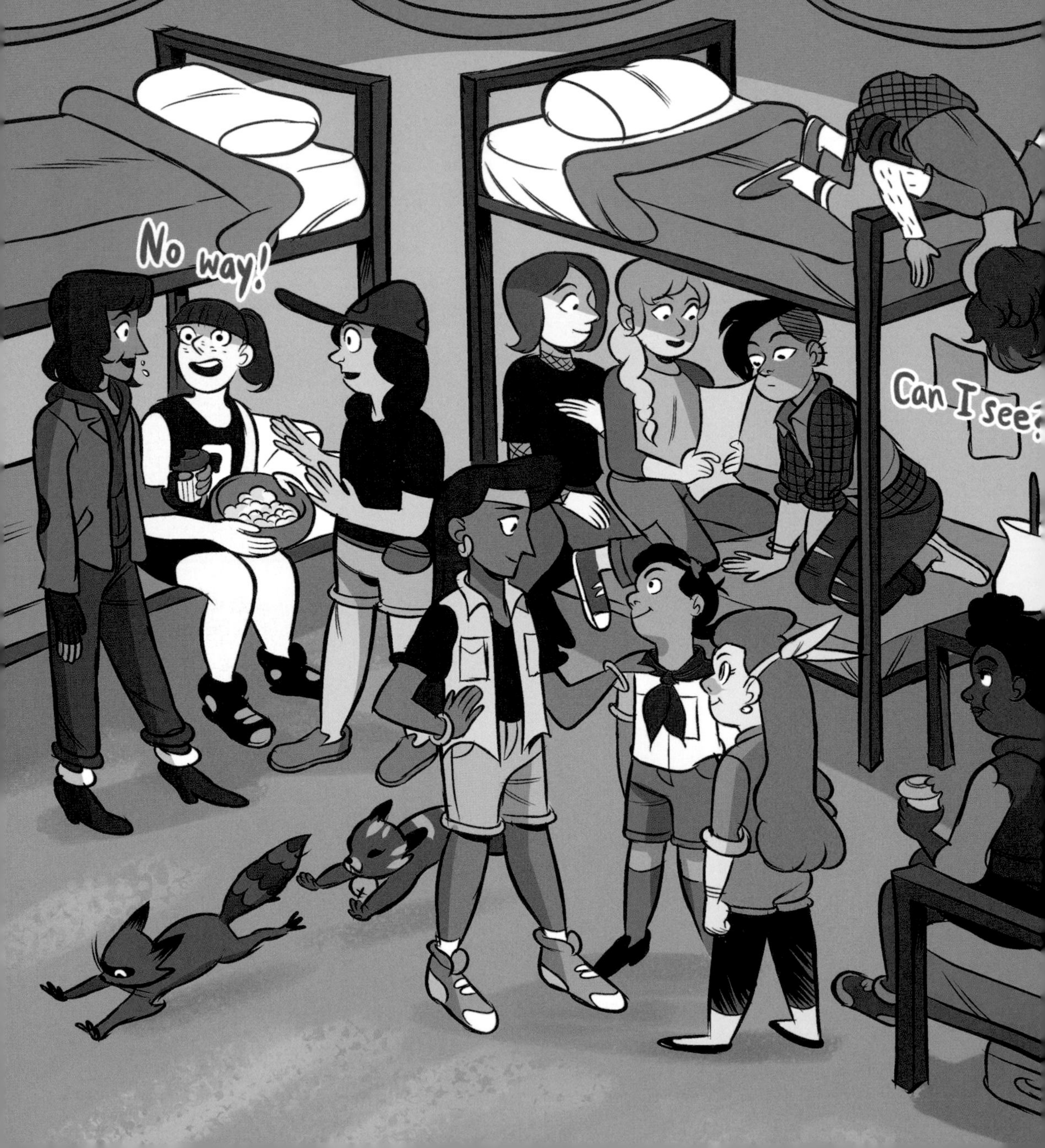

No way!
Can I see?

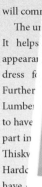

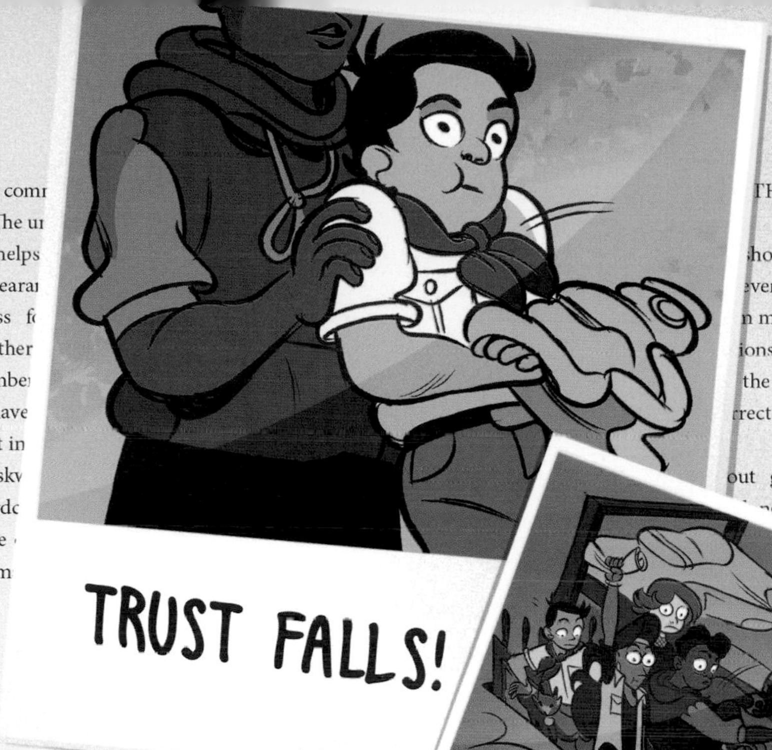
TRUST FALLS!

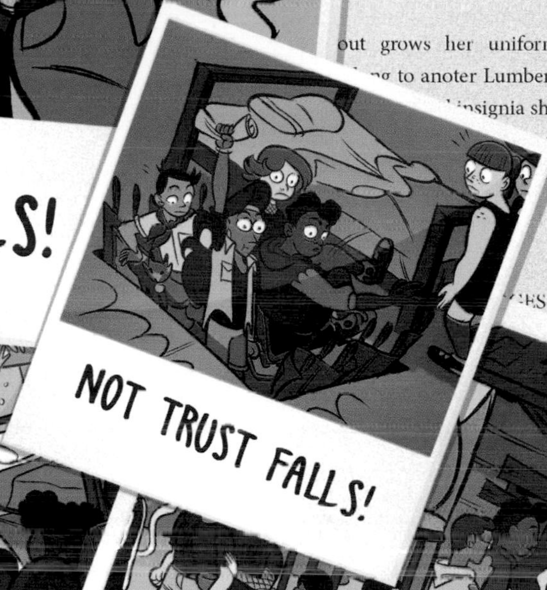
NOT TRUST FALLS!

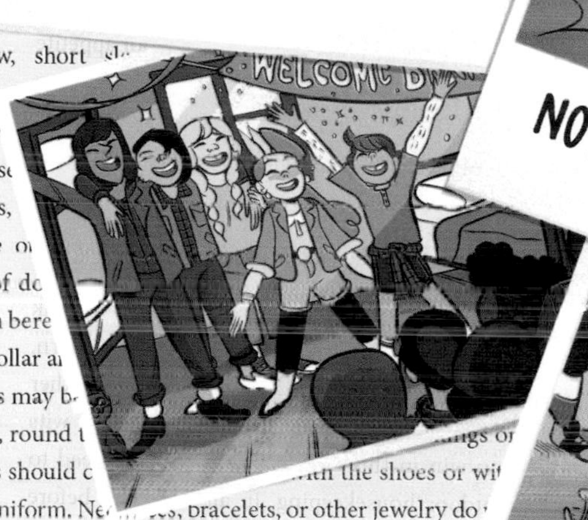
WELCOME

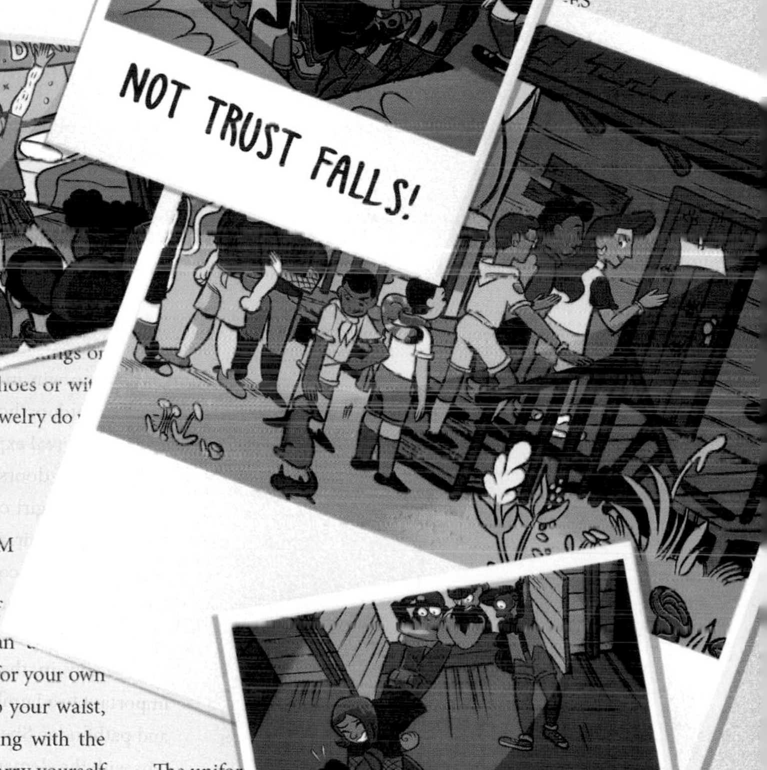

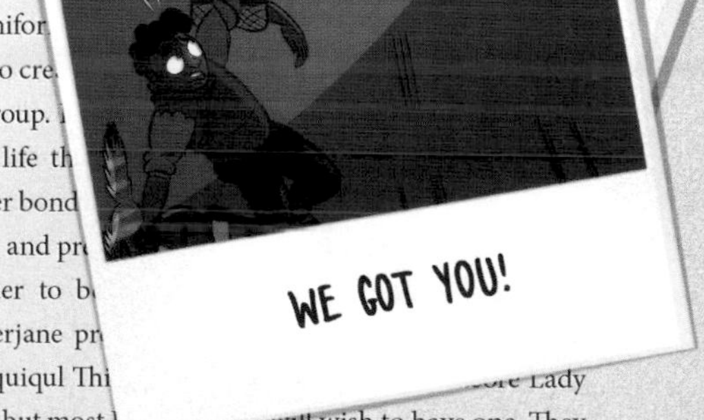
WE GOT YOU!

will comr
The ur
It helps
appearai
dress fc
Further
Lumbe
to have
part in
Thiskv
Hardc
have
them

THE UNIFORM

should be worn at camp
events when Lumberjanes
n may also be worn at other
ions. It should be worn as a
the uniform dress with
rrect shoes, and stocking or

out grows her uniform or
ng to anoter Lumberjane.
insignia she has
her
f her

The
yellow, short sl
emb
the w
choose
slacks,
made o
out of do
green bere
the collar a
Shoes may b
heels, round t ... ings or
socks should c ... with the shoes or wi
the uniform. Ne... , bracelets, or other jewelry do
belong with a Lumberjane uniform.

HOW TO WEAR THE UNIFORM

To look well in a uniform demands first of
uniform be kept in good condition—clean
pressed. See that the skirt is the right length for your own height and build, that the belt is adjusted to your waist, that your shoes and stockings are in keeping with the uniform, that you watch your posture and carry yourself with dignity and grace. If the beret is removed indoors, be sure that your hair is neat and kept in place with an insonspicuous clip or ribbon. When you wear a Lumberjane uniform you are identified as a member of this organization and you should be doubly careful to conduct yourself in a way that will show everyone that courtesy and thoughtfullness are part of being a Lumberjane. People are likely to judge a whole nation by the selfishness of a few individuals, to criticize a whole family because of the misconduct of one member, and to feel unkindly toward and organization because of the

The unifor
helps to cre
in a group.
active life th
another bond
future, and pr
in order to b
Lumberjane pr
Penniquiqul Thi
Types, but most ... will wish to have one. They can either buy the uniform, or make it themselves from materials available at the trading post.

LUMBERJANES FIELD MANUAL

CHAPTER
THIRTY-FOUR

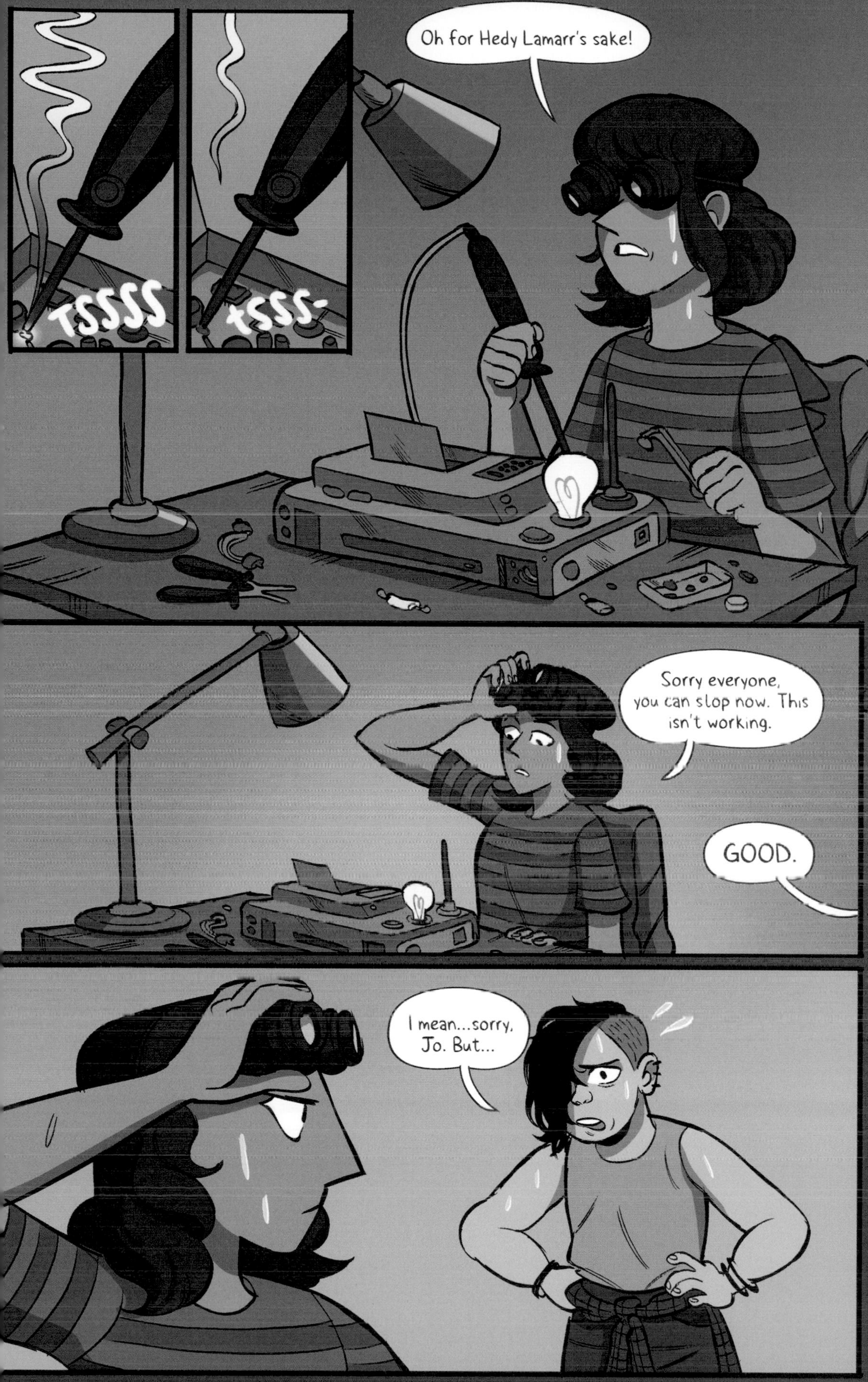
TSSSS
tSSS-
Oh for Hedy Lamarr's sake!
Sorry everyone, you can slop now. This isn't working.
GOOD.
I mean...sorry, Jo. But...

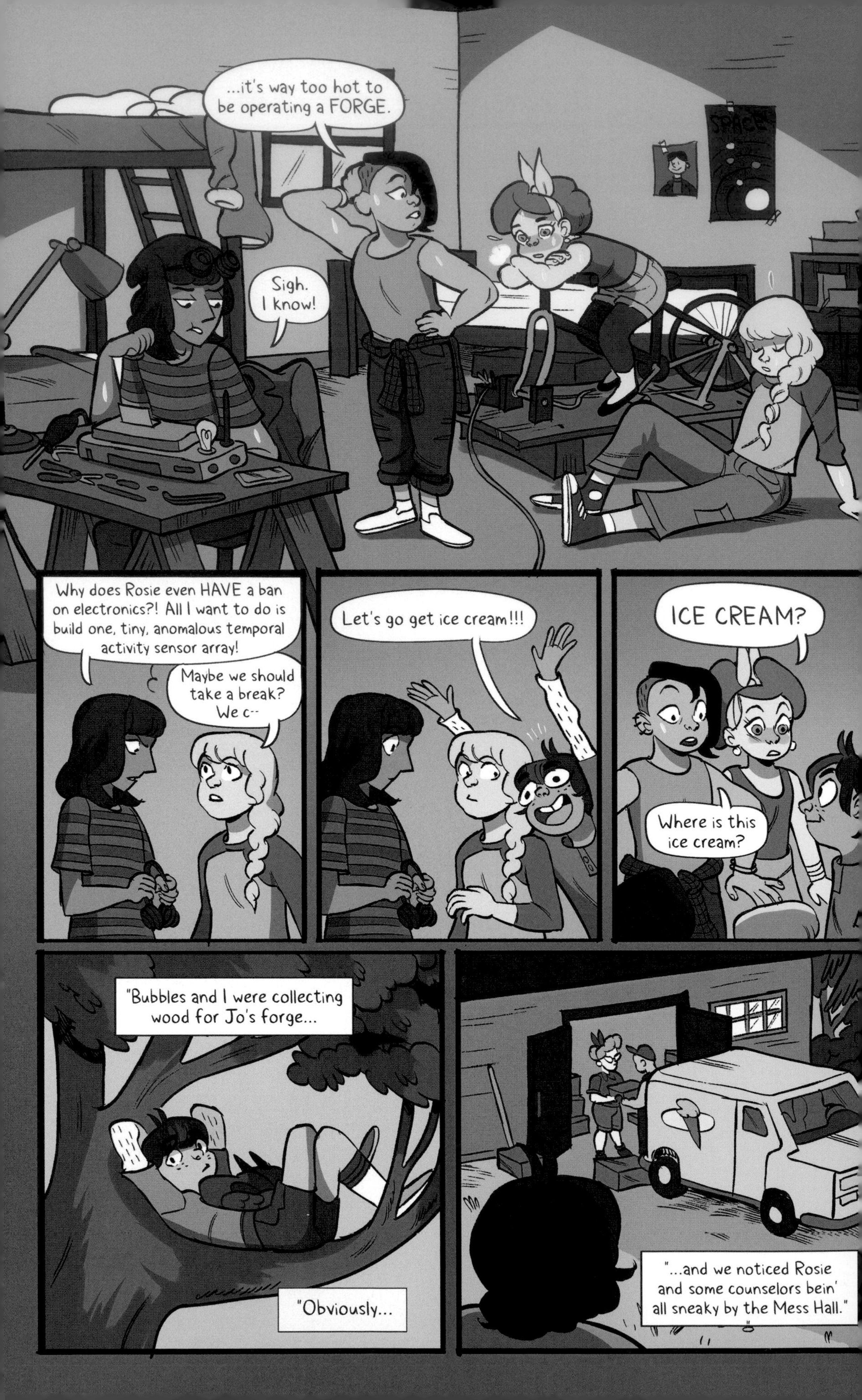
...it's way too hot to be operating a FORGE.
Sigh. I know!
Why does Rosie even HAVE a ban on electronics?! All I want to do is build one, tiny, anomalous temporal activity sensor array!
Maybe we should take a break? We c--
Let's go get ice cream!!!
ICE CREAM?
Where is this ice cream?
"Bubbles and I were collecting wood for Jo's forge...
"Obviously...
"...and we noticed Rosie and some counselors bein' all sneaky by the Mess Hall."
SPACE

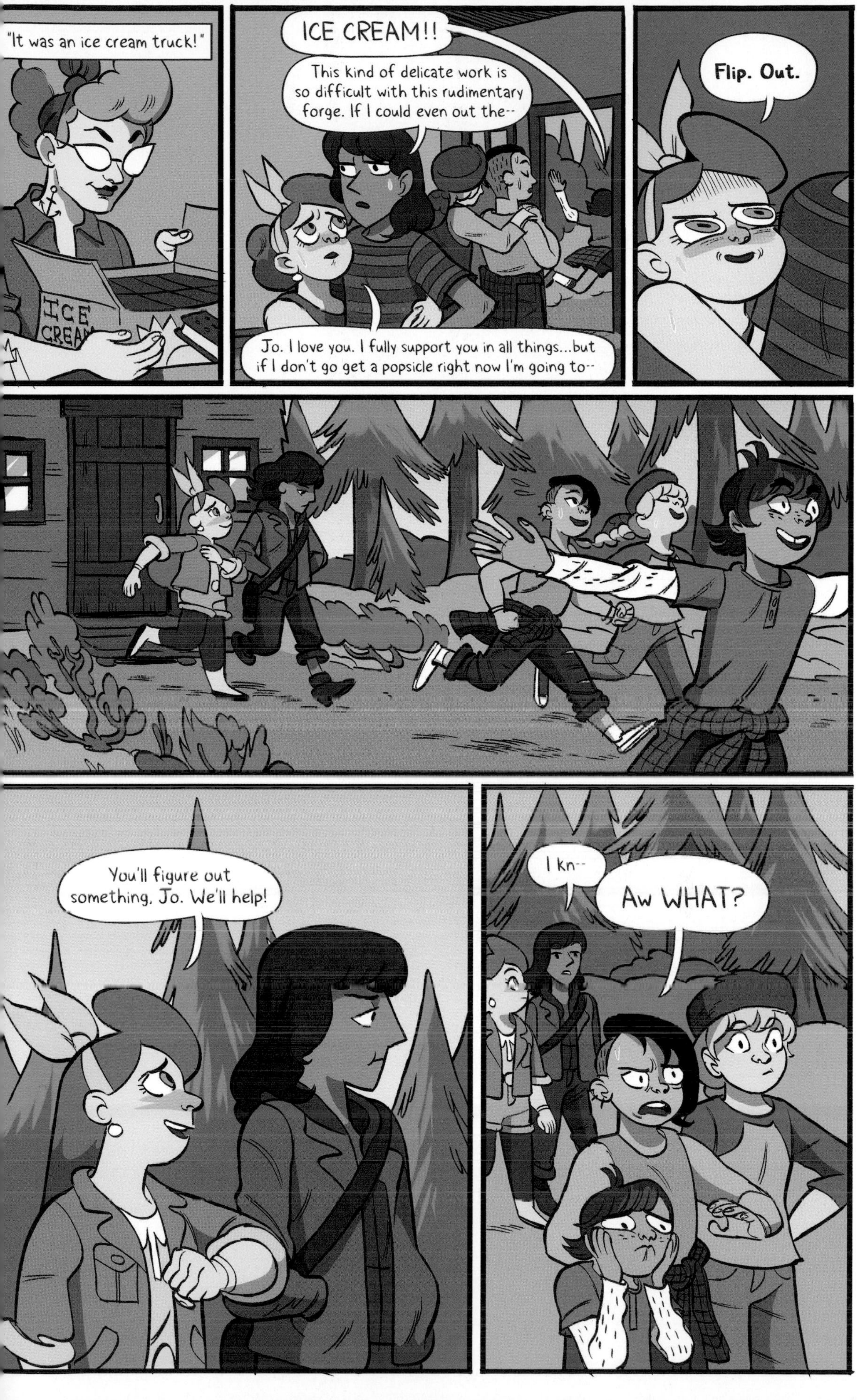
"It was an ice cream truck!"
ICE CREAM
ICE CREAM!!
This kind of delicate work is so difficult with this rudimentary forge. If I could even out the--
Jo. I love you. I fully support you in all things...but if I don't go get a popsicle right now I'm going to--
Flip. Out.
You'll figure out something, Jo. We'll help!
I kn--
Aw WHAT?

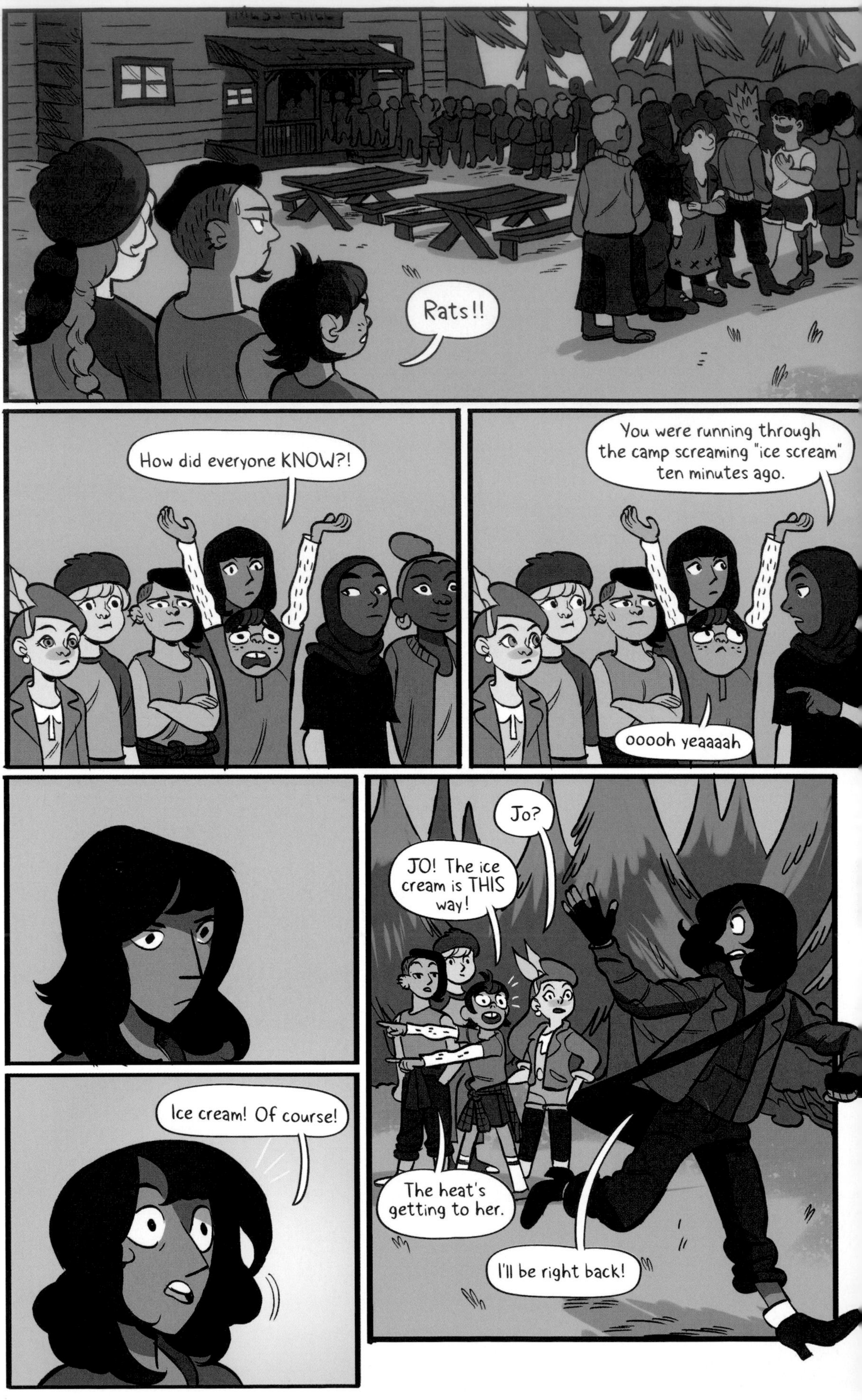
Rats!!
How did everyone KNOW?!
You were running through the camp screaming "ice scream" ten minutes ago.
ooooh yeaaaah
Ice cream! Of course!
Jo?
JO! The ice cream is THIS way!
The heat's getting to her.
I'll be right back!

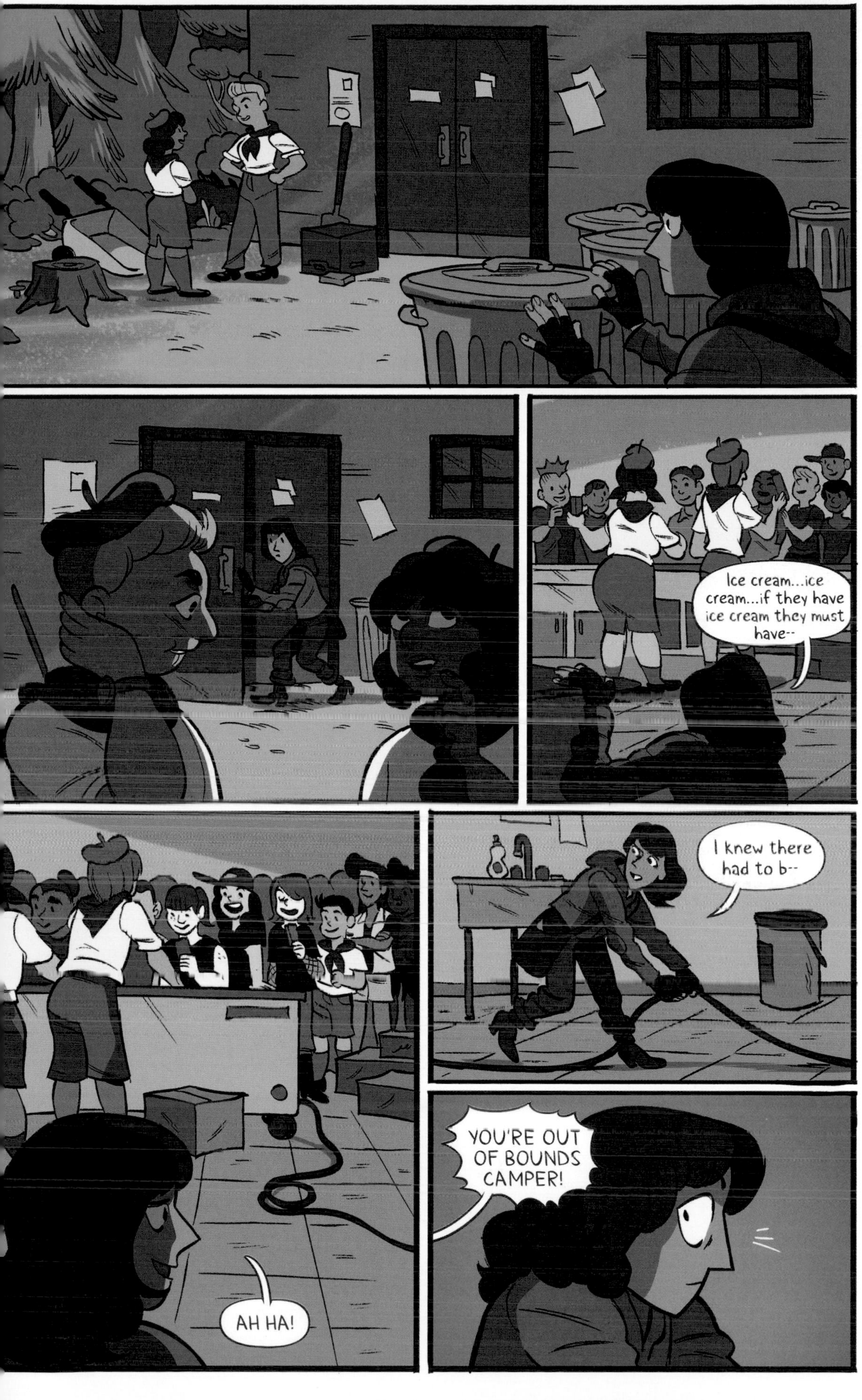
Ice cream...ice cream...if they have ice cream they must have--
I knew there had to b--
AH HA!
YOU'RE OUT OF BOUNDS CAMPER!

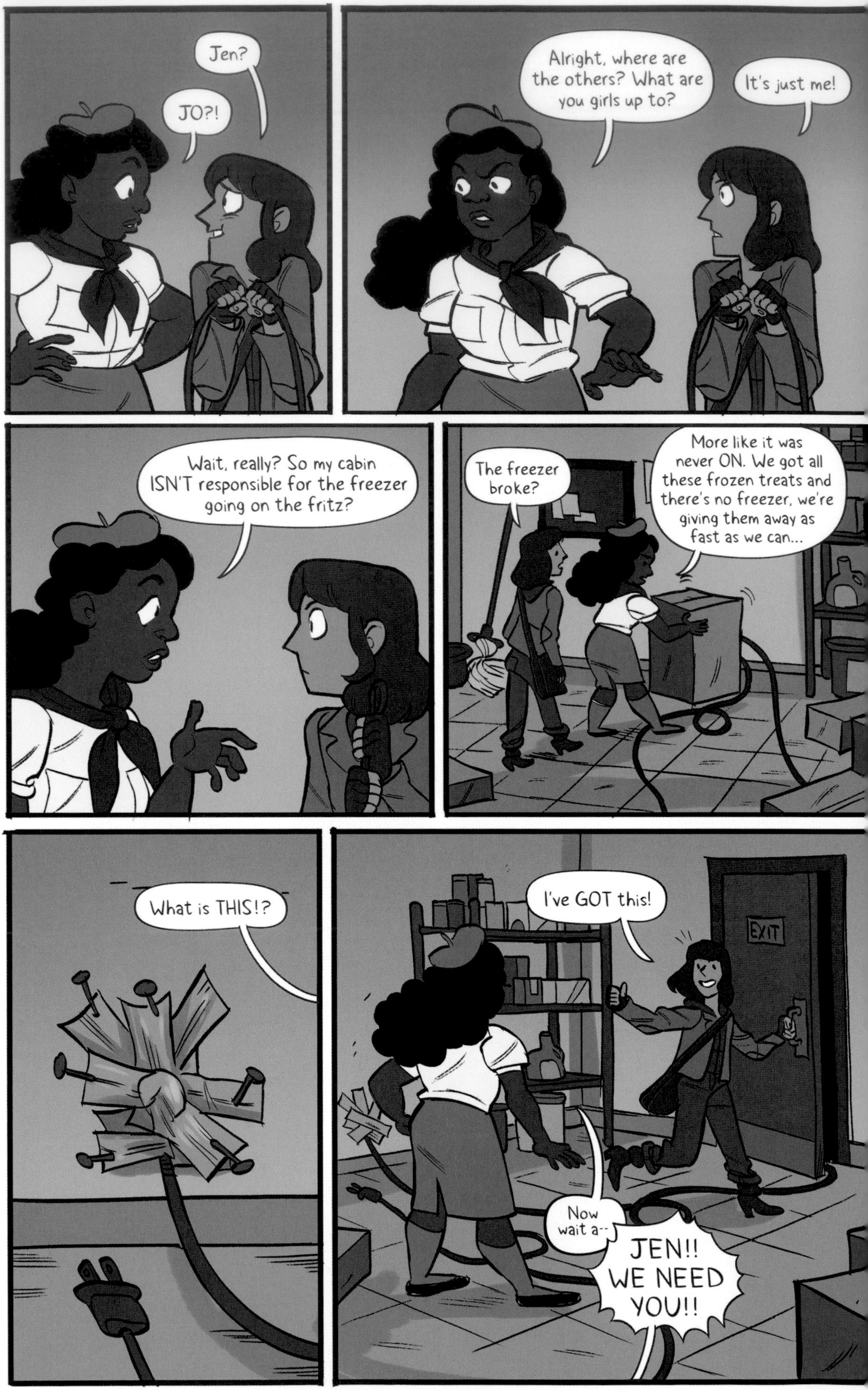
JO?!
Jen?
Alright, where are the others? What are you girls up to?
It's just me!
Wait, really? So my cabin ISN'T responsible for the freezer going on the fritz?
The freezer broke?
More like it was never ON. We got all these frozen treats and there's no freezer, we're giving them away as fast as we can...
What is THIS!?
I've GOT this!
EXIT
Now wait a--
JEN!! WE NEED YOU!!

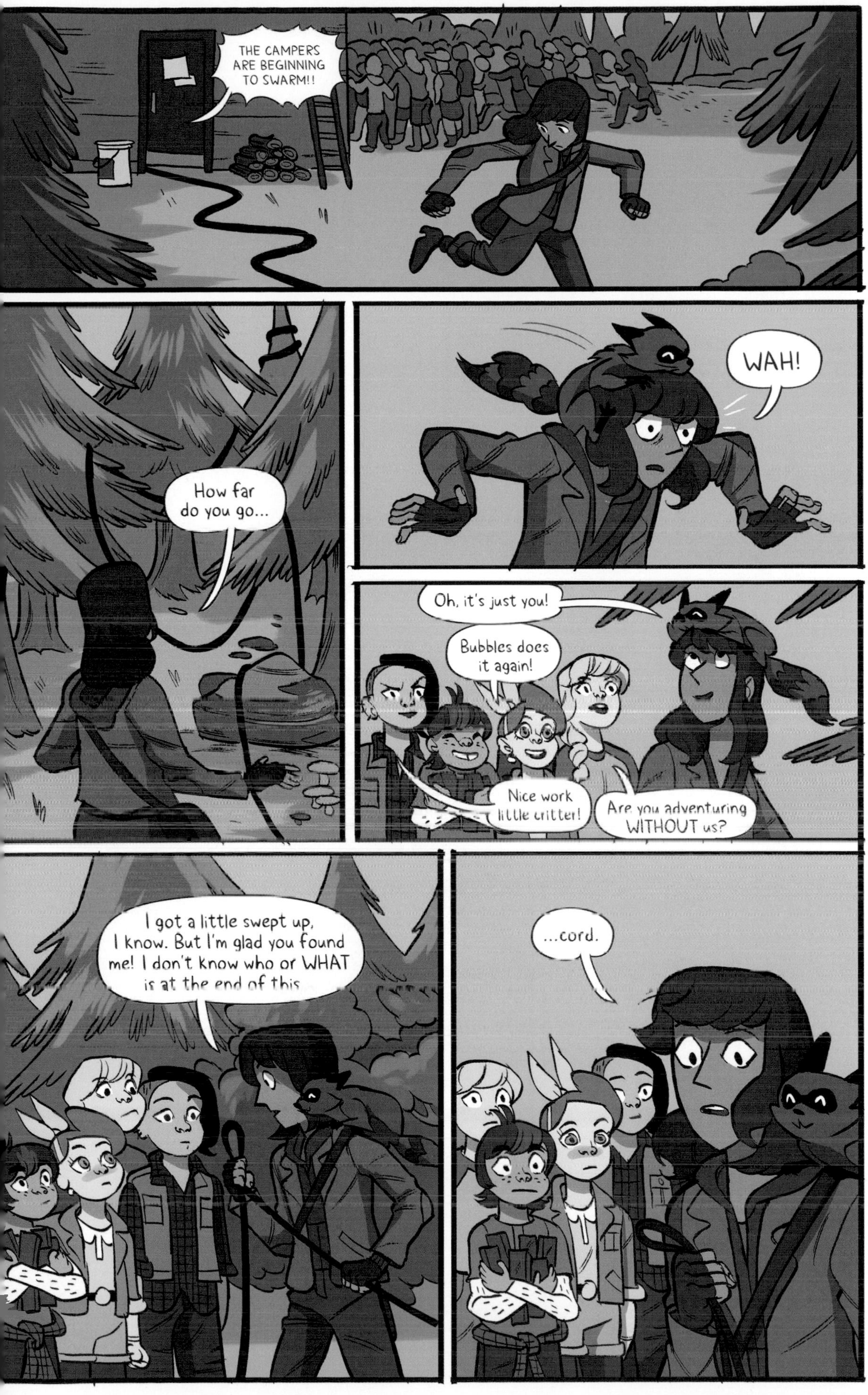
THE CAMPERS ARE BEGINNING TO SWARM!!
How far do you go...
WAH!
Oh, it's just you!
Bubbles does it again!
Nice work little critter!
Are you adventuring WITHOUT us?
I got a little swept up, I know. But I'm glad you found me! I don't know who or WHAT is at the end of this
...cord.

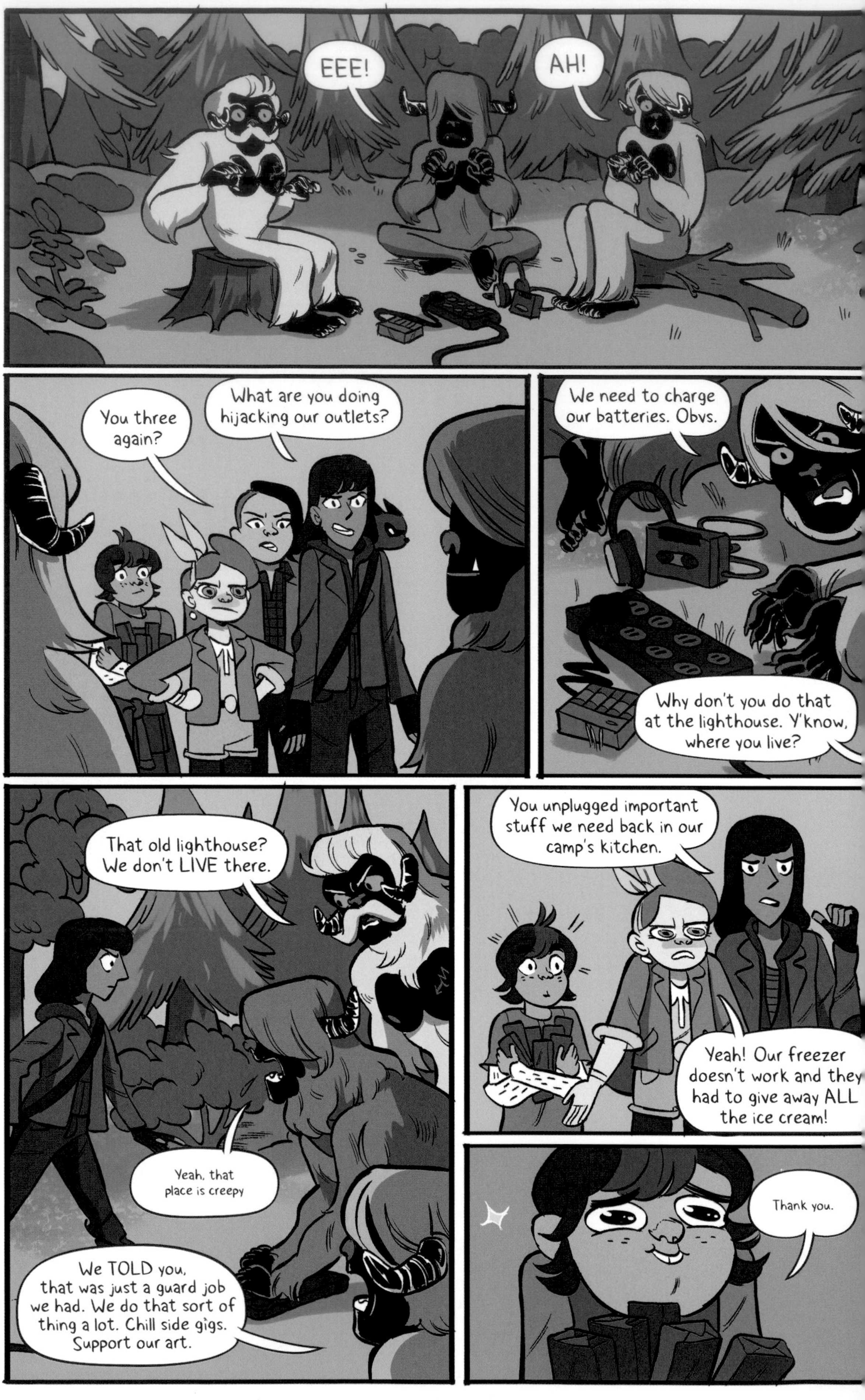
EEE!
AH!
You three again?
What are you doing hijacking our outlets?
We need to charge our batteries. Obvs.
Why don't you do that at the lighthouse. Y'know, where you live?
That old lighthouse? We don't LIVE there.
Yeah, that place is creepy
We TOLD you, that was just a guard job we had. We do that sort of thing a lot. Chill side gigs. Support our art.
You unplugged important stuff we need back in our camp's kitchen.
Yeah! Our freezer doesn't work and they had to give away ALL the ice cream!
Thank you.

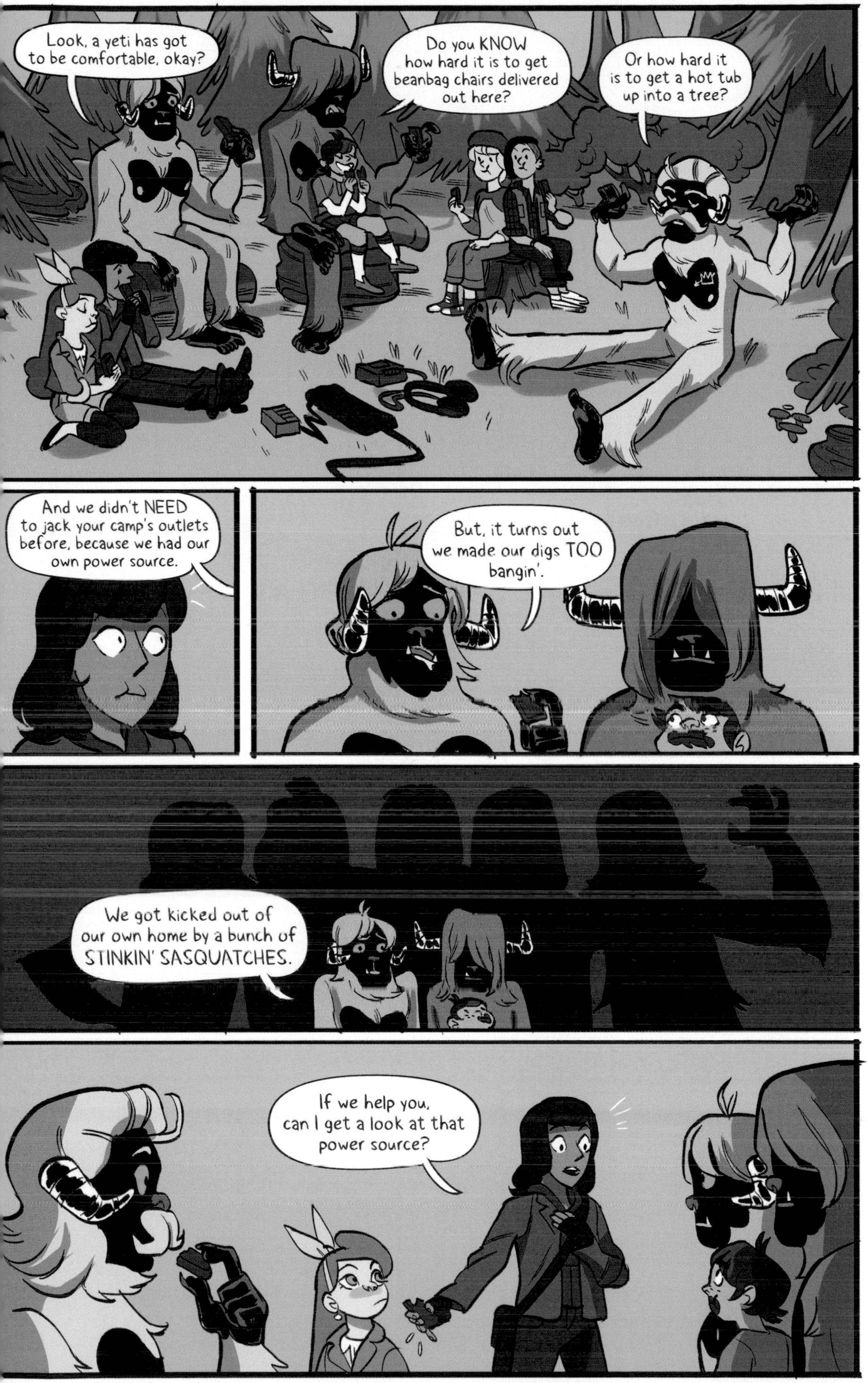
Look, a yeti has got to be comfortable, okay?
Do you KNOW how hard it is to get beanbag chairs delivered out here?
Or how hard it is to get a hot tub up into a tree?
And we didn't NEED to jack your camp's outlets before, because we had our own power source.
But, it turns out we made our digs TOO bangin'.
We got kicked out of our own home by a bunch of STINKIN' SASQUATCHES.
If we help you, can I get a look at that power source?

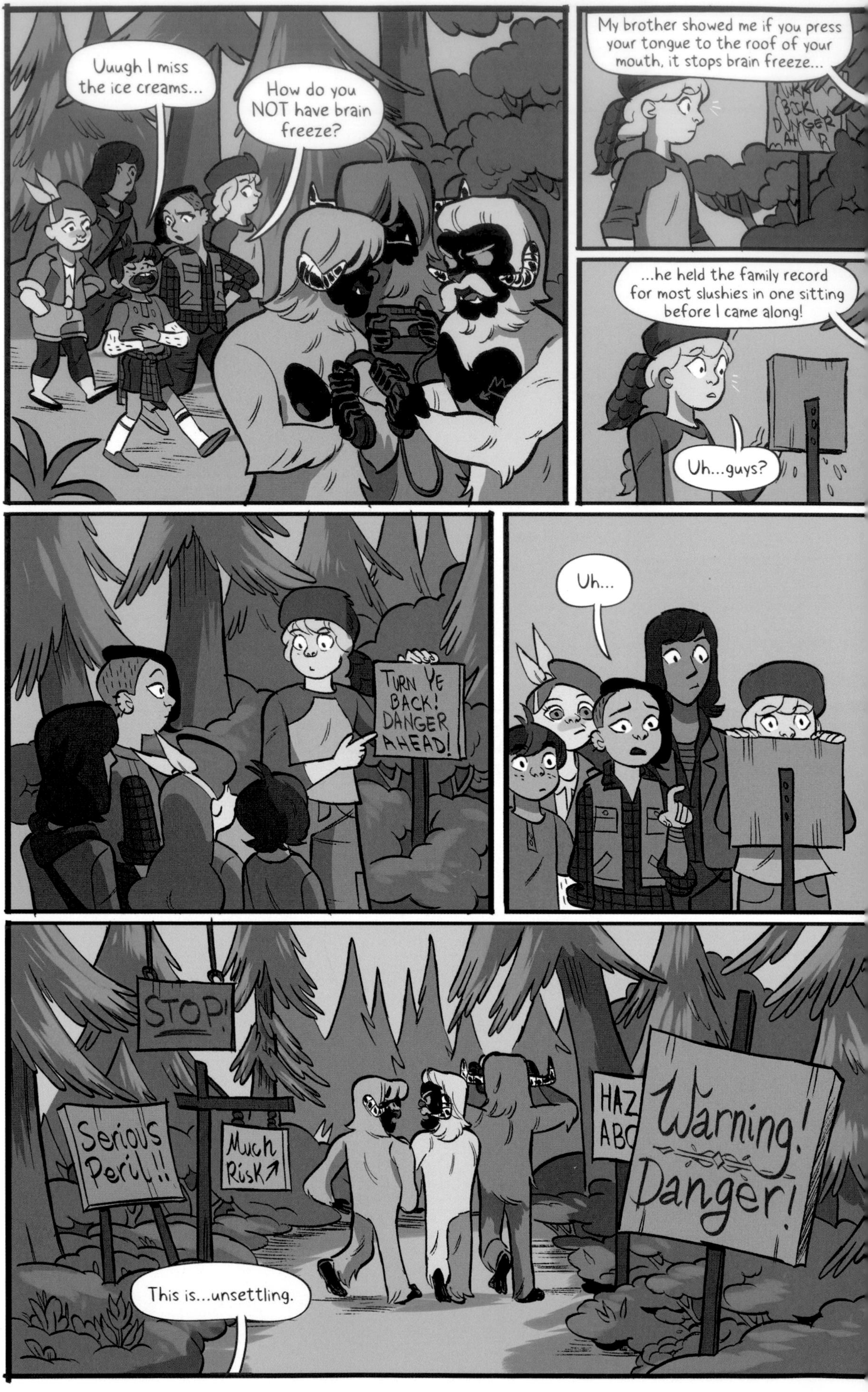
Uuugh I miss the ice creams...
How do you NOT have brain freeze?
My brother showed me if you press your tongue to the roof of your mouth, it stops brain freeze...
...he held the family record for most slushies in one sitting before I came along!
Uh...guys?
TURN YE BACK! DANGER AHEAD!
Uh...
STOP!
Serious Peril!!
Much Risk
Warning! Danger!
This is...unsettling.

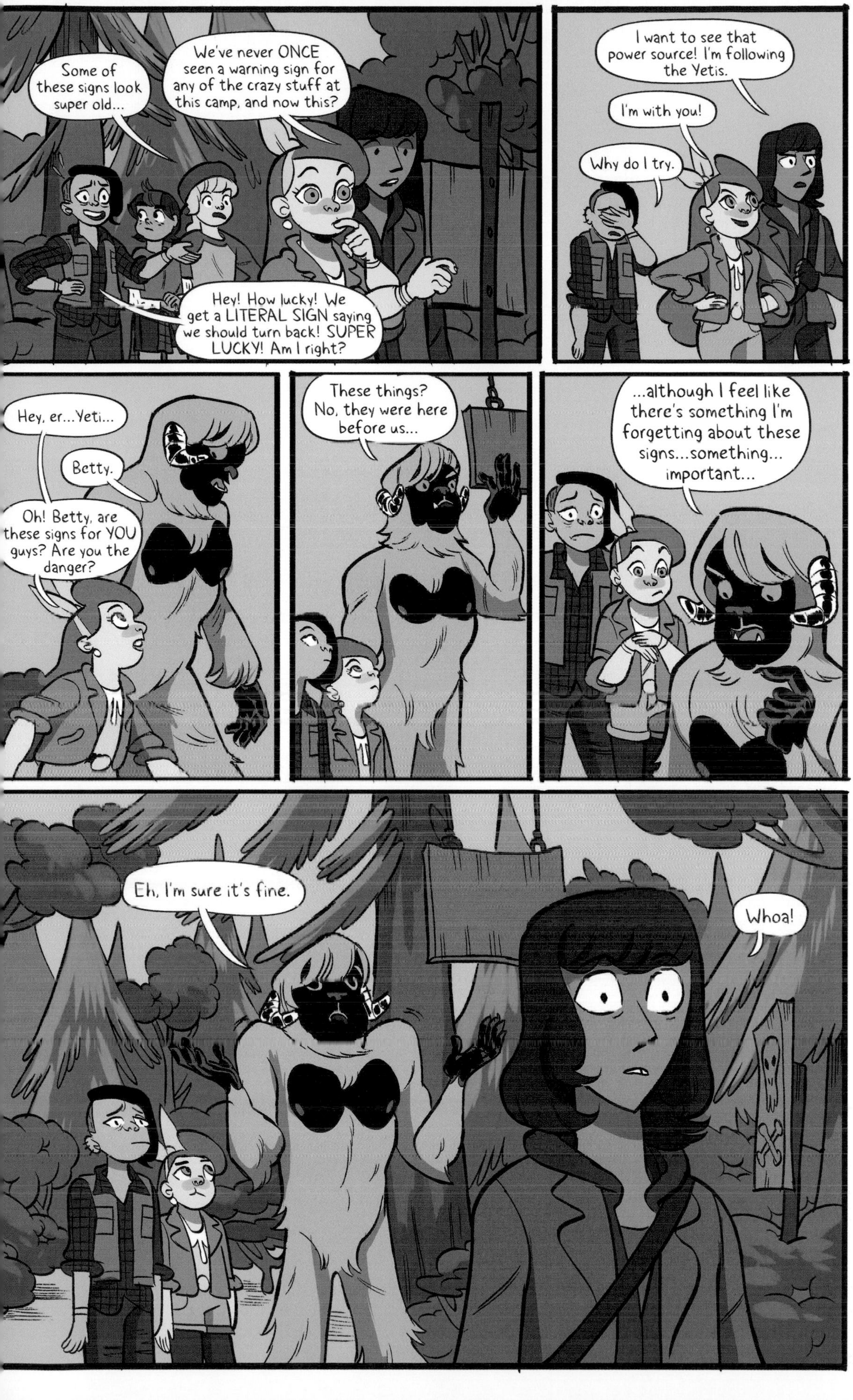
Some of these signs look super old...
We've never ONCE seen a warning sign for any of the crazy stuff at this camp, and now this?
Hey! How lucky! We get a LITERAL SIGN saying we should turn back! SUPER LUCKY! Am I right?
I want to see that power source! I'm following the Yetis.
I'm with you!
Why do I try.
Hey, er...Yeti...
Betty.
Oh! Betty, are these signs for YOU guys? Are you the danger?
These things? No, they were here before us...
...although I feel like there's something I'm forgetting about these signs...something... important...
Eh, I'm sure it's fine.
Whoa!

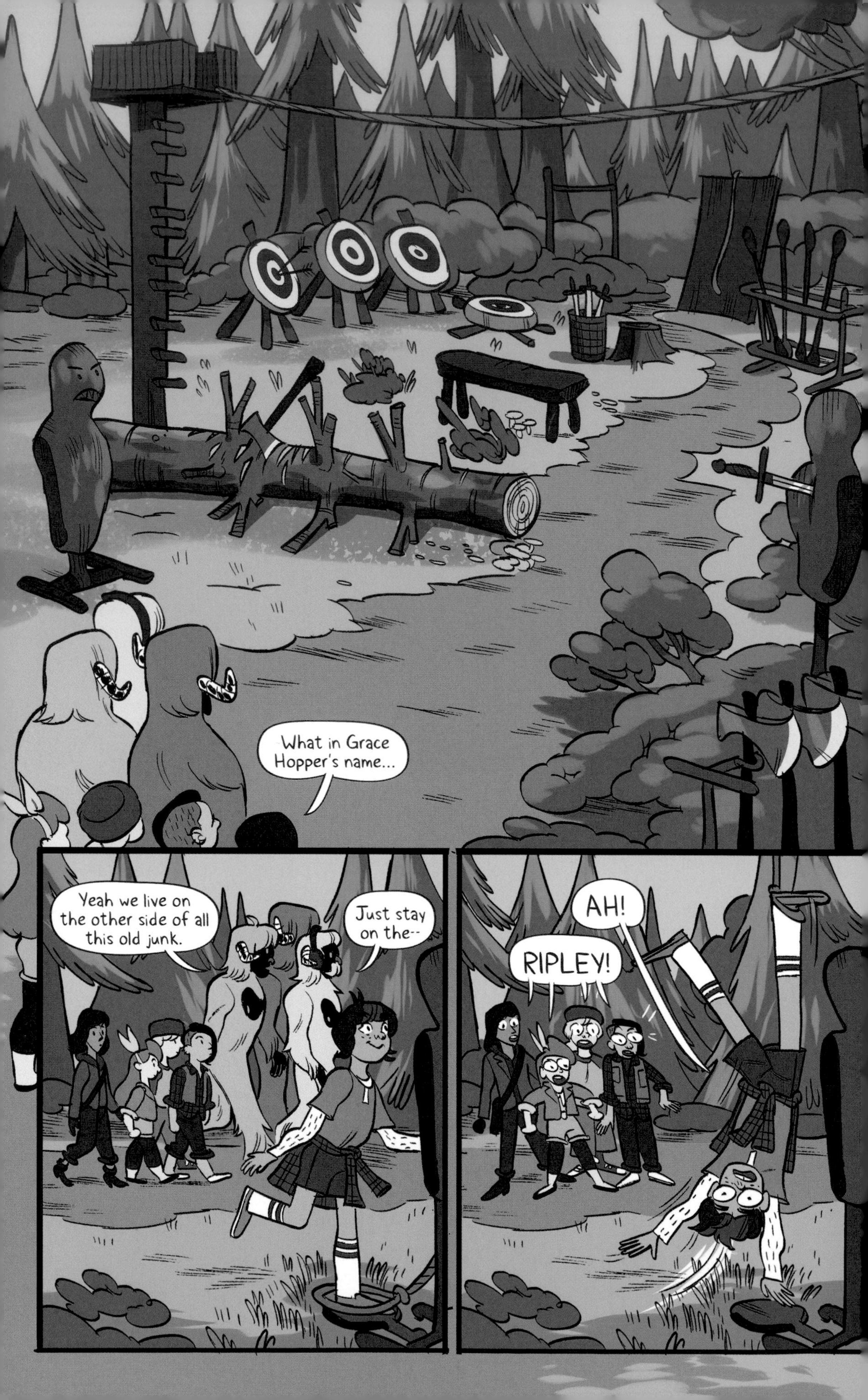
What in Grace Hopper's name...
Yeah we live on the other side of all this old junk.
Just stay on the--
AH!
RIPLEY!

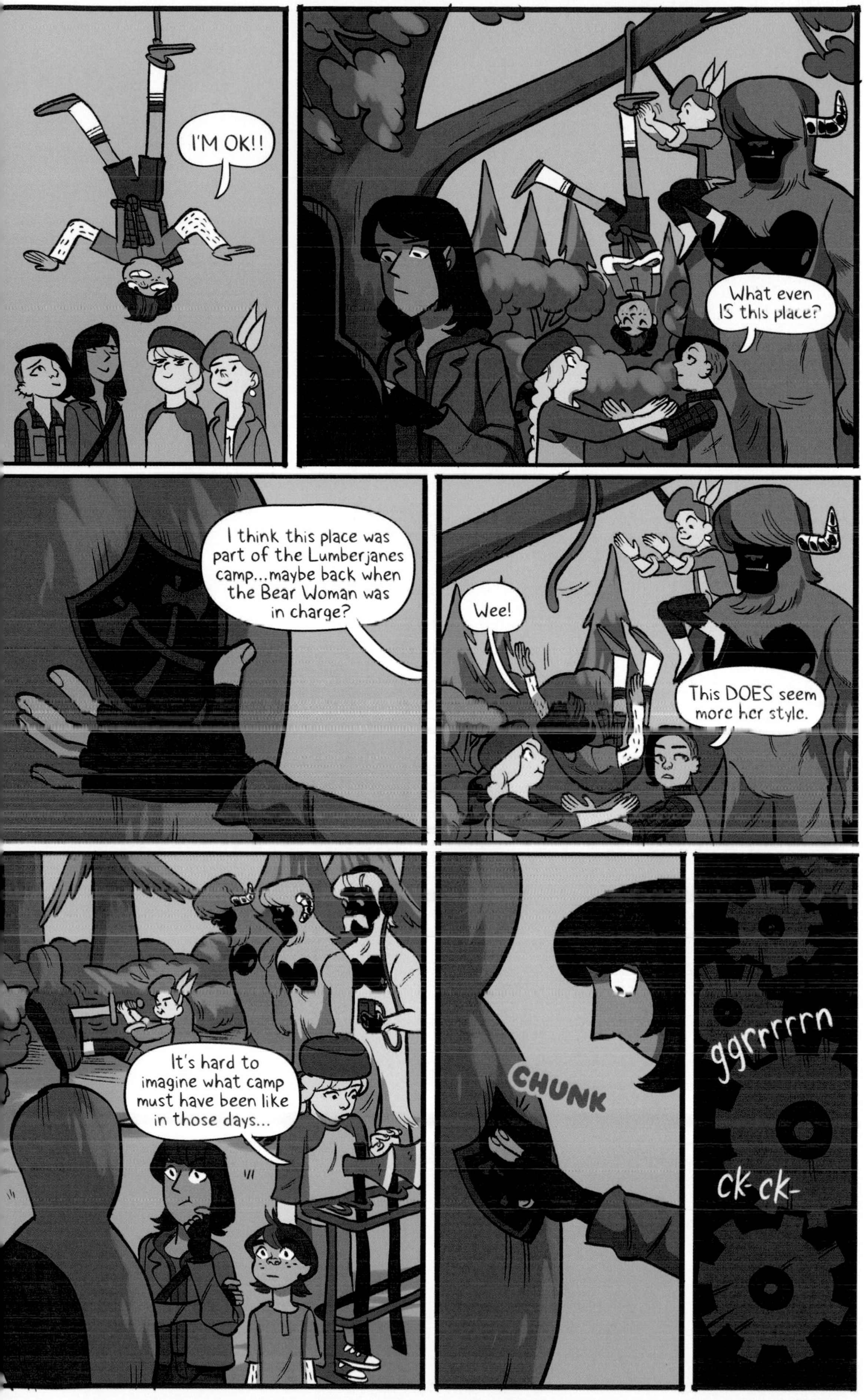
I'M OK!!
What even IS this place?
I think this place was part of the Lumberjanes camp...maybe back when the Bear Woman was in charge?
Wee!
This DOES seem more her style.
It's hard to imagine what camp must have been like in those days...
CHUNK
ggrrrrrn
ck-ck-

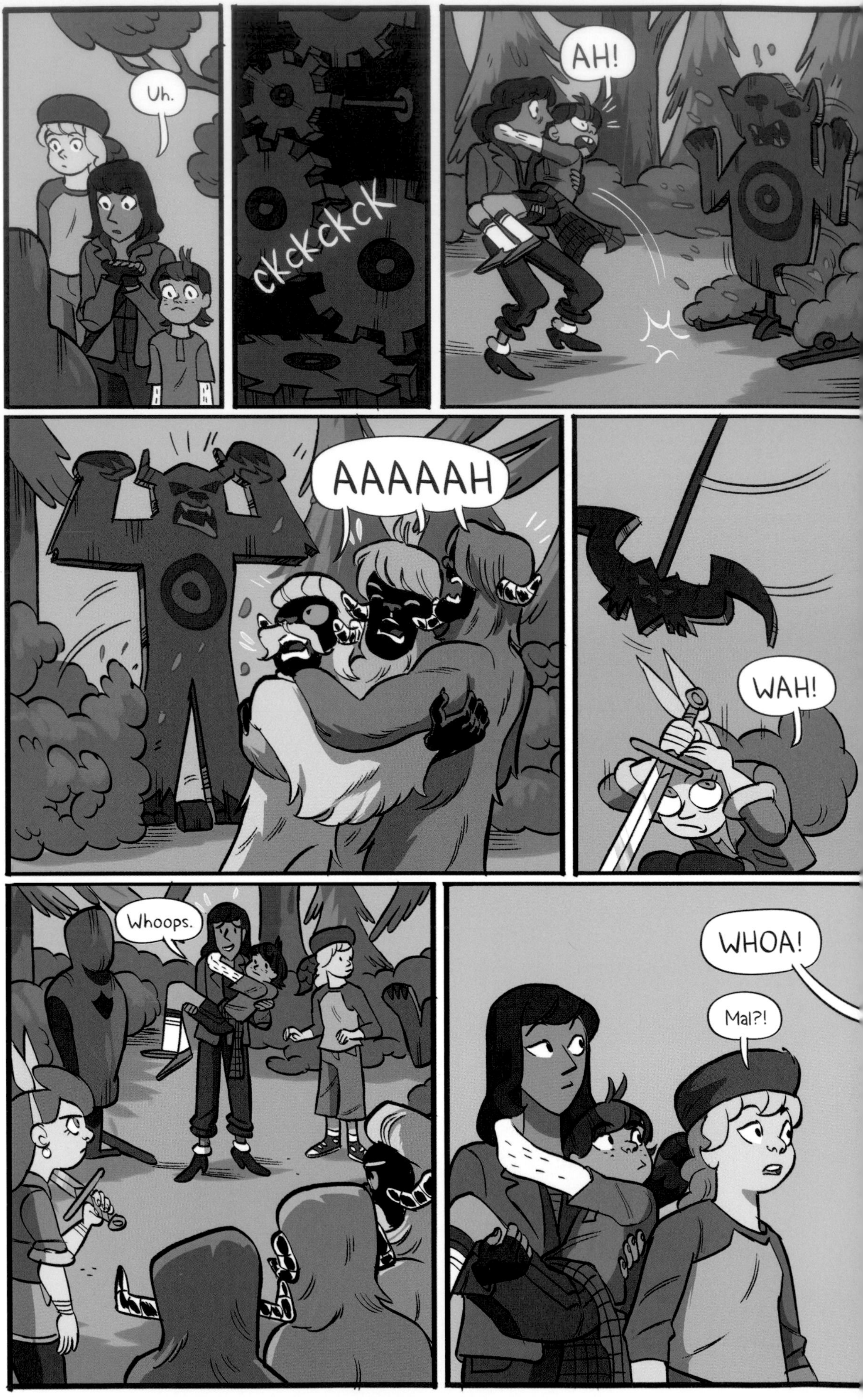
Uh.
CKCKCKCK
AH!
AAAAAH
WAH!
Whoops.
WHOA!
Mal?!

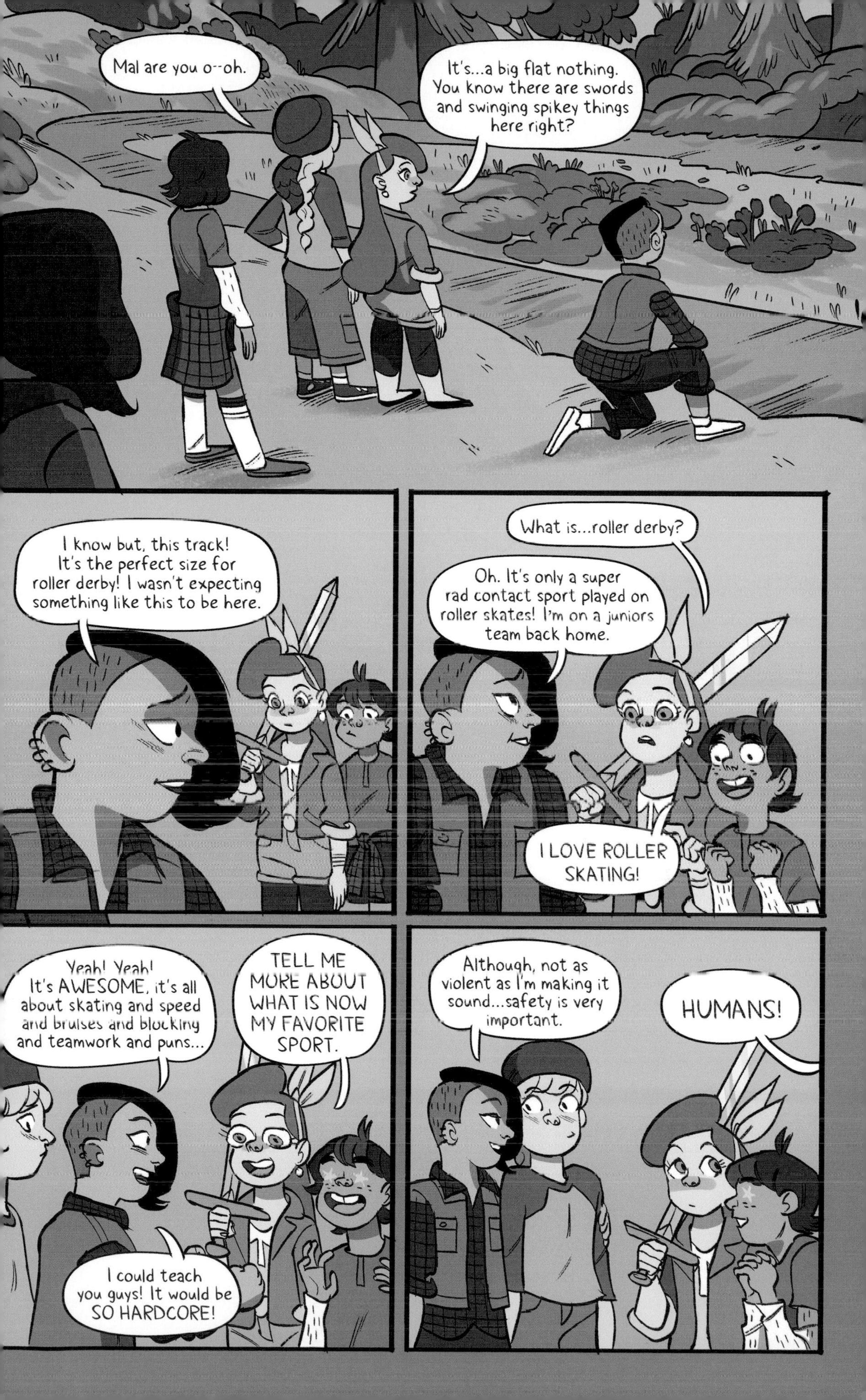
Mal are you o--oh.
It's...a big flat nothing. You know there are swords and swinging spikey things here right?
I know but, this track! It's the perfect size for roller derby! I wasn't expecting something like this to be here.
What is...roller derby?
Oh. It's only a super rad contact sport played on roller skates! I'm on a juniors team back home.
I LOVE ROLLER SKATING!
Yeah! Yeah! It's AWESOME, it's all about skating and speed and bruises and blocking and teamwork and puns...
TELL ME MORE ABOUT WHAT IS NOW MY FAVORITE SPORT.
I could teach you guys! It would be SO HARDCORE!
Although, not as violent as I'm making it sound...safety is very important.
HUMANS!

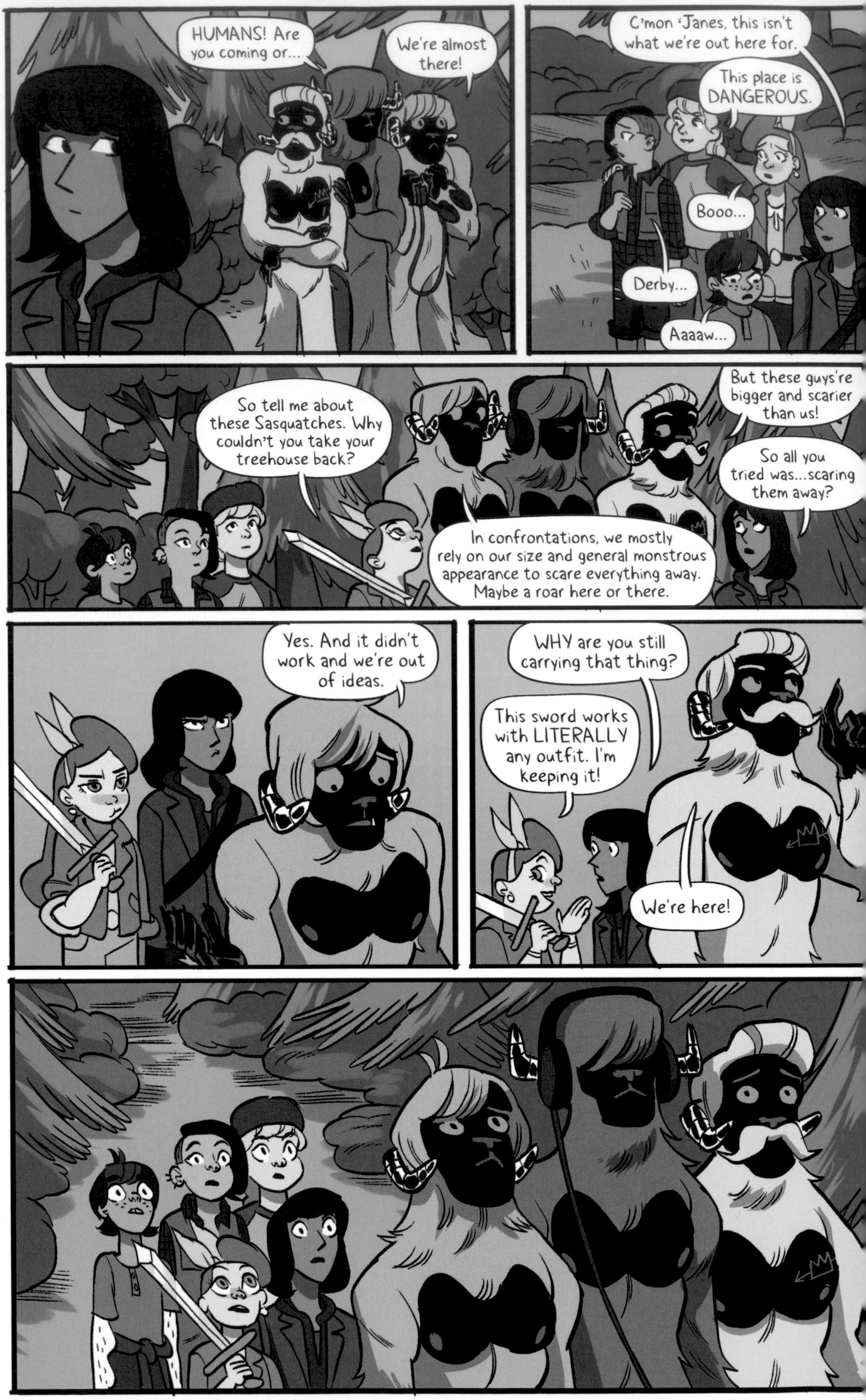
HUMANS! Are you coming or...
We're almost there!
C'mon 'Janes, this isn't what we're out here for.
This place is DANGEROUS.
Booo...
Derby...
Aaaaw...
So tell me about these Sasquatches. Why couldn't you take your treehouse back?
In confrontations, we mostly rely on our size and general monstrous appearance to scare everything away. Maybe a roar here or there.
But these guys're bigger and scarier than us!
So all you tried was...scaring them away?
Yes. And it didn't work and we're out of ideas.
WHY are you still carrying that thing?
This sword works with LITERALLY any outfit. I'm keeping it!
We're here!

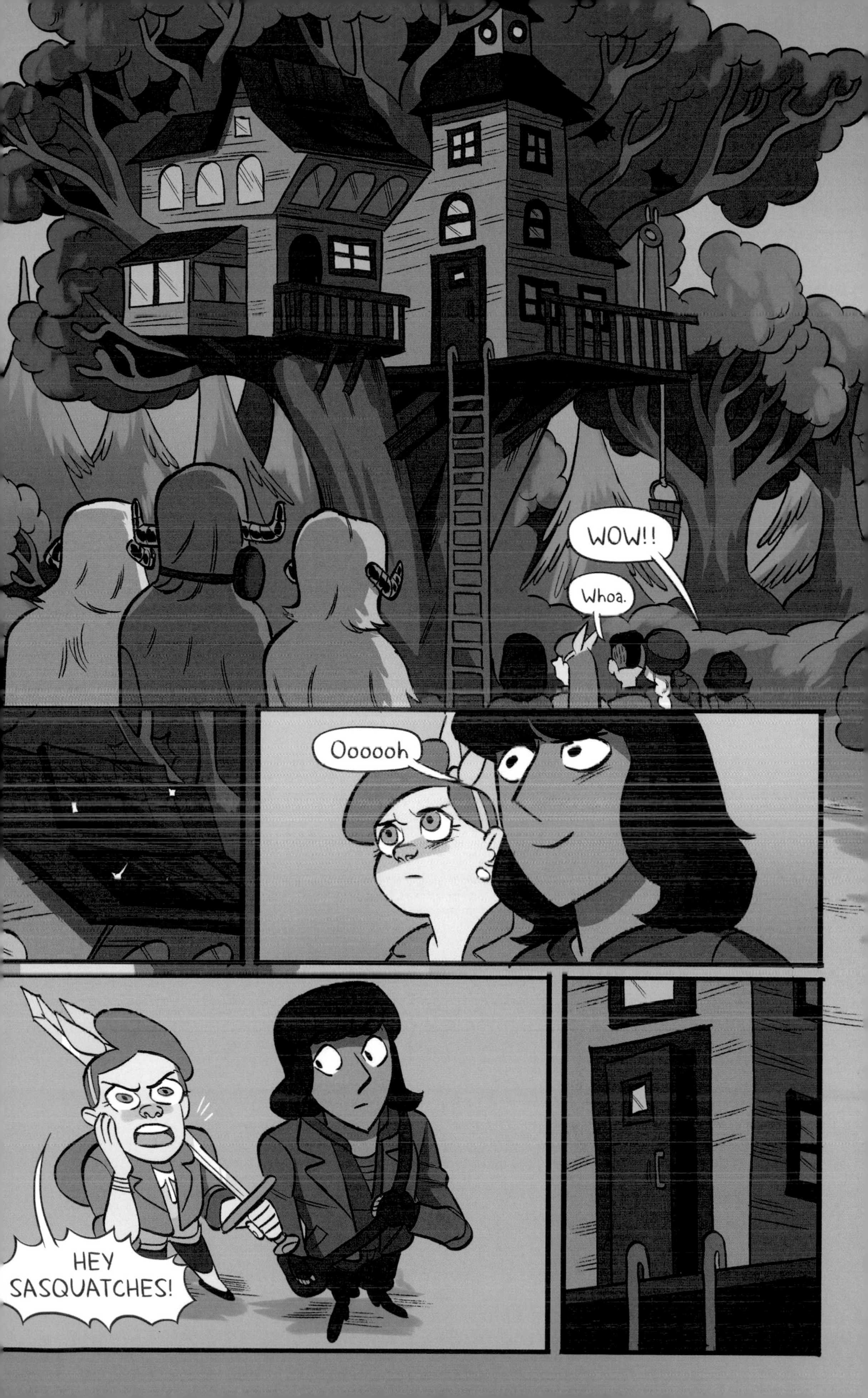
WOW!!
Whoa.
Oooooh
HEY SASQUATCHES!

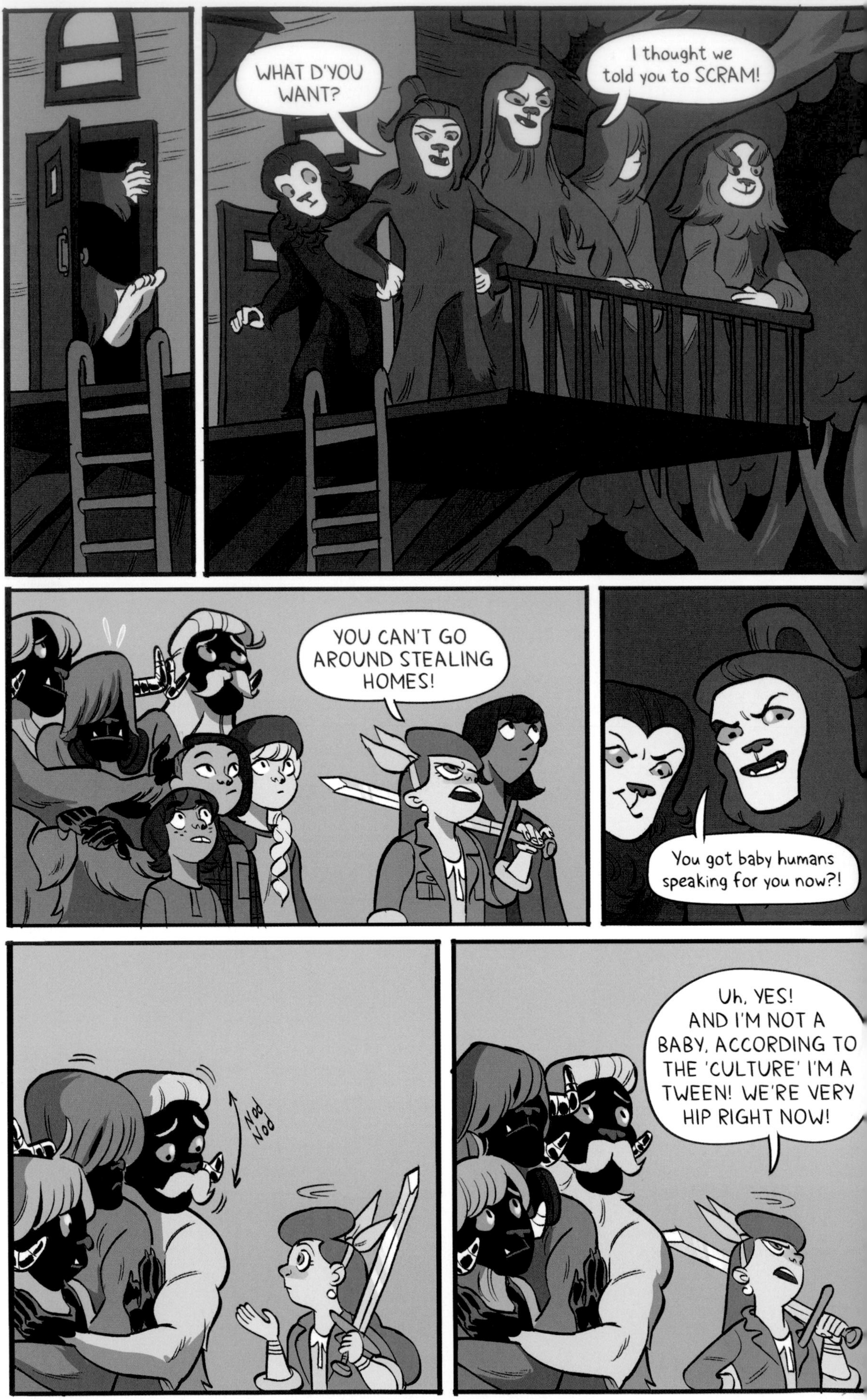
WHAT D'YOU WANT?
I thought we told you to SCRAM!
YOU CAN'T GO AROUND STEALING HOMES!
You got baby humans speaking for you now?!
NOD NOD
Uh, YES! AND I'M NOT A BABY, ACCORDING TO THE 'CULTURE' I'M A TWEEN! WE'RE VERY HIP RIGHT NOW!

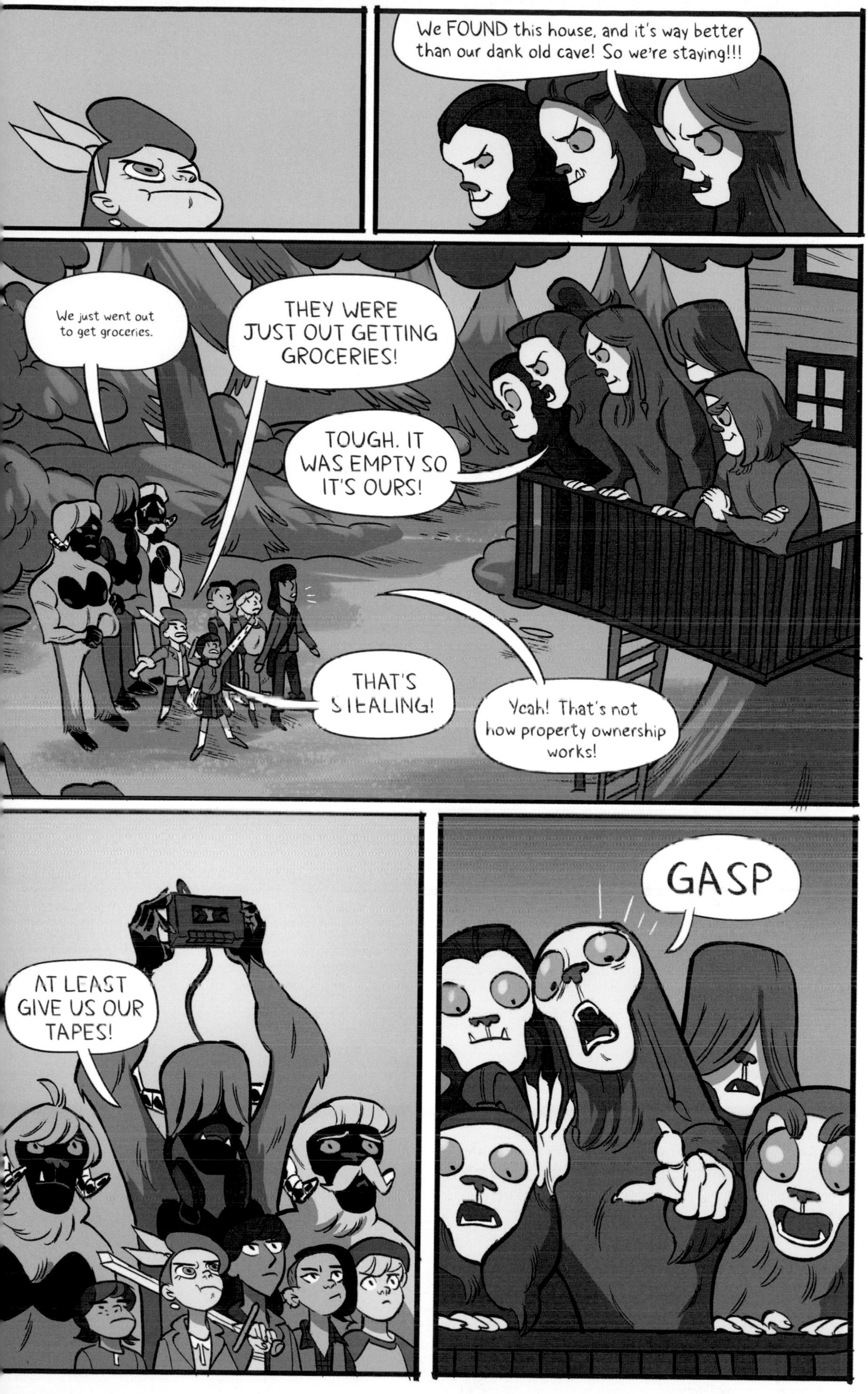
We FOUND this house, and it's way better than our dank old cave! So we're staying!!!
We just went out to get groceries.
THEY WERE JUST OUT GETTING GROCERIES!
TOUGH. IT WAS EMPTY SO IT'S OURS!
THAT'S STEALING!
Yeah! That's not how property ownership works!
AT LEAST GIVE US OUR TAPES!
GASP

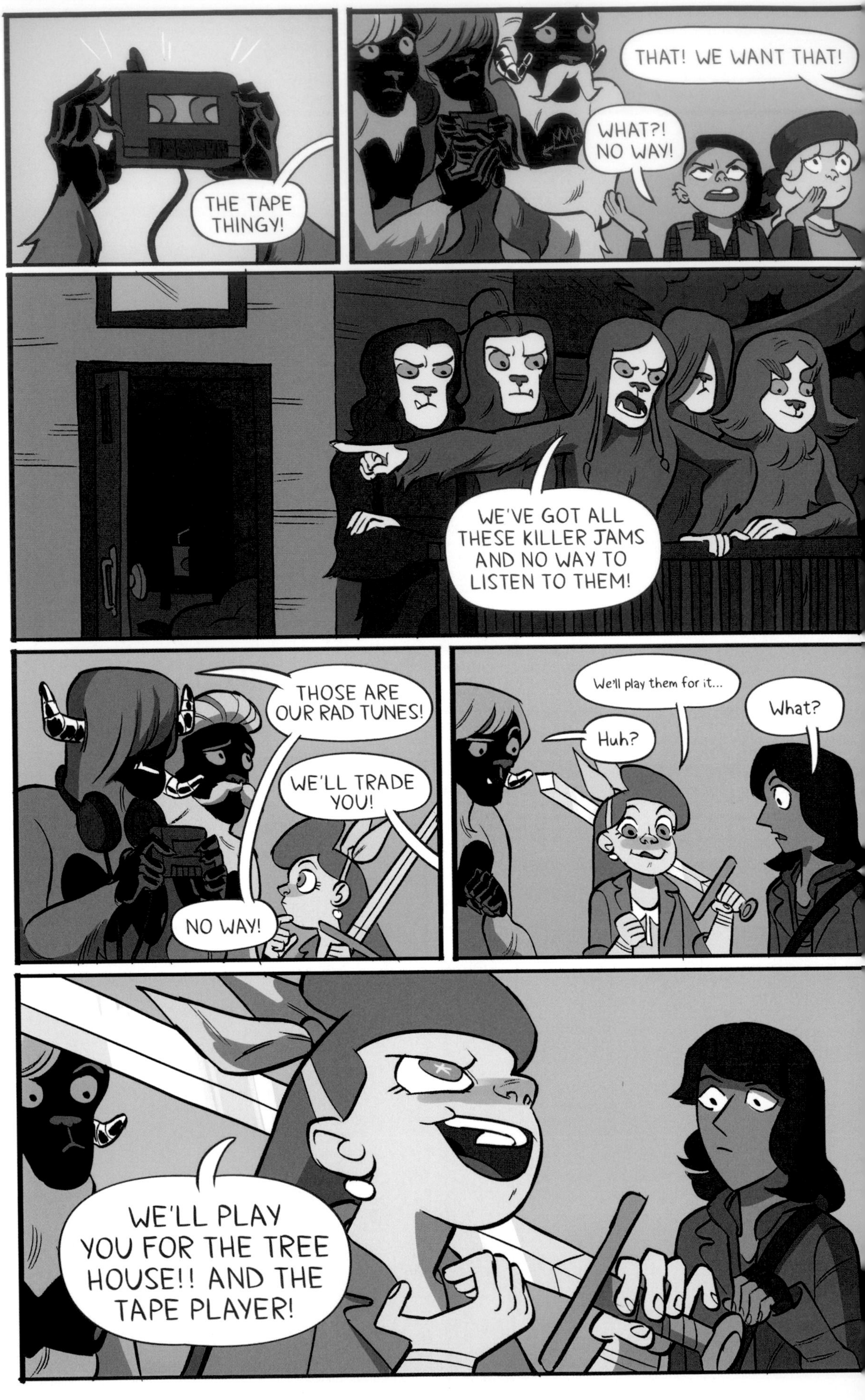
THE TAPE THINGY!
THAT! WE WANT THAT!
WHAT?! NO WAY!
WE'VE GOT ALL THESE KILLER JAMS AND NO WAY TO LISTEN TO THEM!
THOSE ARE OUR RAD TUNES!
WE'LL TRADE YOU!
NO WAY!
We'll play them for it...
Huh?
What?
WE'LL PLAY YOU FOR THE TREE HOUSE!! AND THE TAPE PLAYER!

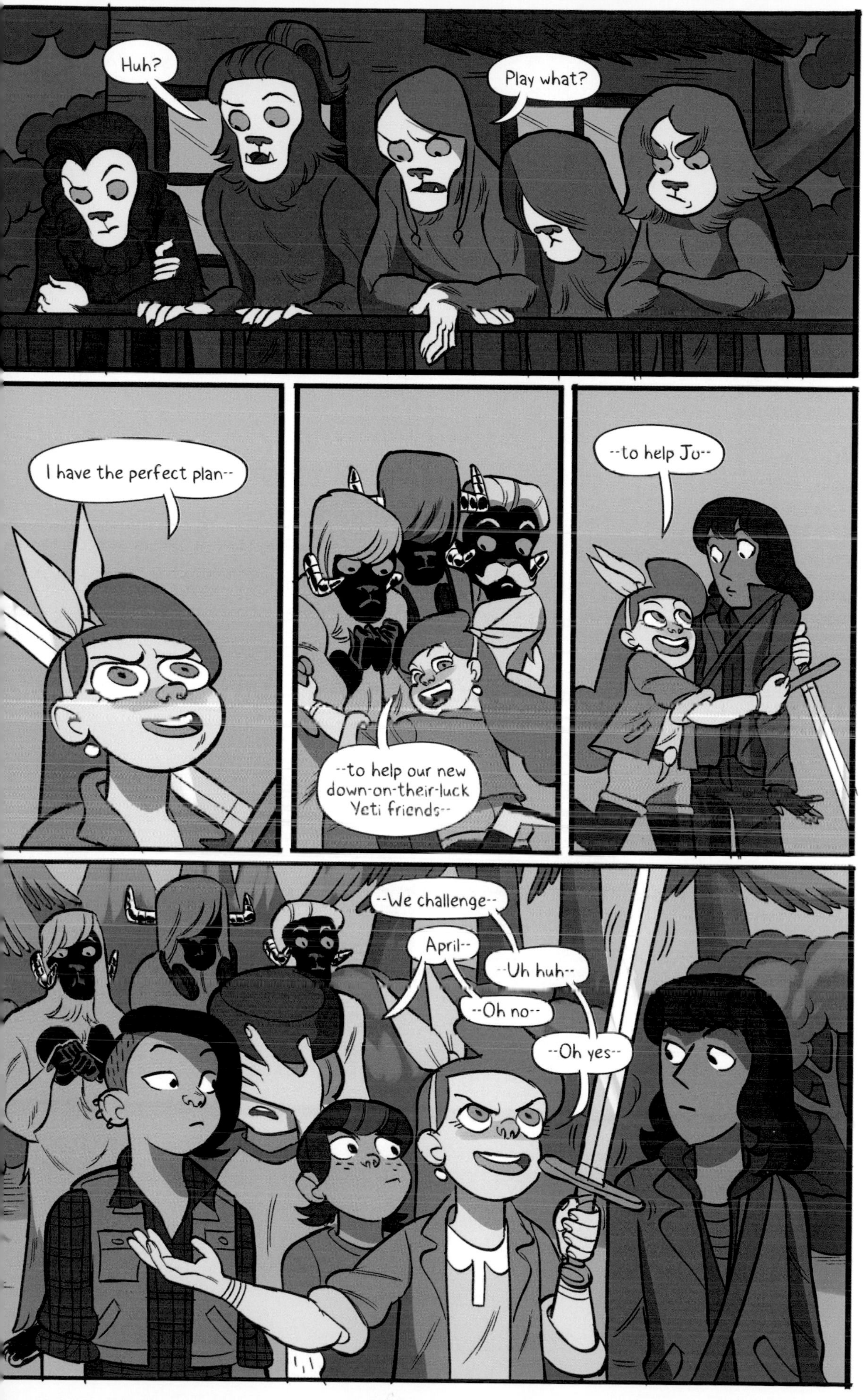
Huh?
Play what?
I have the perfect plan--
--to help our new down-on-their-luck Yeti friends--
--to help Jo--
--We challenge--
April--
--Uh huh--
--Oh no--
--Oh yes--

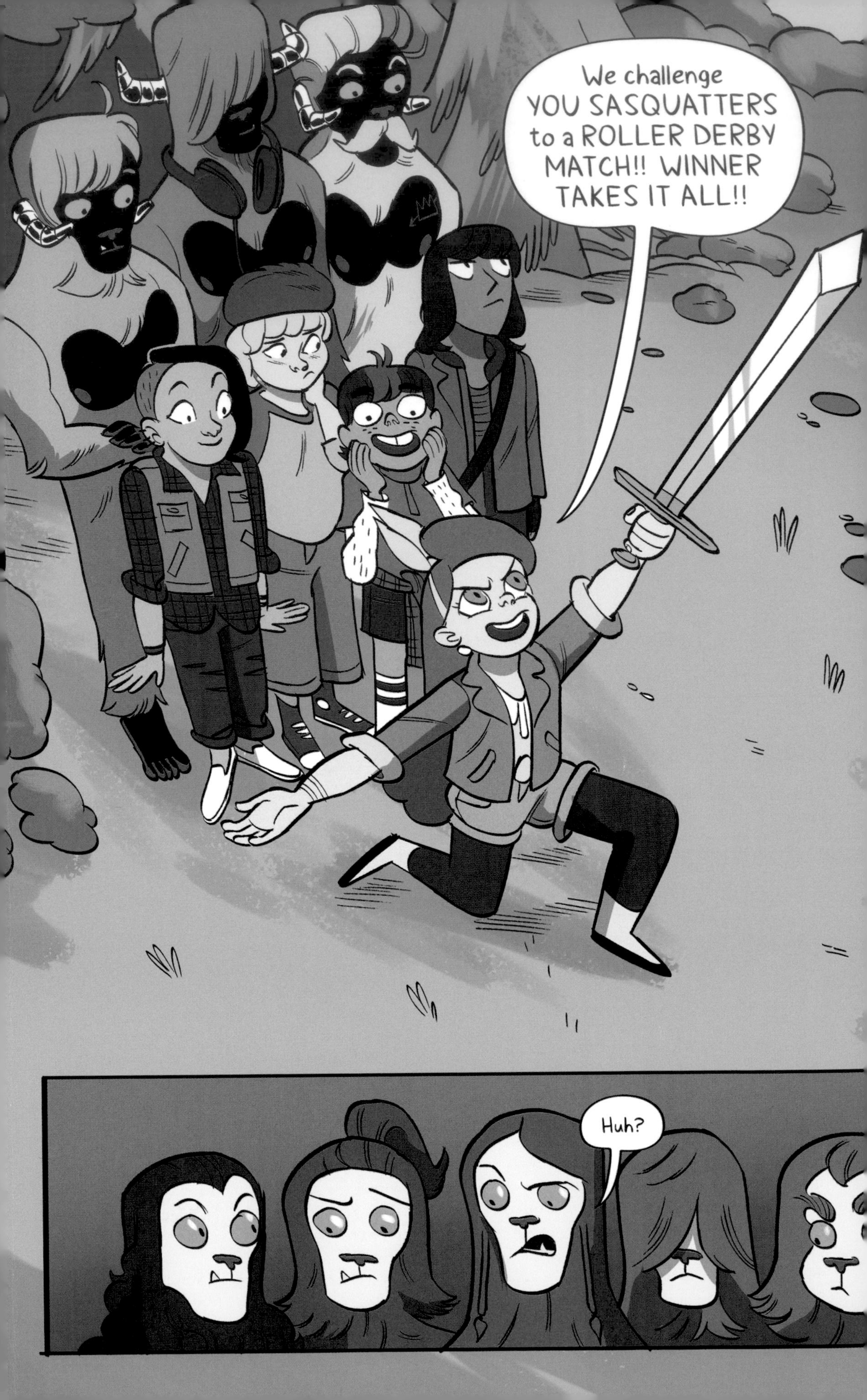
We challenge YOU SASQUATTERS to a ROLLER DERBY MATCH!! WINNER TAKES IT ALL!!
Huh?

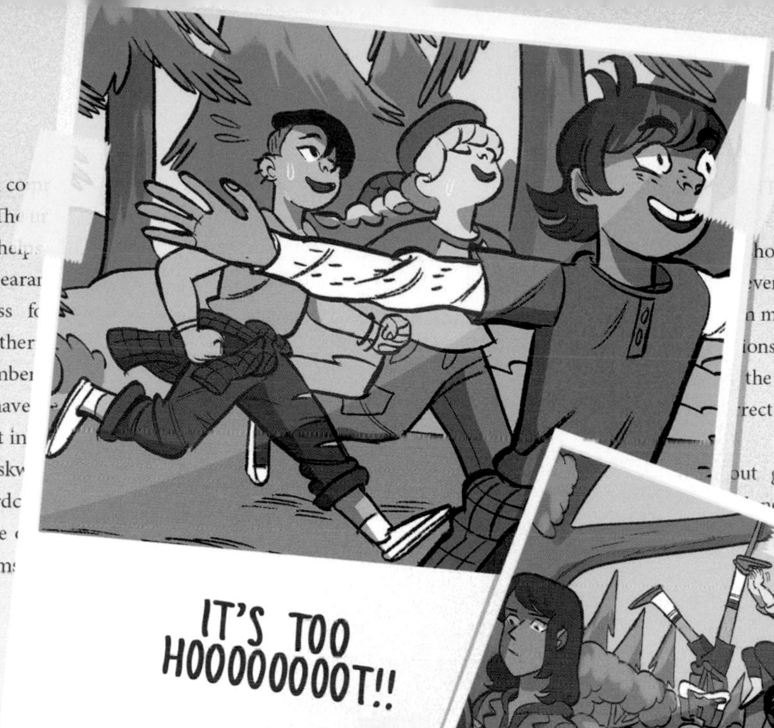
IT'S TOO HOOOOOOOOT!!

will co

Th

It he

appearar

dress fo

Further

Lumber

to have

part in

Thiskw

Hardc

have

thems

HE UNIFORM

hould be worn at camp events when Lumberjanes n may also be worn at other ions. It should be worn as a the uniform dress with rect shoes, and stocking or

out grows her uniform or ter Lumberjane. a she has her her

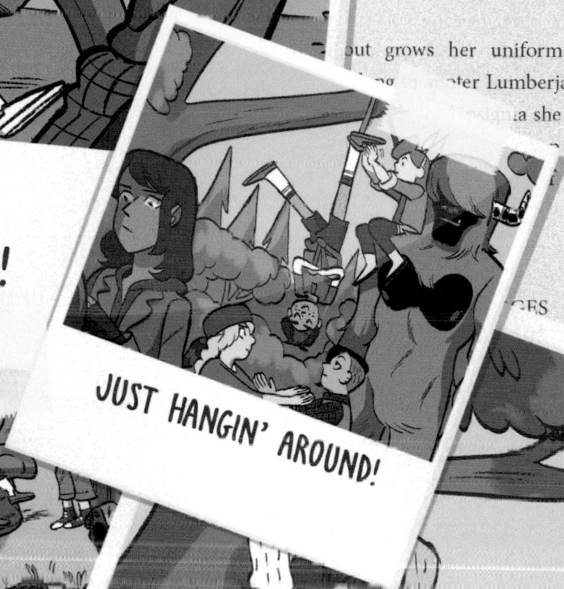
JUST HANGIN' AROUND!

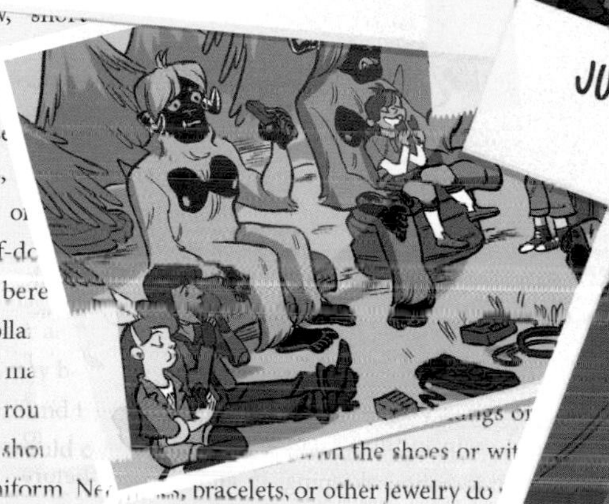

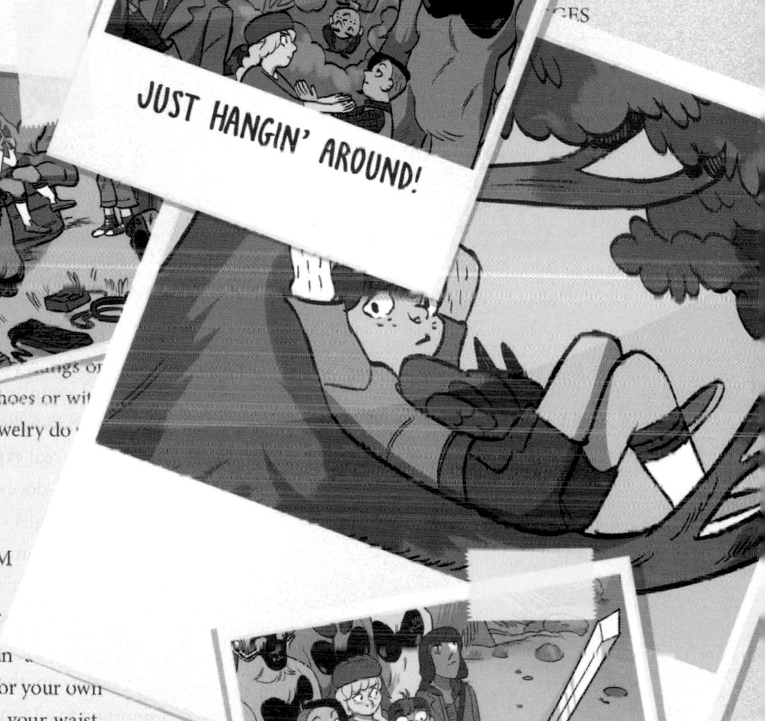

The yellow, emb the w choose slacks, made o out-of-do green bere the colla Shoes ma heels, rou ngs or socks shou th the shoes or wi the uniform Ne bracelets, or other jewelry do belong with a Lumberjane uniform.

HOW TO WEAR THE UNIFORM

To look well in a uniform demands first of uniform be kept in good condition—clean pressed. See that the skirt is the right length for your own height and build, that the belt is adjusted to your waist, that your shoes and stockings are in keeping with the uniform, that you watch your posture and carry yourself with dignity and grace. If the beret is removed indoors, be sure that your hair is neat and kept in place with an insonspicuous clip or ribbon. When you wear a Lumberjane uniform you are identified as a member of this organization and you should be doubly careful to conduct yourself in a way that will show everyone that courtesy and thoughtfullness are part of being a Lumberjane. People are likely to judge a whole nation by the selfishness of a few individuals, to criticize a whole family because of the misconduct of one member, and to feel unkindly toward and organization because of the

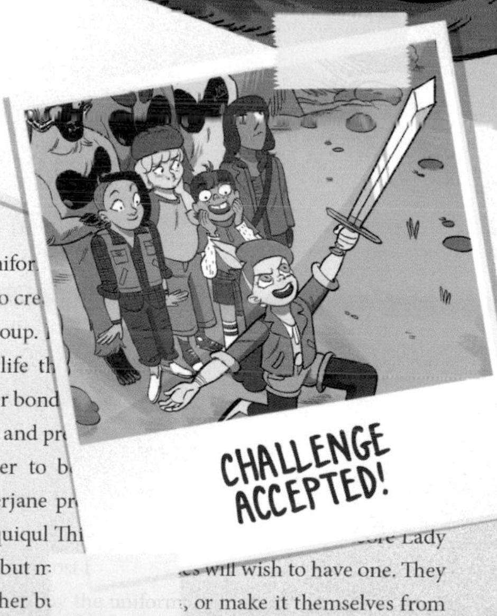
CHALLENGE ACCEPTED!

The unifor helps to cre in a group. active life th another bond future, and pr in order to b Lumberjane pr Penniquiqul Thi Types, but m will wish to have one. They can either bu the uniform, or make it themselves from materials available at the trading post.

LUMBERJANES FIELD MANUAL

CHAPTER
THIRTY-FIVE

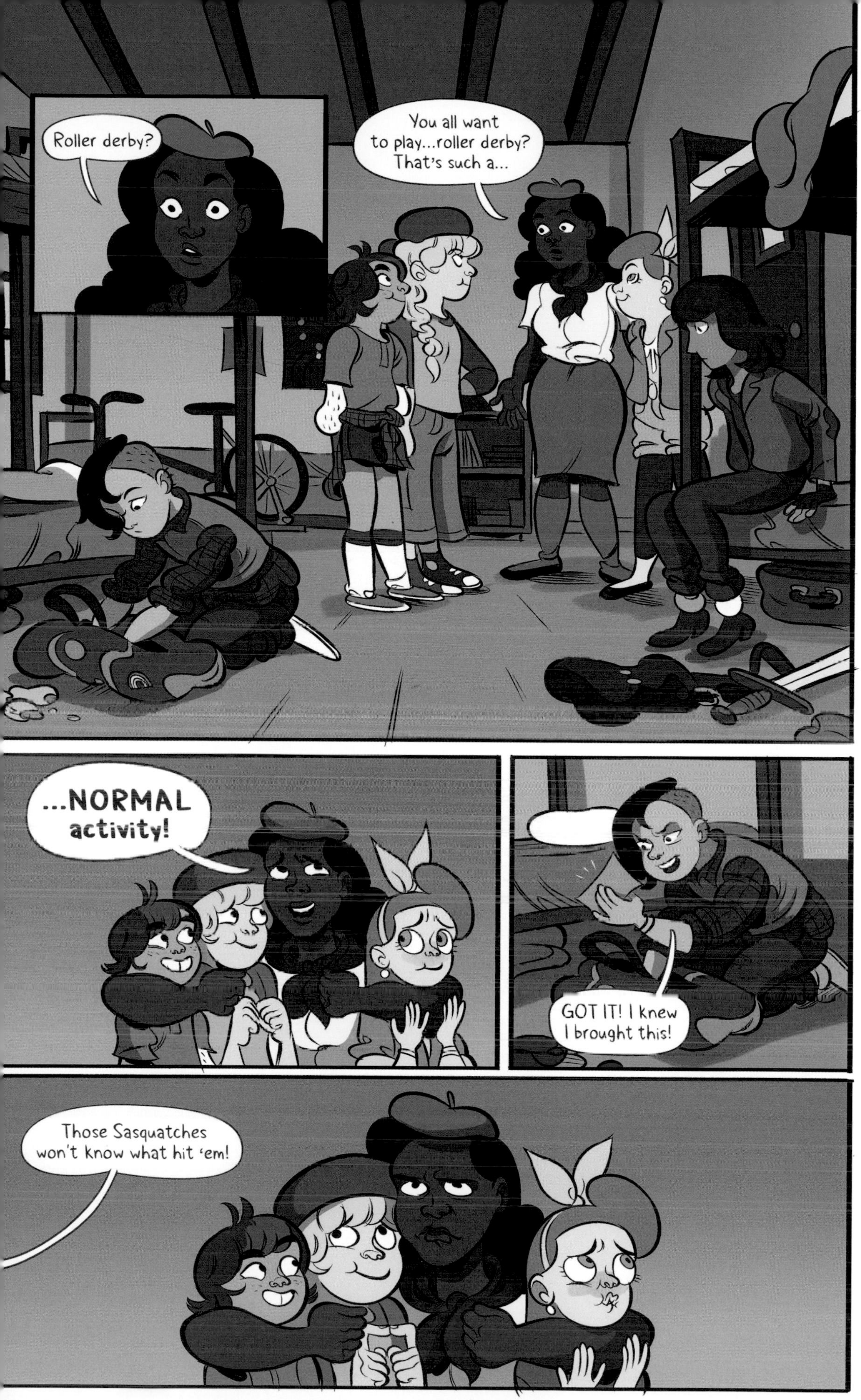

Roller derby?
You all want to play...roller derby? That's such a...
...NORMAL activity!
GOT IT! I knew I brought this!
Those Sasquatches won't know what hit 'em!

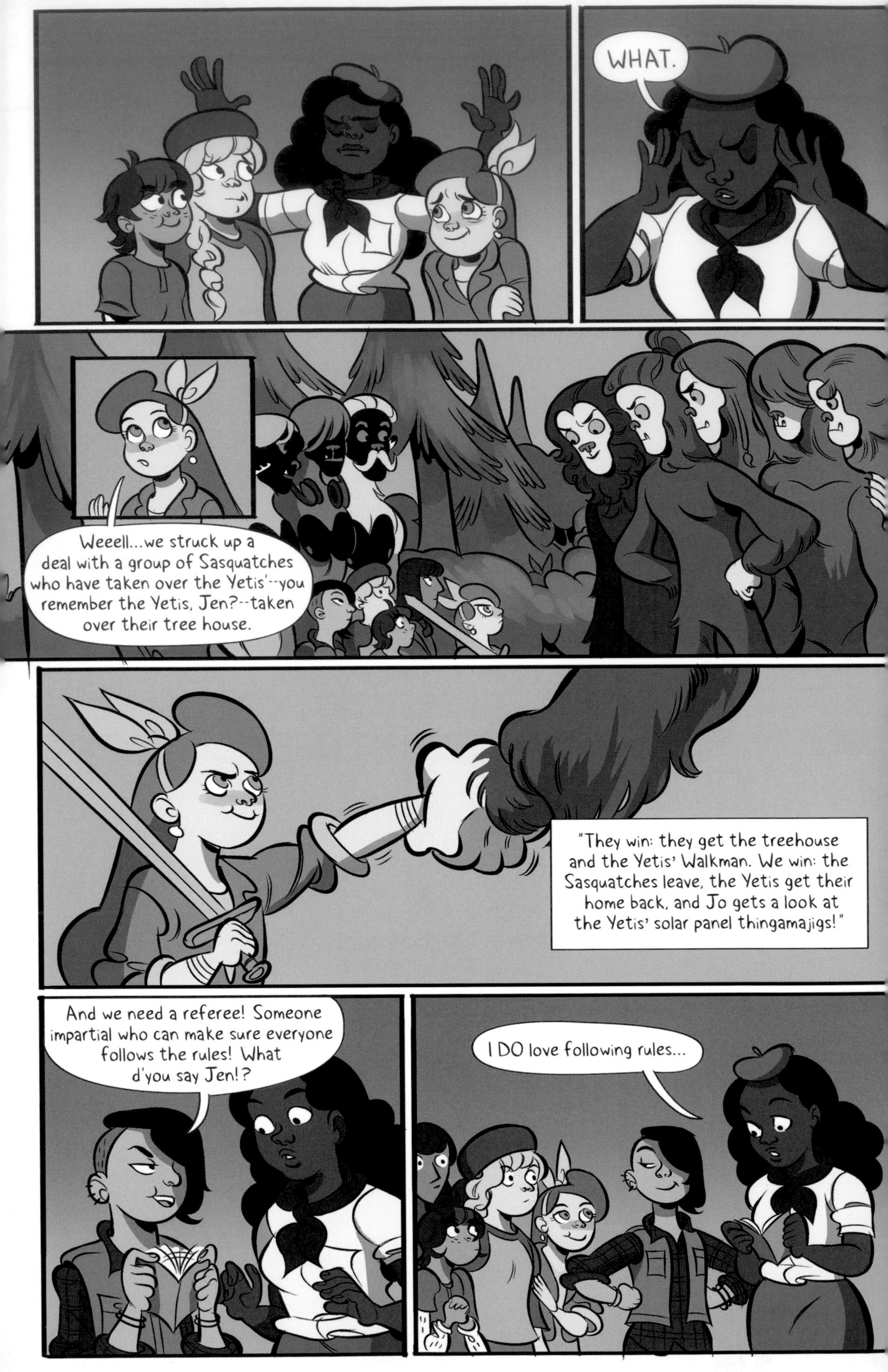
WHAT.
Weeell...we struck up a deal with a group of Sasquatches who have taken over the Yetis'--you remember the Yetis, Jen?--taken over their tree house.
"They win: they get the treehouse and the Yetis' Walkman. We win: the Sasquatches leave, the Yetis get their home back, and Jo gets a look at the Yetis' solar panel thingamajigs!"
And we need a referee! Someone impartial who can make sure everyone follows the rules! What d'you say Jen!?
I DO love following rules...

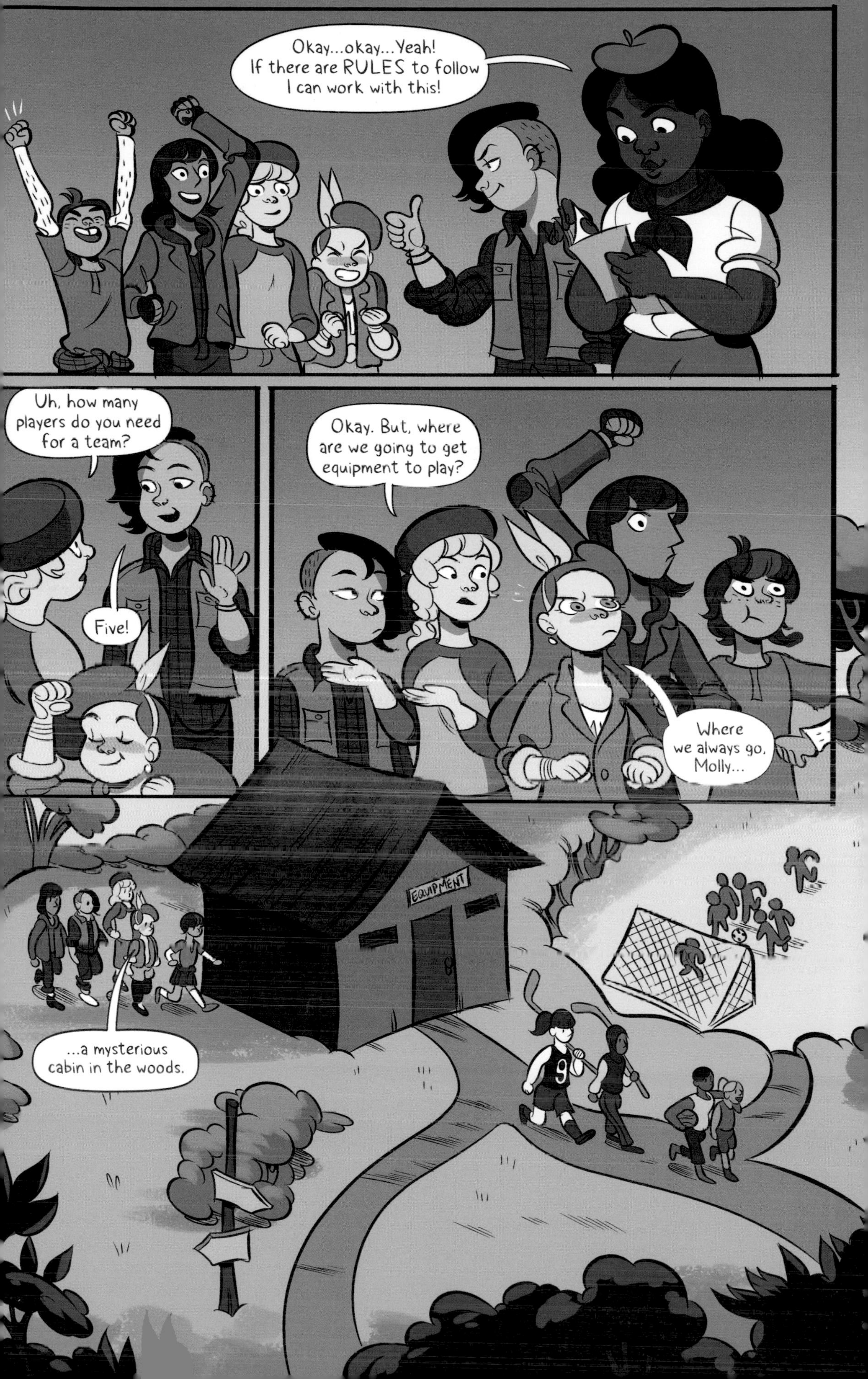
Okay...okay...Yeah! If there are RULES to follow I can work with this!
Uh, how many players do you need for a team?
Five!
Okay. But, where are we going to get equipment to play?
Where we always go, Molly...
...a mysterious cabin in the woods.
EQUIPMENT

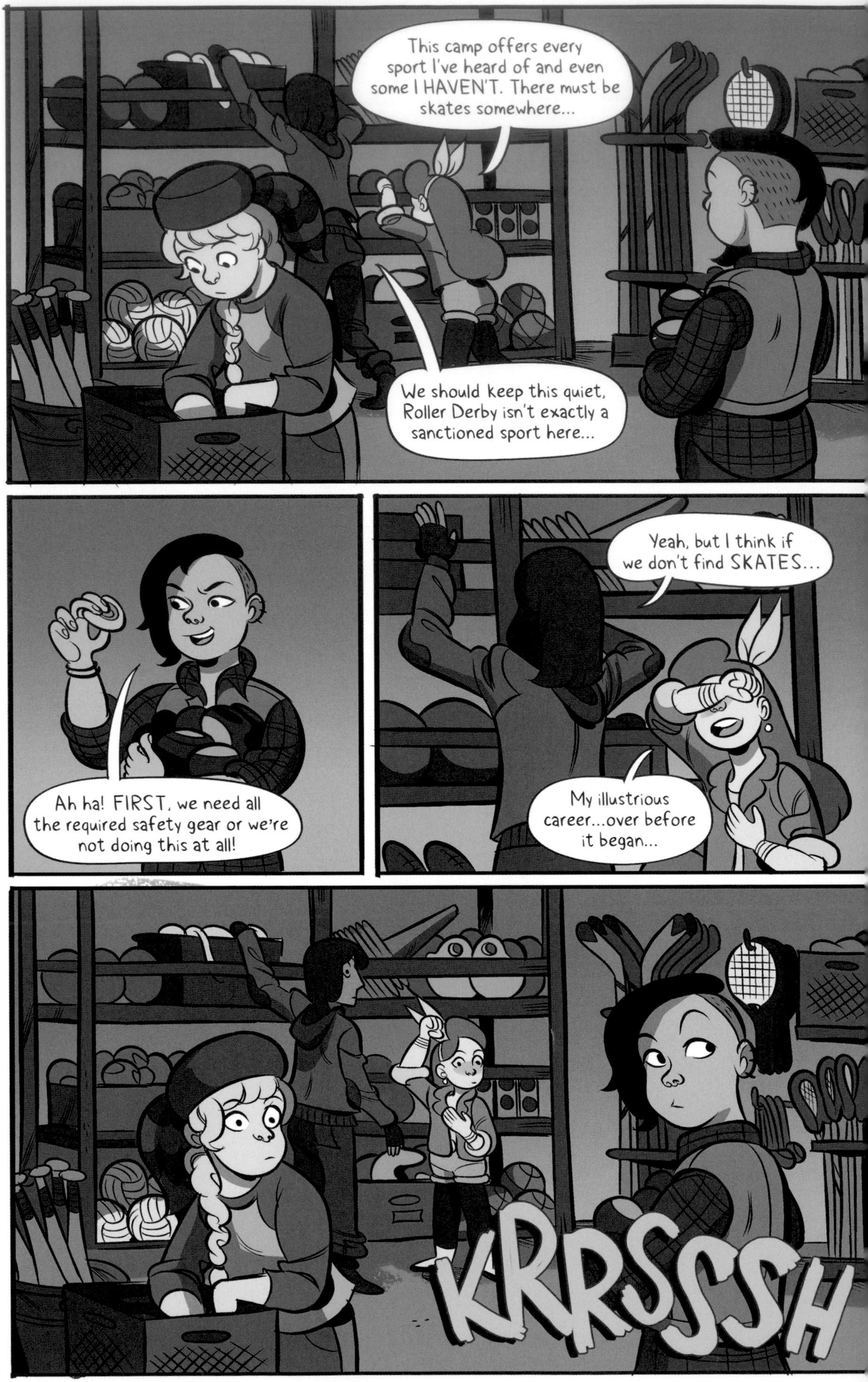
This camp offers every sport I've heard of and even some I HAVEN'T. There must be skates somewhere...
We should keep this quiet, Roller Derby isn't exactly a sanctioned sport here...
Ah ha! FIRST, we need all the required safety gear or we're not doing this at all!
Yeah, but I think if we don't find SKATES...
My illustrious career...over before it began...
KRRSSSH

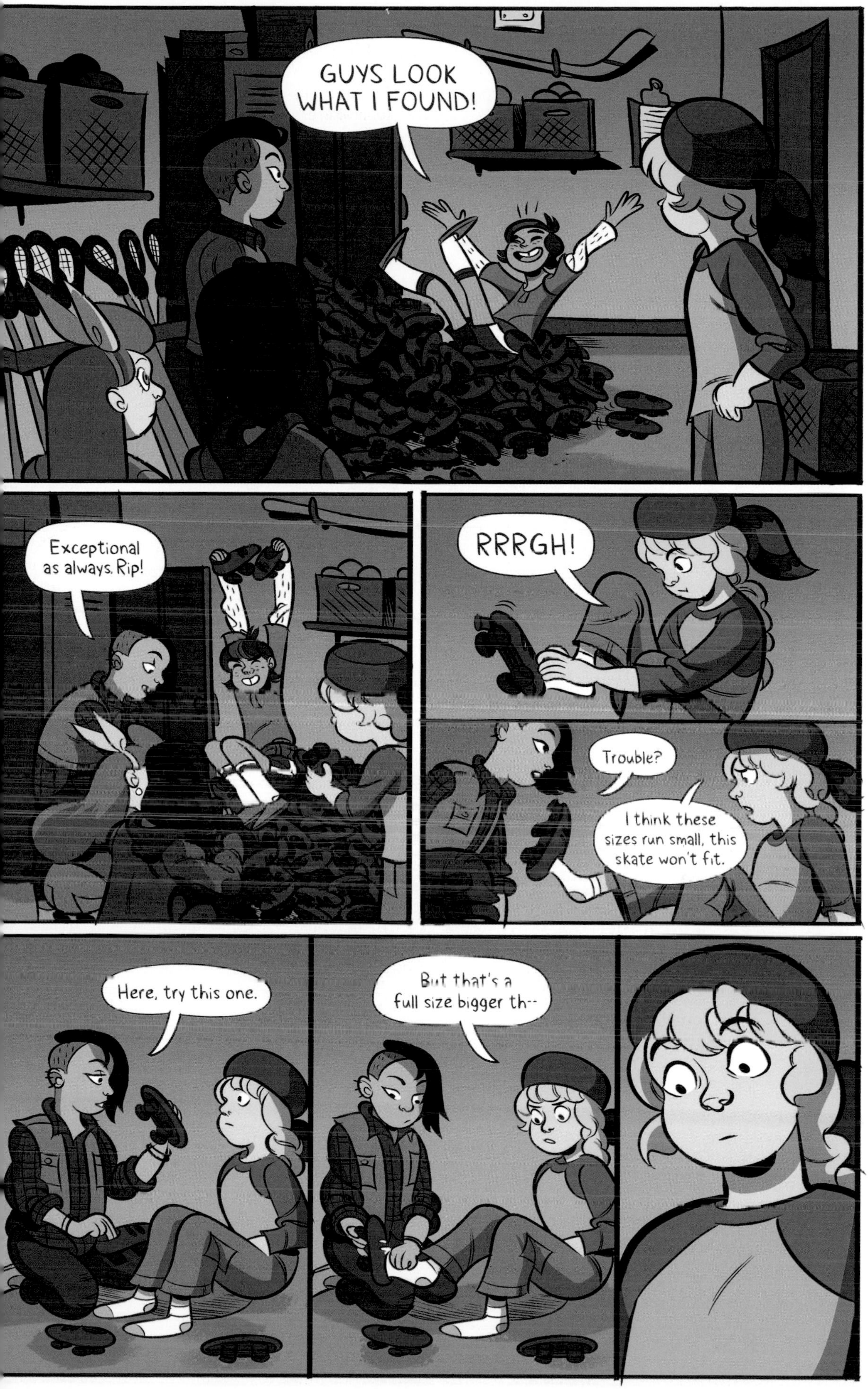
GUYS LOOK WHAT I FOUND!
Exceptional as always, Rip!
RRRGH!
Trouble?
I think these sizes run small, this skate won't fit.
Here, try this one.
But that's a full size bigger th--

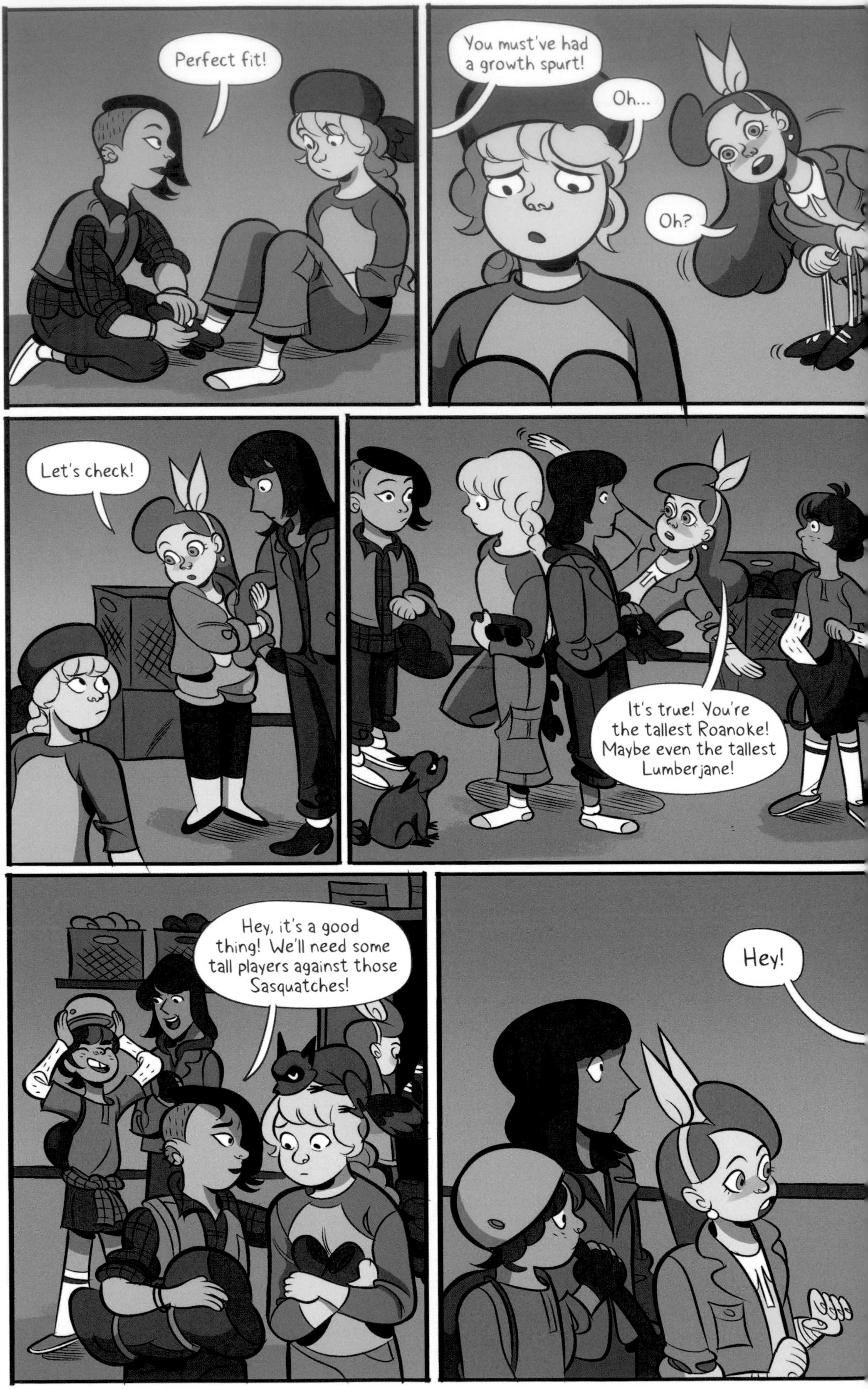
Perfect fit!
You must've had a growth spurt!
Oh...
Oh?
Let's check!
It's true! You're the tallest Roanoke! Maybe even the tallest Lumberjane!
Hey, it's a good thing! We'll need some tall players against those Sasquatches!
Hey!

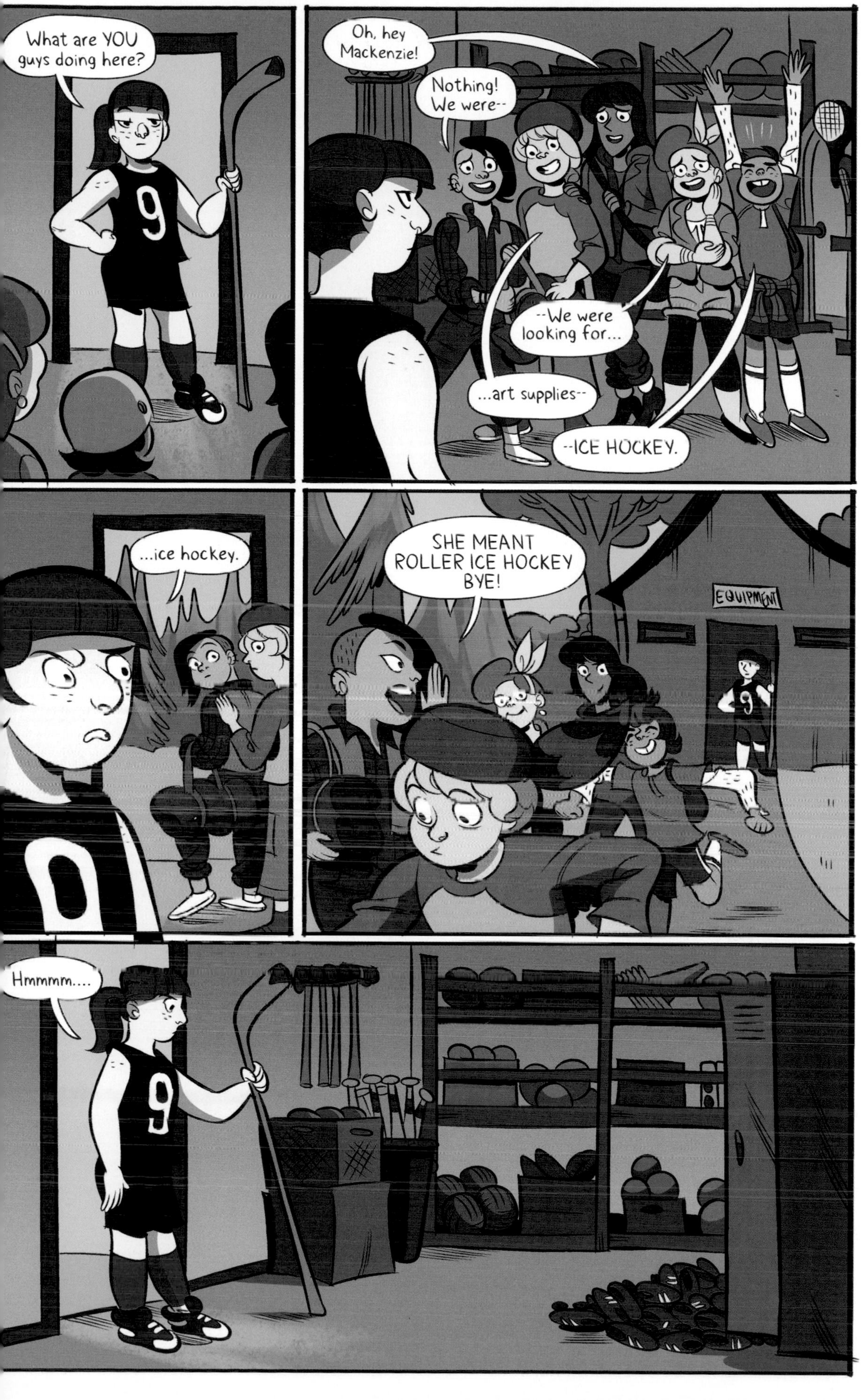
What are YOU guys doing here?
Oh, hey Mackenzie!
Nothing! We were--
--We were looking for...
...art supplies--
--ICE HOCKEY.
...ice hockey.
SHE MEANT ROLLER ICE HOCKEY BYE!
EQUIPMENT
Hmmmm....

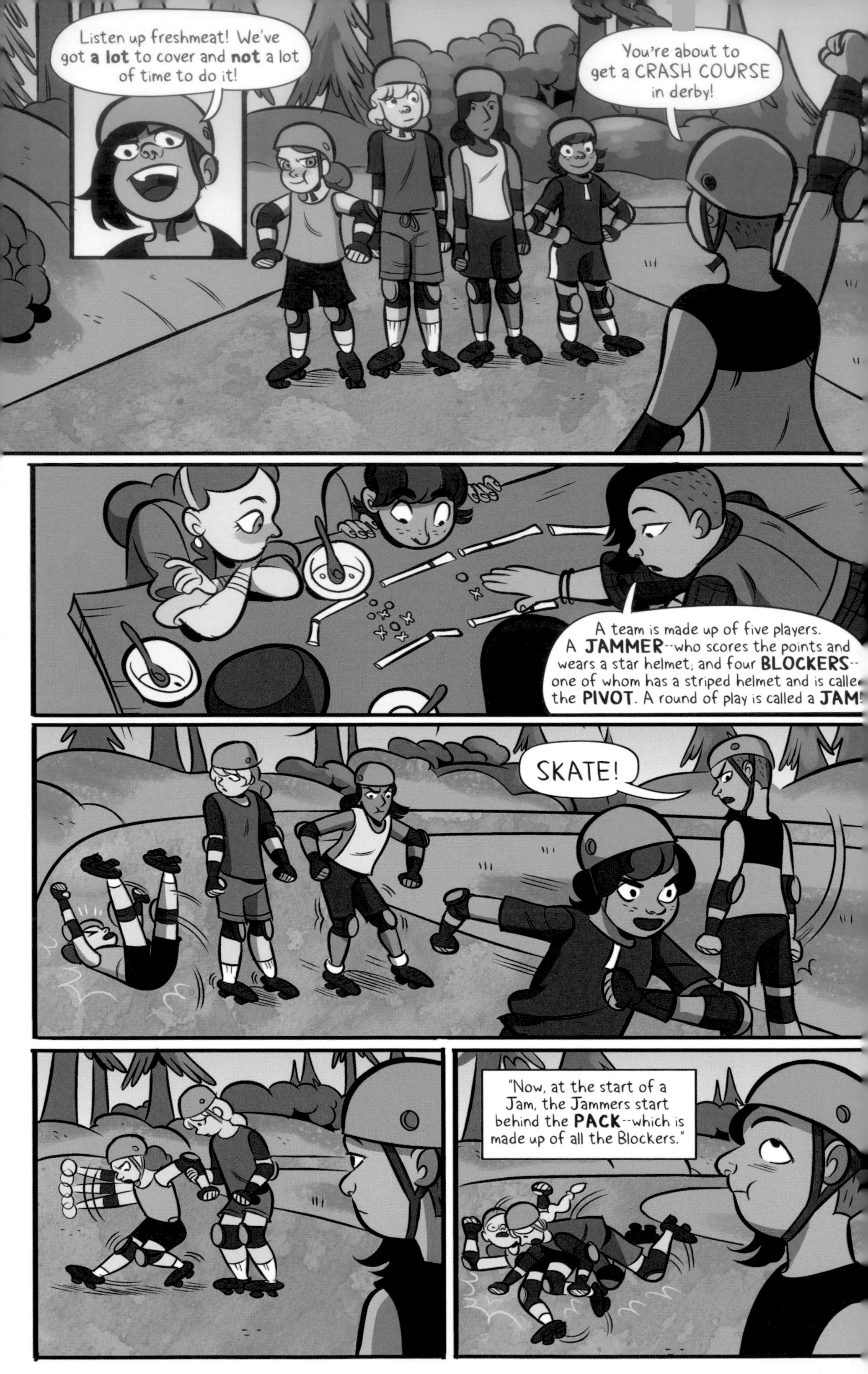
Listen up freshmeat! We've got **a lot** to cover and **not** a lot of time to do it!
You're about to get a CRASH COURSE in derby!
A team is made up of five players. A **JAMMER**--who scores the points and wears a star helmet; and four **BLOCKERS**--one of whom has a striped helmet and is calle the **PIVOT**. A round of play is called a **JAM**
SKATE!
"Now, at the start of a Jam, the Jammers start behind the **PACK**--which is made up of all the Blockers."

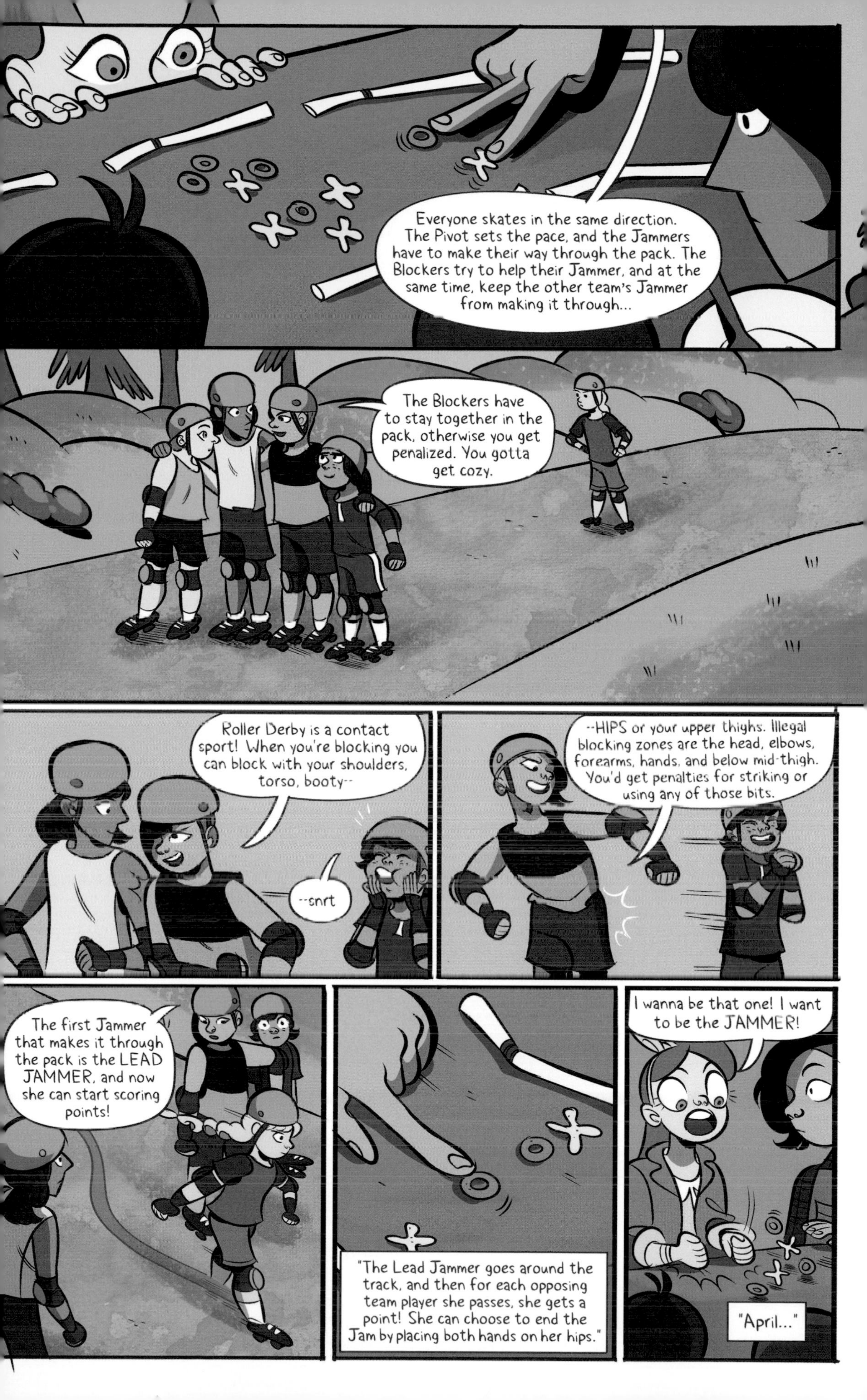
Everyone skates in the same direction. The Pivot sets the pace, and the Jammers have to make their way through the pack. The Blockers try to help their Jammer, and at the same time, keep the other team's Jammer from making it through...
The Blockers have to stay together in the pack, otherwise you get penalized. You gotta get cozy.
Roller Derby is a contact sport! When you're blocking you can block with your shoulders, torso, booty--
--snrt
--HIPS or your upper thighs. Illegal blocking zones are the head, elbows, forearms, hands, and below mid-thigh. You'd get penalties for striking or using any of those bits.
The first Jammer that makes it through the pack is the LEAD JAMMER, and now she can start scoring points!
"The Lead Jammer goes around the track, and then for each opposing team player she passes, she gets a point! She can choose to end the Jam by placing both hands on her hips."
I wanna be that one! I want to be the JAMMER!
"April..."

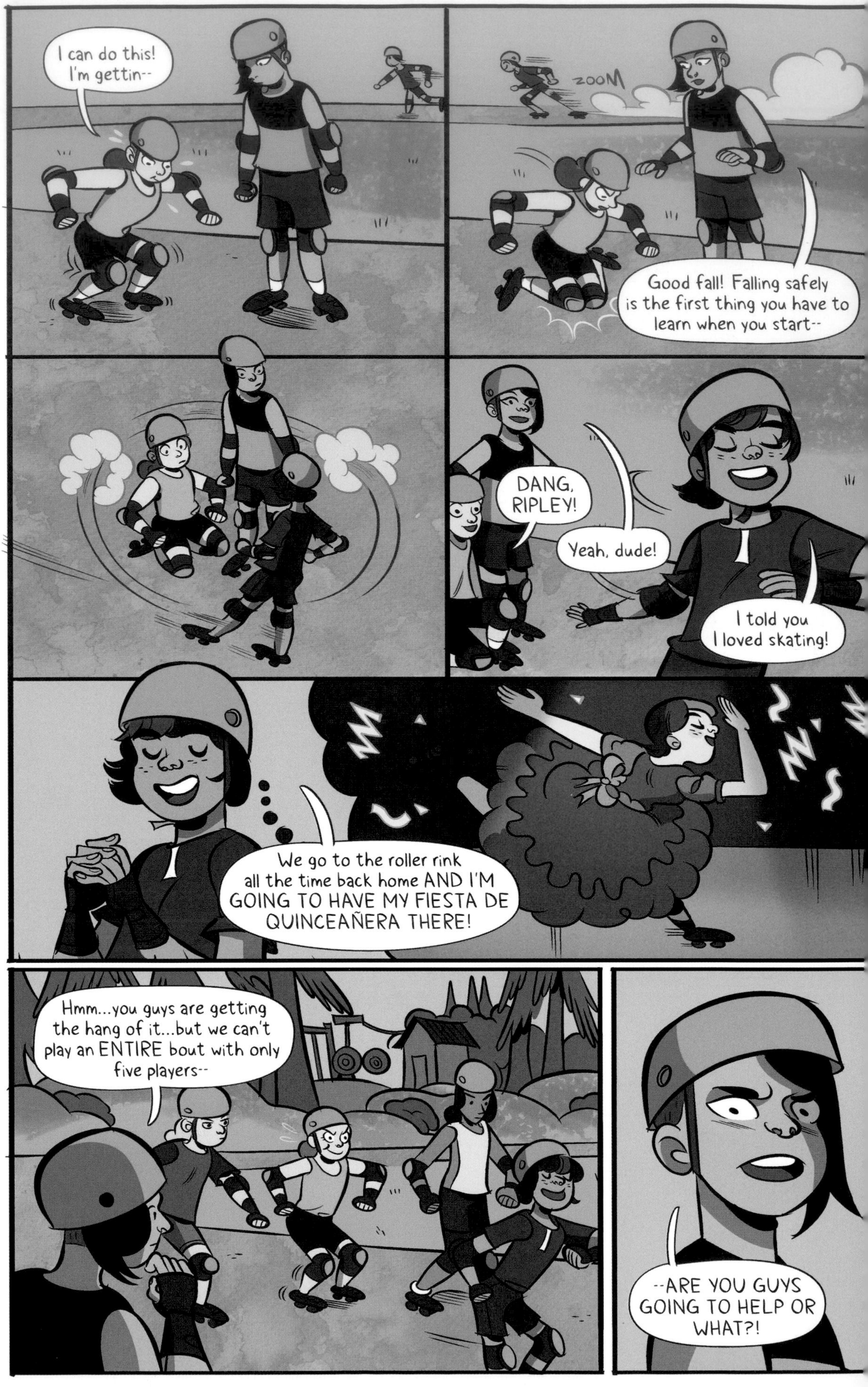
I can do this! I'm gettin--
zooM
Good fall! Falling safely is the first thing you have to learn when you start--
DANG, RIPLEY!
Yeah, dude!
I told you I loved skating!
We go to the roller rink all the time back home AND I'M GOING TO HAVE MY FIESTA DE QUINCEAÑERA THERE!
Hmm...you guys are getting the hang of it...but we can't play an ENTIRE bout with only five players--
--ARE YOU GUYS GOING TO HELP OR WHAT?!

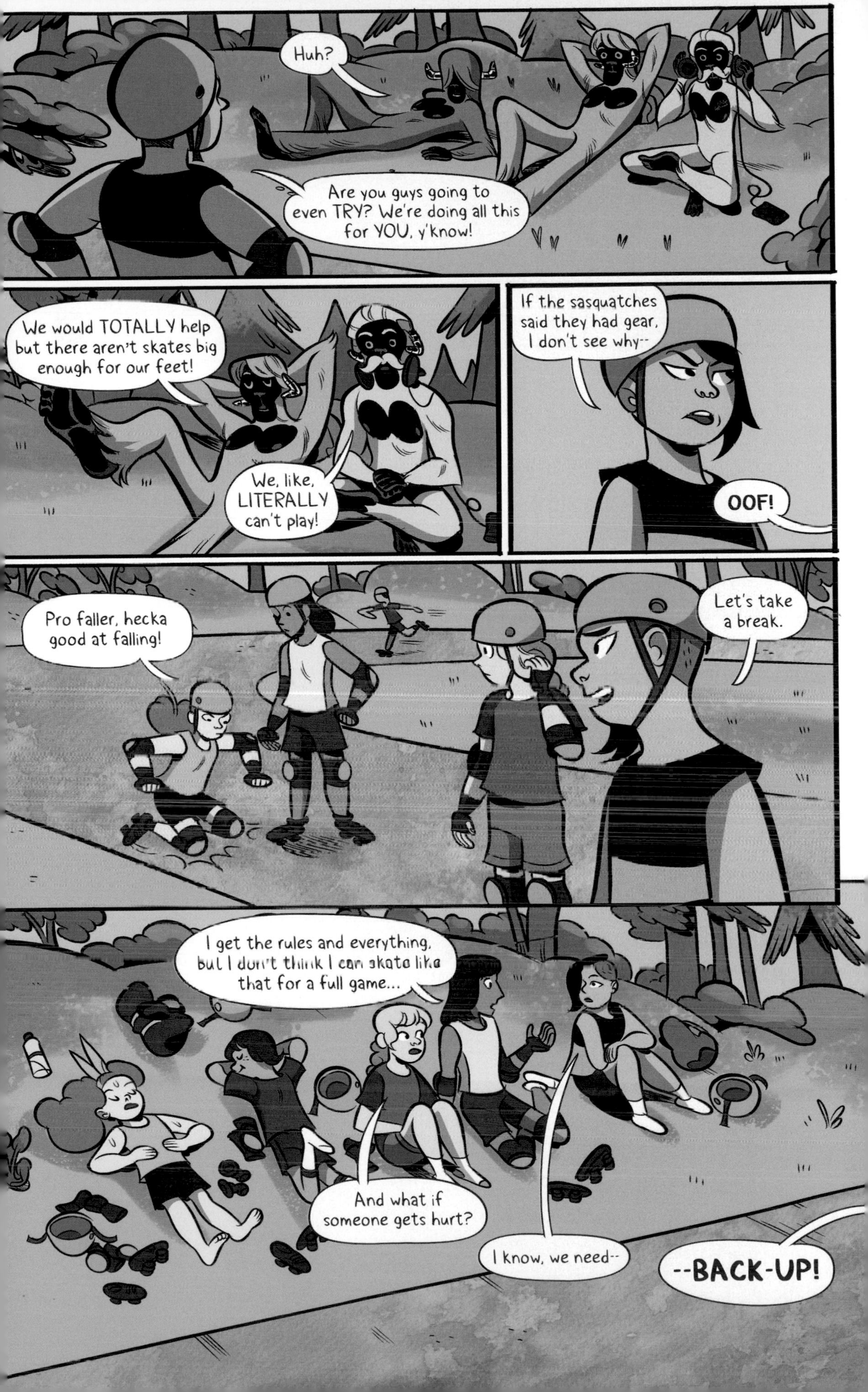
Huh?
Are you guys going to even TRY? We're doing all this for YOU, y'know!
We would TOTALLY help but there aren't skates big enough for our feet!
We, like, LITERALLY can't play!
If the sasquatches said they had gear, I don't see why--
OOF!
Pro faller, hecka good at falling!
Let's take a break.
I get the rules and everything, but I don't think I can skate like that for a full game...
And what if someone gets hurt?
I know, we need--
--BACK-UP!

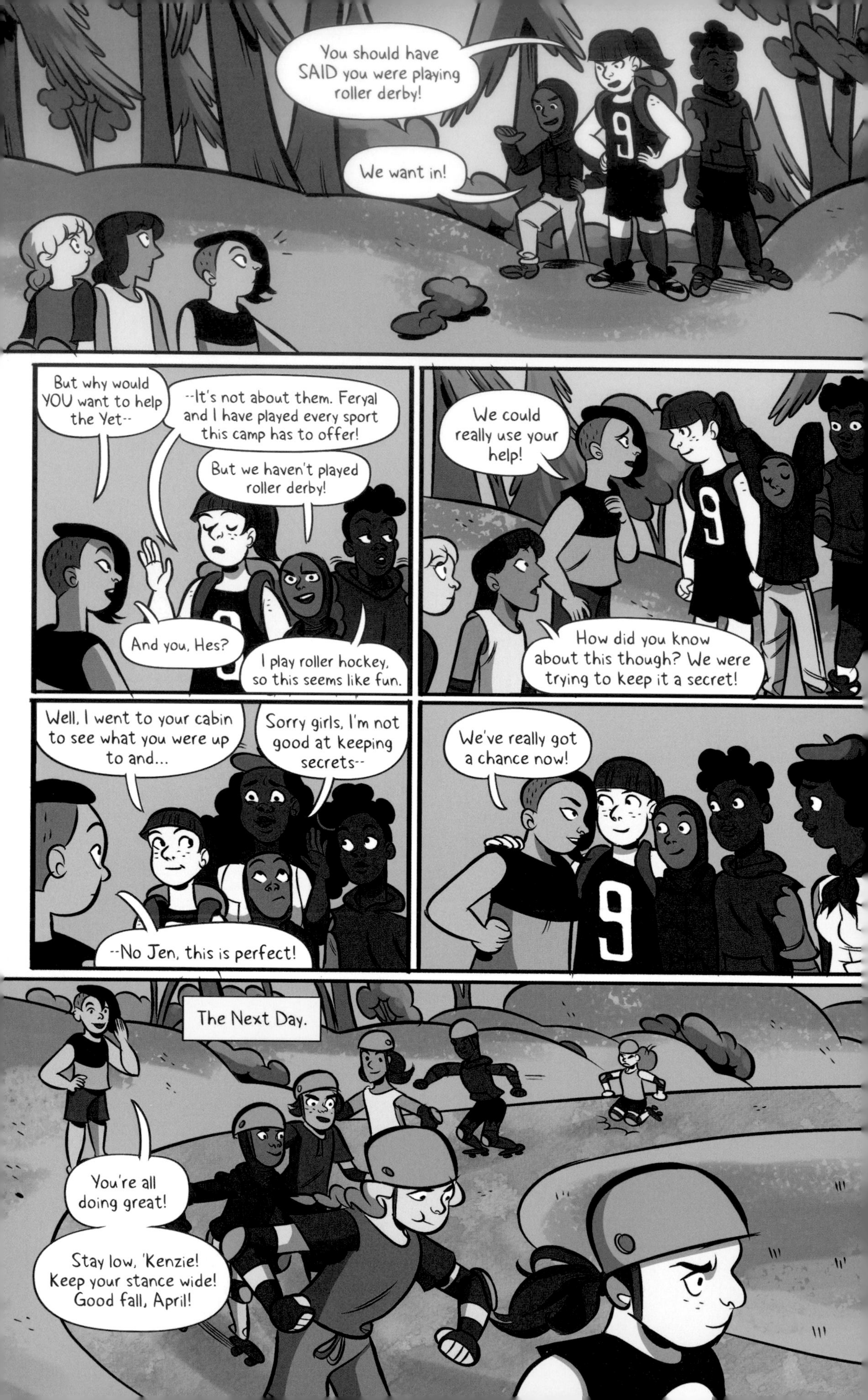
You should have SAID you were playing roller derby!
We want in!
But why would YOU want to help the Yet--
--It's not about them. Feryal and I have played every sport this camp has to offer!
But we haven't played roller derby!
And you, Hes?
I play roller hockey, so this seems like fun.
We could really use your help!
How did you know about this though? We were trying to keep it a secret!
Well, I went to your cabin to see what you were up to and...
Sorry girls, I'm not good at keeping secrets--
--No Jen, this is perfect!
We've really got a chance now!
The Next Day.
You're all doing great!
Stay low, 'Kenzie! Keep your stance wide! Good fall, April!

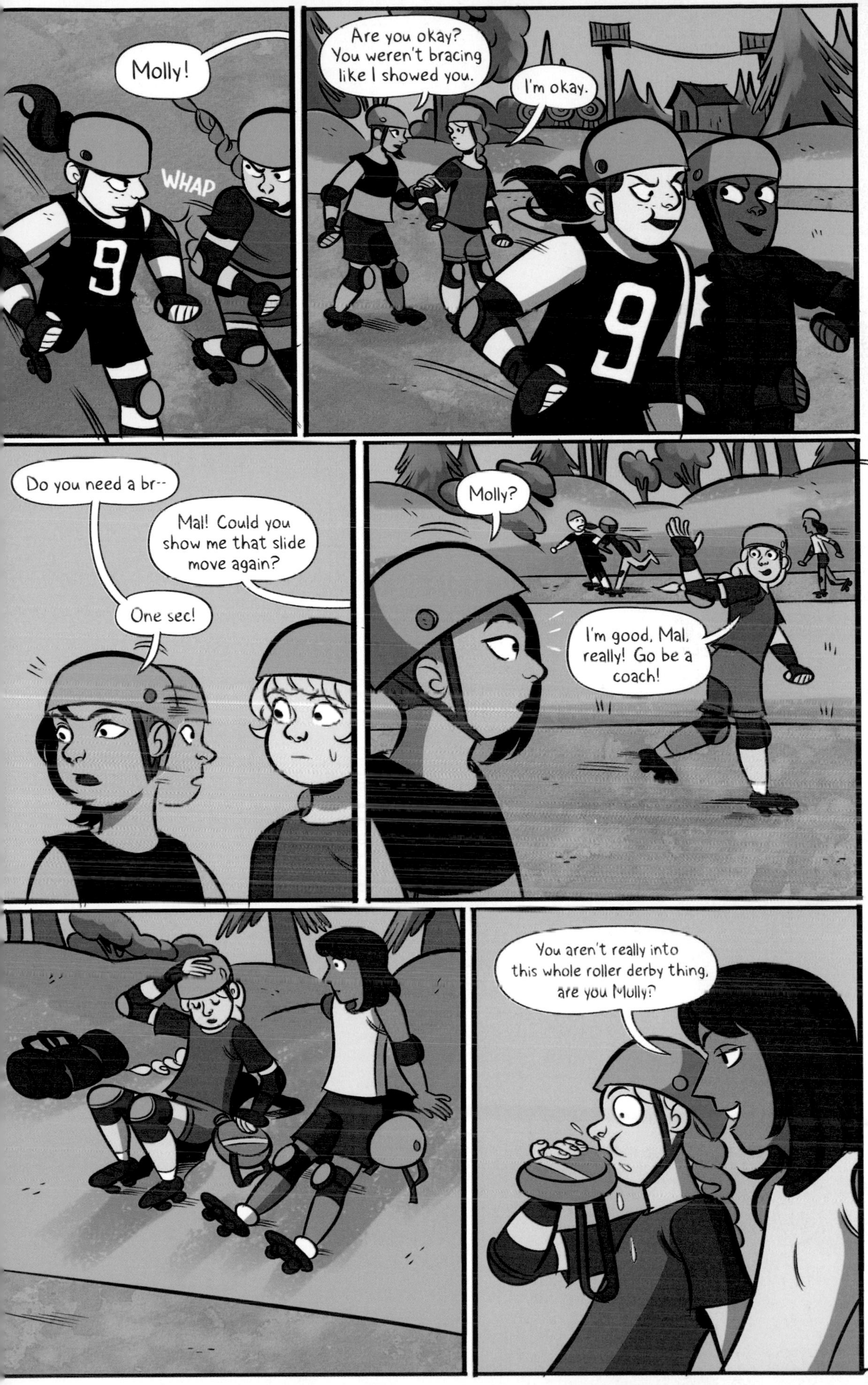
Molly!
WHAP
Are you okay? You weren't bracing like I showed you.
I'm okay.
Do you need a br--
Mal! Could you show me that slide move again?
One sec!
Molly?
I'm good, Mal, really! Go be a coach!
You aren't really into this whole roller derby thing, are you Molly?

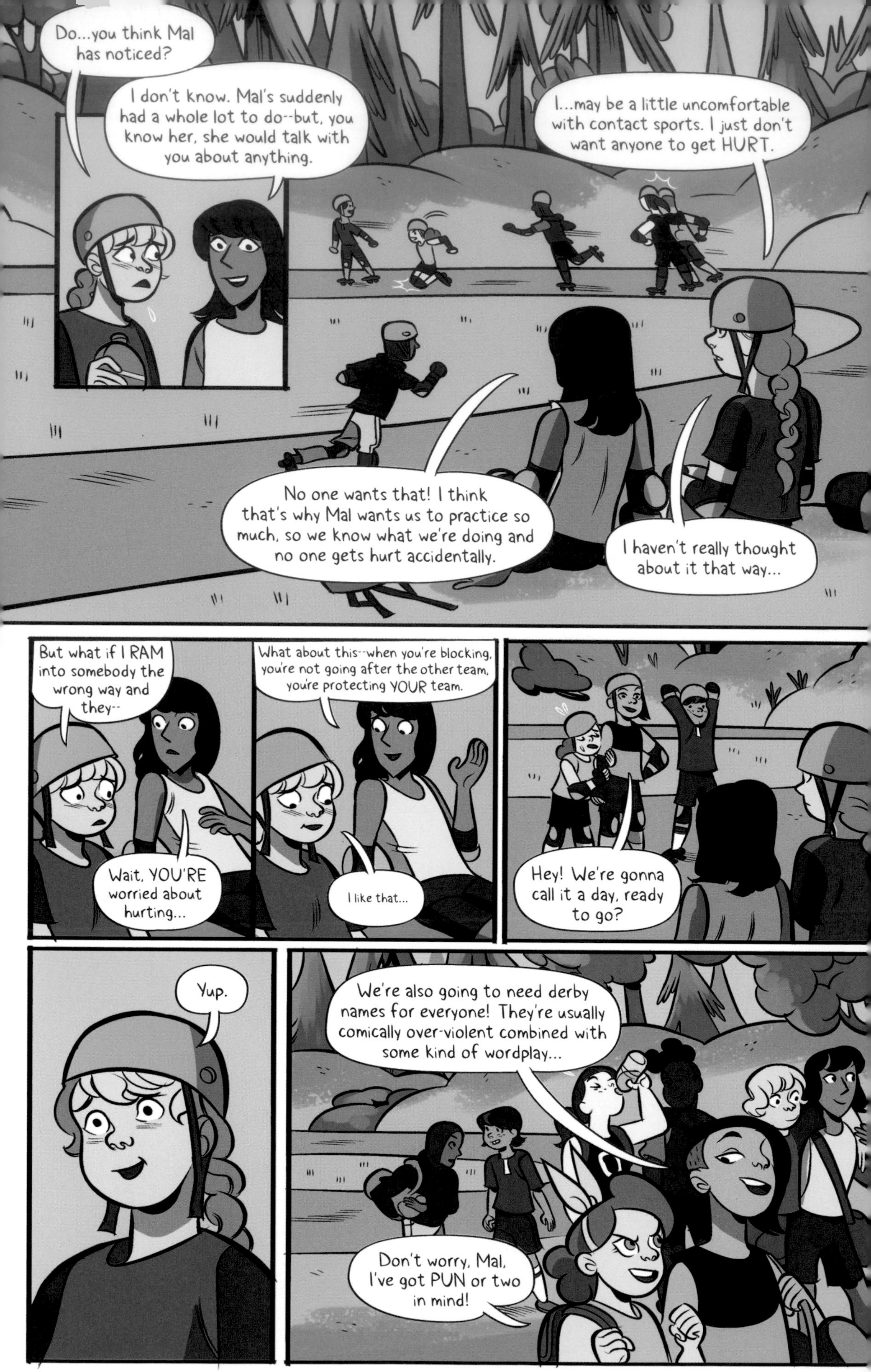
Do...you think Mal has noticed?
I don't know. Mal's suddenly had a whole lot to do--but, you know her, she would talk with you about anything.
I...may be a little uncomfortable with contact sports. I just don't want anyone to get HURT.
No one wants that! I think that's why Mal wants us to practice so much, so we know what we're doing and no one gets hurt accidentally.
I haven't really thought about it that way...
But what if I RAM into somebody the wrong way and they--
Wait, YOU'RE worried about hurting...
What about this--when you're blocking, you're not going after the other team, you're protecting YOUR team.
I like that...
Hey! We're gonna call it a day, ready to go?
Yup.
We're also going to need derby names for everyone! They're usually comically over-violent combined with some kind of wordplay...
Don't worry, Mal, I've got PUN or two in mind!

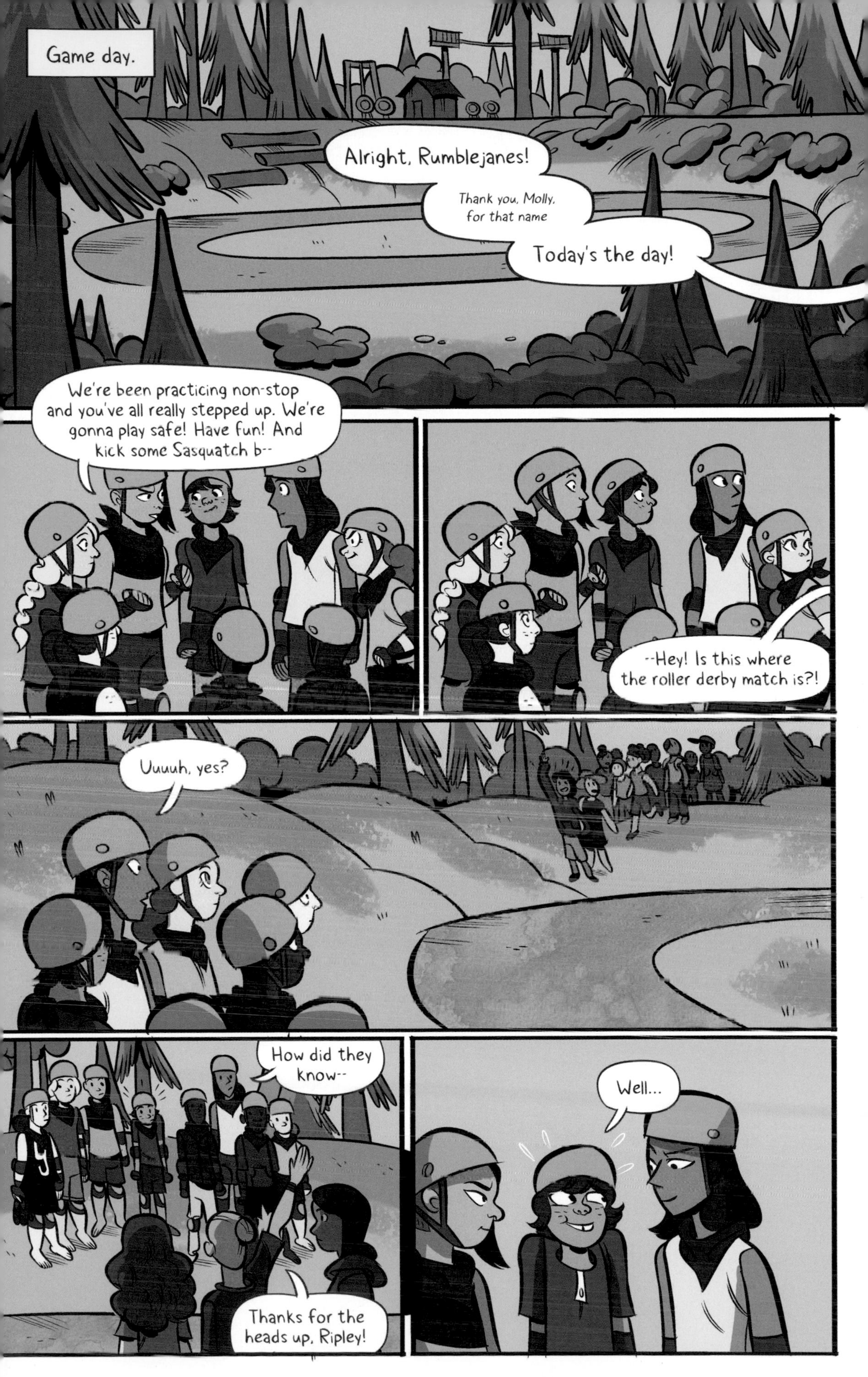
Game day.
Alright, Rumblejanes!
Thank you, Molly, for that name
Today's the day!
We're been practicing non-stop and you've all really stepped up. We're gonna play safe! Have fun! And kick some Sasquatch b--
--Hey! Is this where the roller derby match is?!
Uuuuh, yes?
How did they know--
Thanks for the heads up, Ripley!
Well...

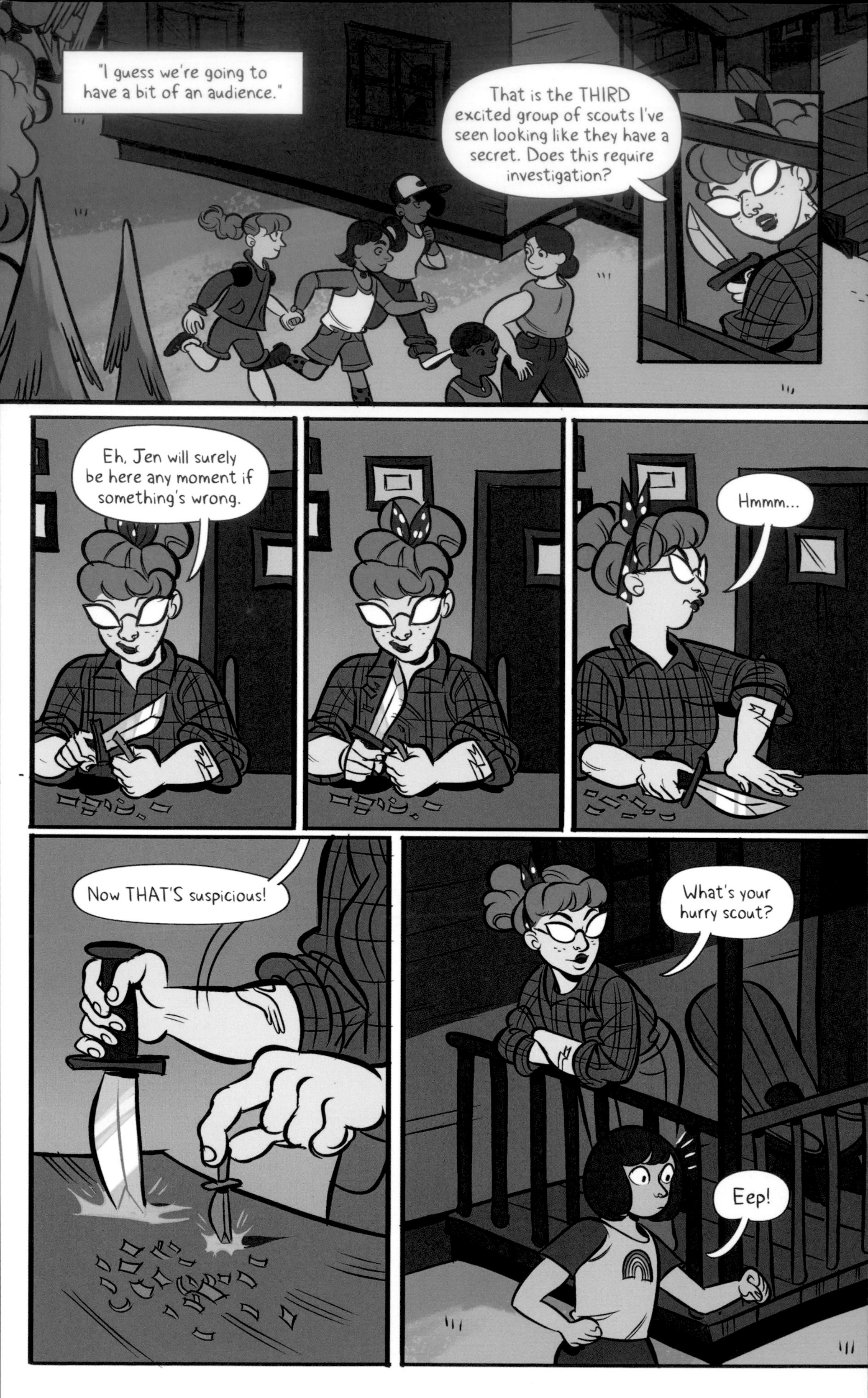
"I guess we're going to have a bit of an audience."
That is the THIRD excited group of scouts I've seen looking like they have a secret. Does this require investigation?
Eh, Jen will surely be here any moment if something's wrong.
Hmmm...
Now THAT'S suspicious!
What's your hurry scout?
Eep!

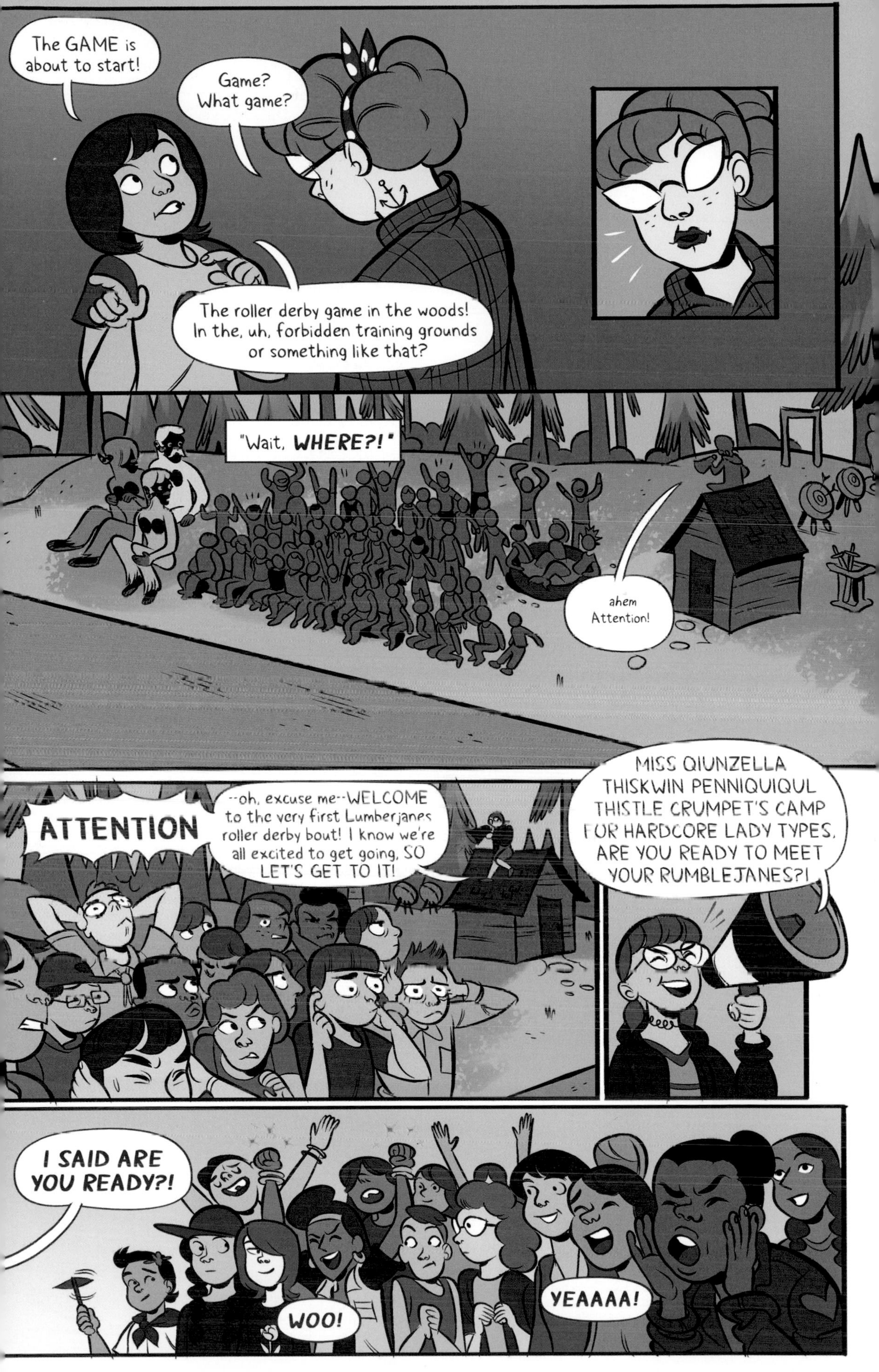
The GAME is about to start!
Game? What game?
The roller derby game in the woods! In the, uh, forbidden training grounds or something like that?
"Wait, WHERE?!"
ahem Attention!
ATTENTION
--oh, excuse me--WELCOME to the very first Lumberjanes roller derby bout! I know we're all excited to get going, SO LET'S GET TO IT!
MISS QIUNZELLA THISKWIN PENNIQUIQUL THISTLE CRUMPET'S CAMP FOR HARDCORE LADY TYPES, ARE YOU READY TO MEET YOUR RUMBLEJANES?!
I SAID ARE YOU READY?!
WOO!
YEAAAA!

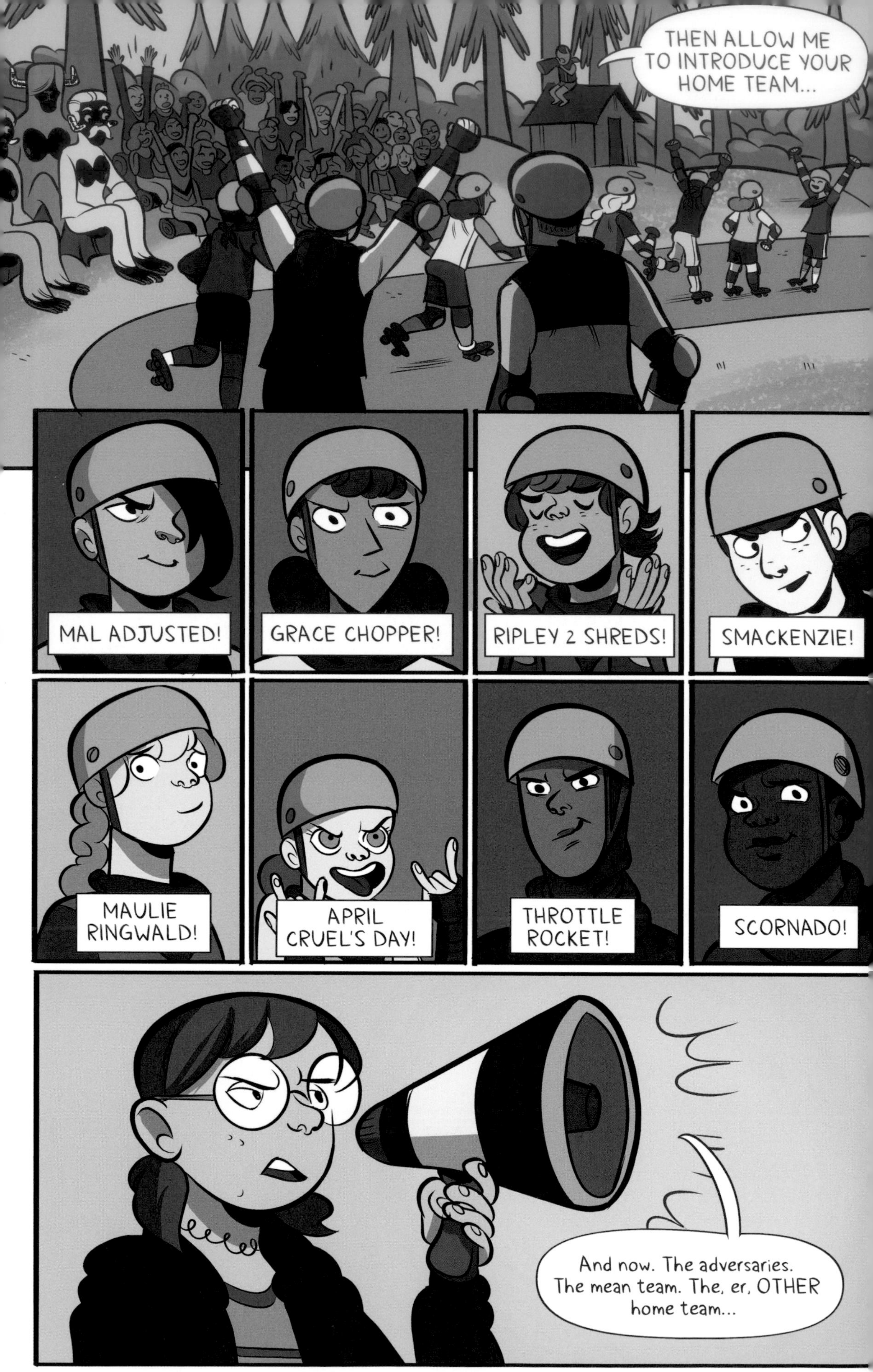
THEN ALLOW ME TO INTRODUCE YOUR HOME TEAM...
MAL ADJUSTED!
GRACE CHOPPER!
RIPLEY 2 SHREDS!
SMACKENZIE!
MAULIE RINGWALD!
APRIL CRUEL'S DAY!
THROTTLE ROCKET!
SCORNADO!
And now. The adversaries. The mean team. The, er, OTHER home team...

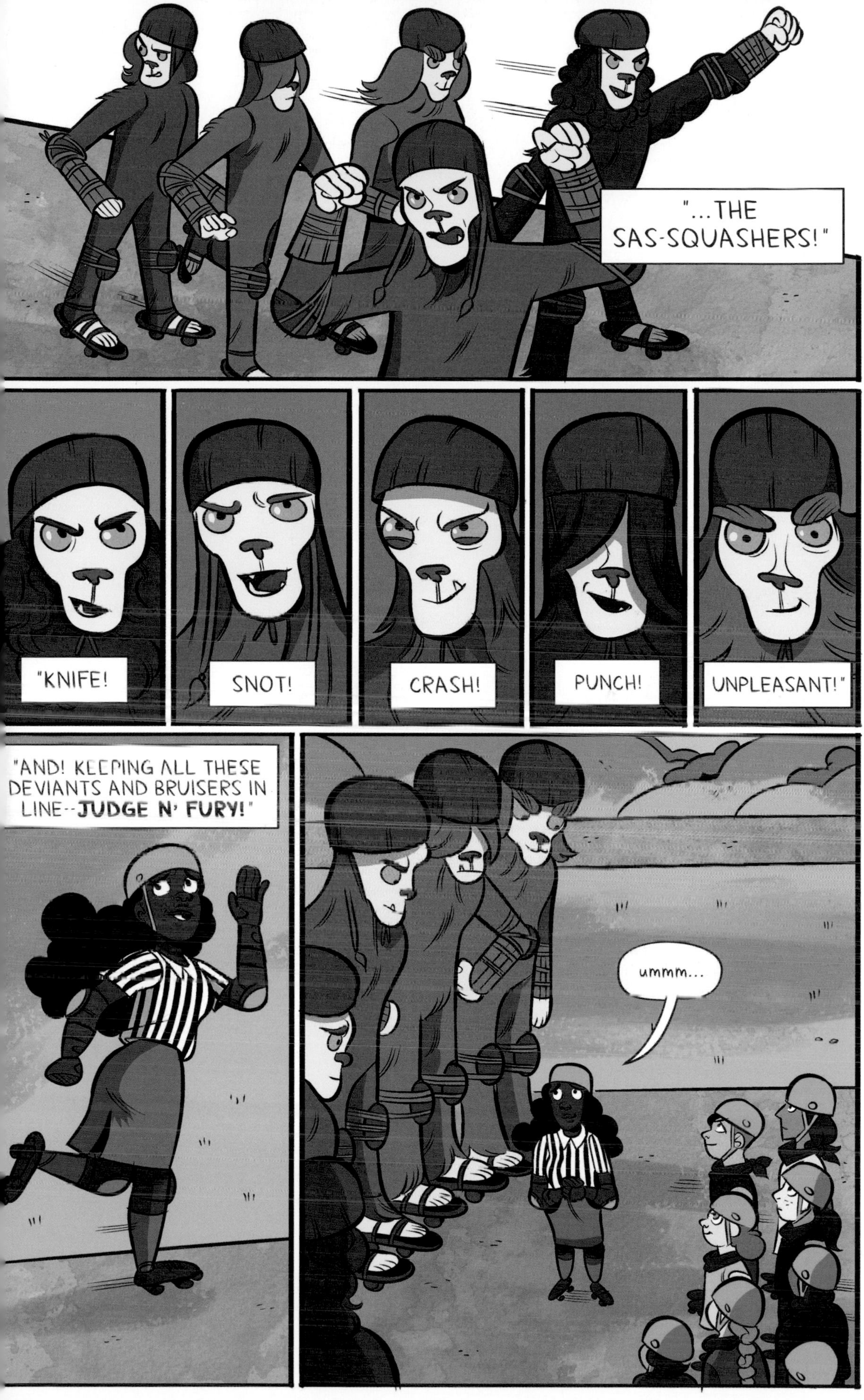
"...THE SAS-SQUASHERS!"
"KNIFE!
SNOT!
CRASH!
PUNCH!
UNPLEASANT!"
"AND! KEEPING ALL THESE DEVIANTS AND BRUISERS IN LINE--JUDGE N' FURY!"
ummm...

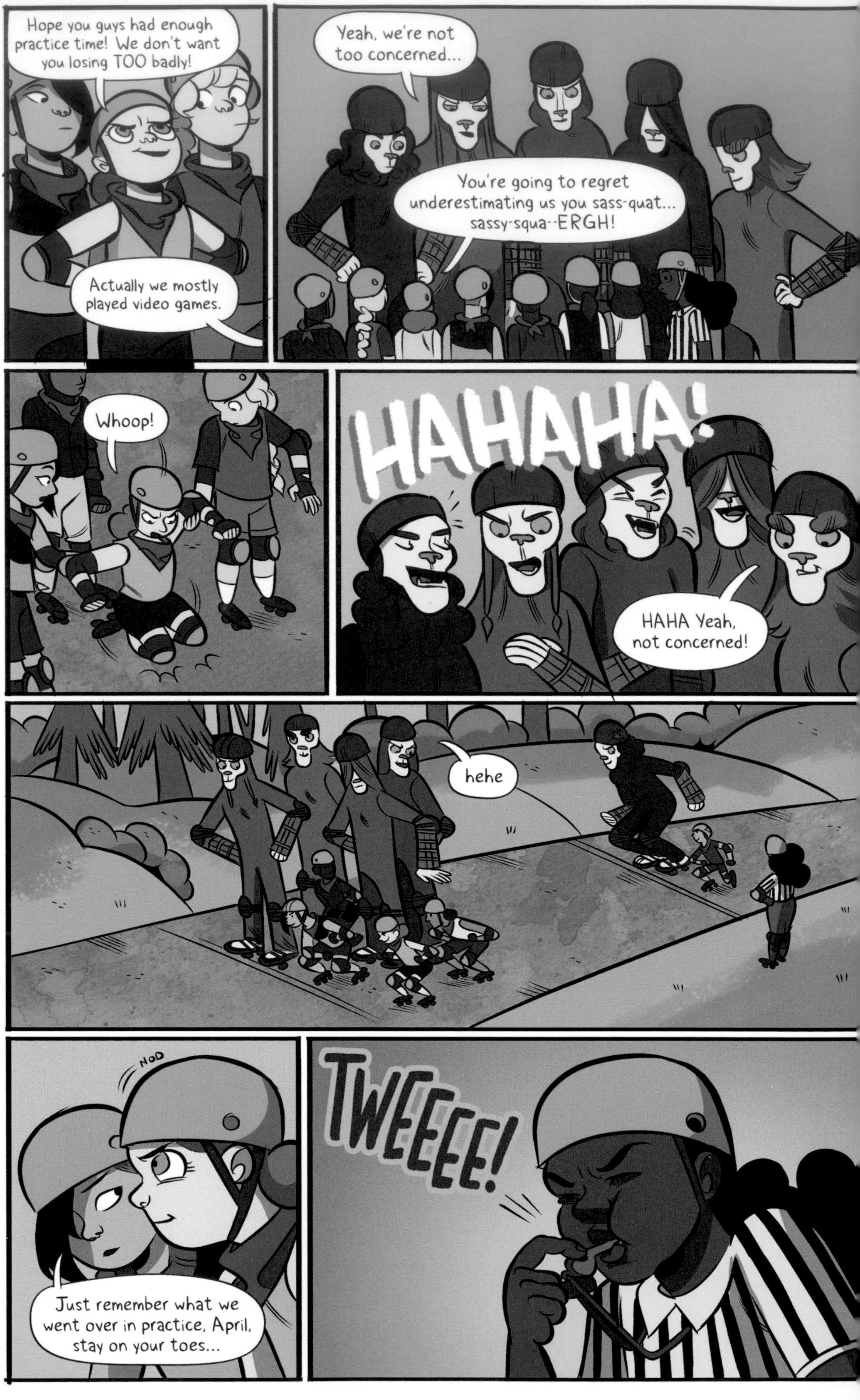
Hope you guys had enough practice time! We don't want you losing TOO badly!
Actually we mostly played video games.
Yeah, we're not too concerned...
You're going to regret underestimating us you sass-quat... sassy-squa--ERGH!
Whoop!
HAHAHA!
HAHA Yeah, not concerned!
hehe
NOD
Just remember what we went over in practice, April, stay on your toes...
TWEEEE!

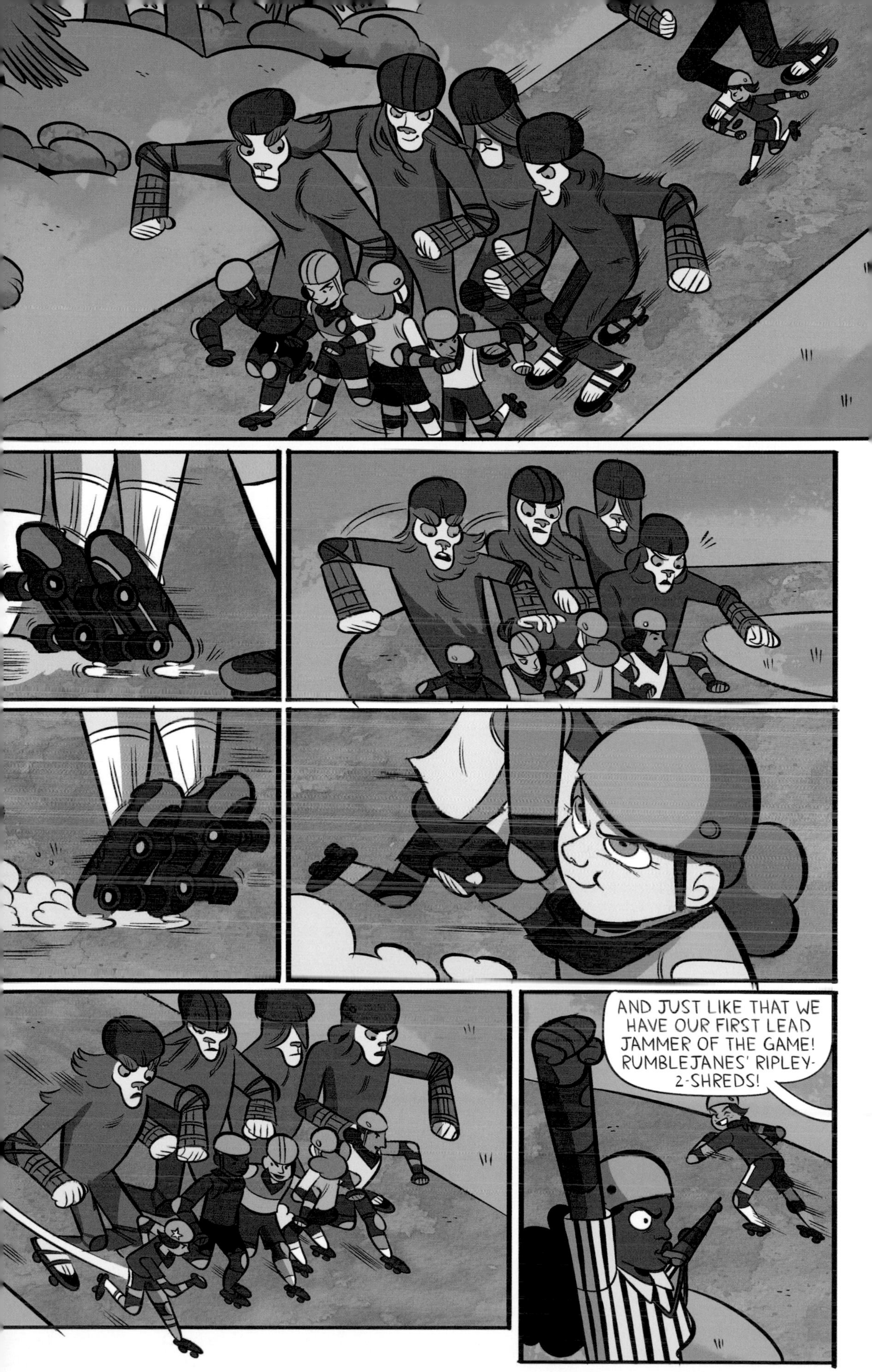
AND JUST LIKE THAT WE HAVE OUR FIRST LEAD JAMMER OF THE GAME! RUMBLEJANES' RIPLEY-2-SHREDS!

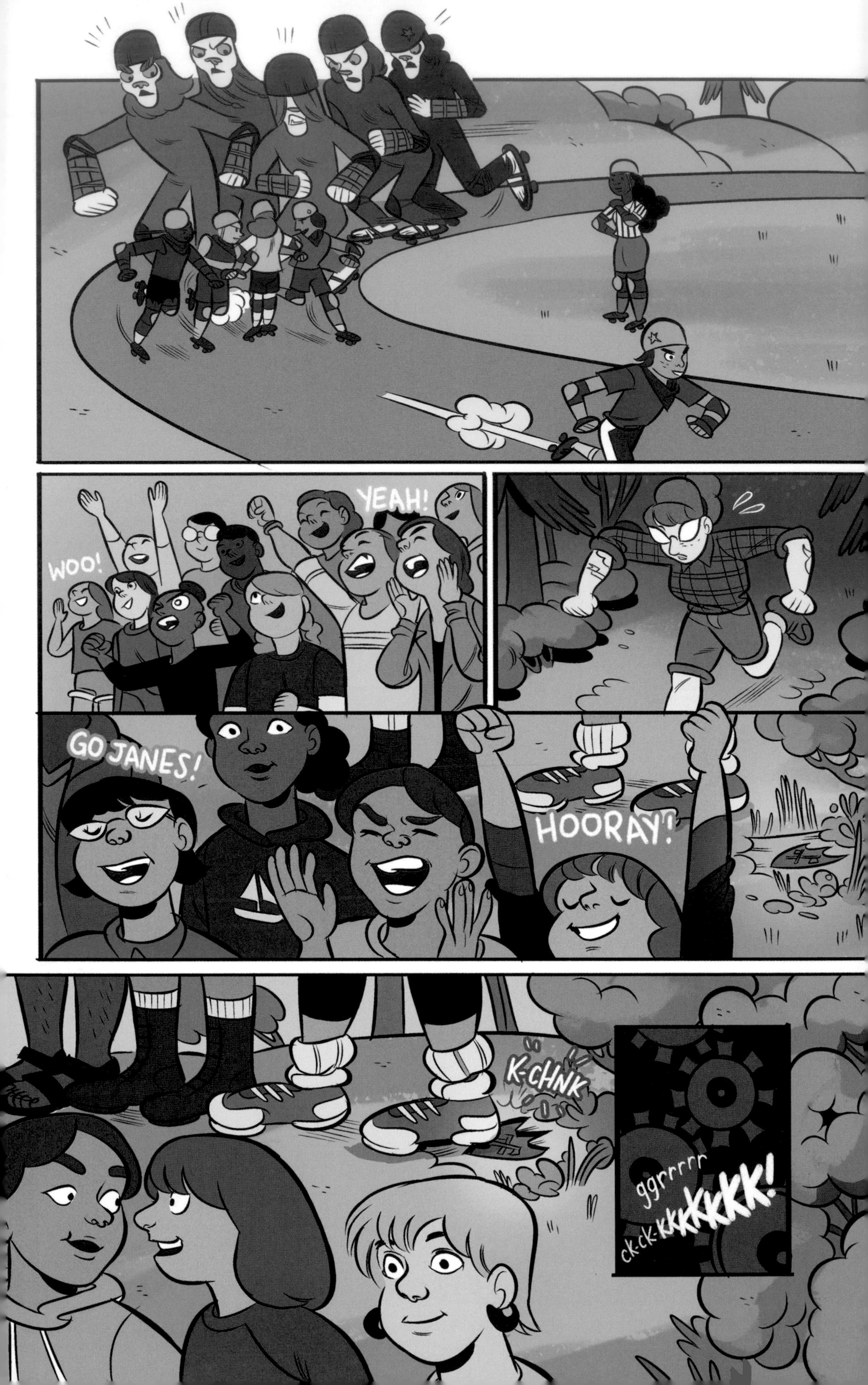

WOO!
YEAH!
GO JANES!
HOORAY!
K-CHNK
ggrrrrr
ck-ck-KKKKKK!

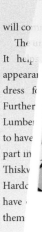

will co…

The…
It help…
appearan…
dress fo…
Further…
Lumber…
to have…
part in…
Thiskv…
Hardc…
have…
them…

JACKPOT!!

GETCHA HEAD IN THE GAME

The…
yellow, short sl…
emb…
the w…
choose…
slacks,…
made o…
out-of-do…
green bere…
the colla…
Shoes m…
heels, rou…
socks should… …th the shoes or wi…
the uniform. Ne… …es, bracelets, or other jewelry do…
belong with a Lumberjane uniform.

HOW TO WEAR THE UNIFORM

To look well in a uniform demands first of…
uniform be kept in good condition—clean…
pressed. See that the skirt is the right length for your own
height and build, that the belt is adjusted to your waist,
that your shoes and stockings are in keeping with the
uniform, that you watch your posture and carry yourself
with dignity and grace. If the beret is removed indoors,
be sure that your hair is neat and kept in place with an
insconspicuous clip or ribbon. When you wear a
Lumberjane uniform you are identified as a member of
this organization and you should be doubly careful to
conduct yourself in a way that will show everyone that
courtesy and thoughtfullness are part of being a
Lumberjane. People are likely to judge a whole nation by
the selfishness of a few individuals, to criticize a whole
family because of the misconduct of one member, and to
feel unkindly toward and organization because of the

…E UNIFORM

should be worn at camp
…vents when Lumberjanes
…n may also be worn at other
…ons. It should be worn as a
…the uniform dress with
…rrect shoes, and stocking or

…ut grows her uniform or
…ter Lumberjane.
…gnia she has
…her
…her

HECK ON WHEELS!

The unifor…
helps to cre…
in a group.…
active life th…
another bond…
future, and pr…
in order to b…
Lumberjane pr…
Penniquiqul Thi… …ore Lady
Types, but m… …es will wish to have one. They
can either b… …e uniform, or make it themselves from
materials available at the trading post.

LUMBERJANES FIELD MANUAL

CHAPTER
THIRTY-SIX

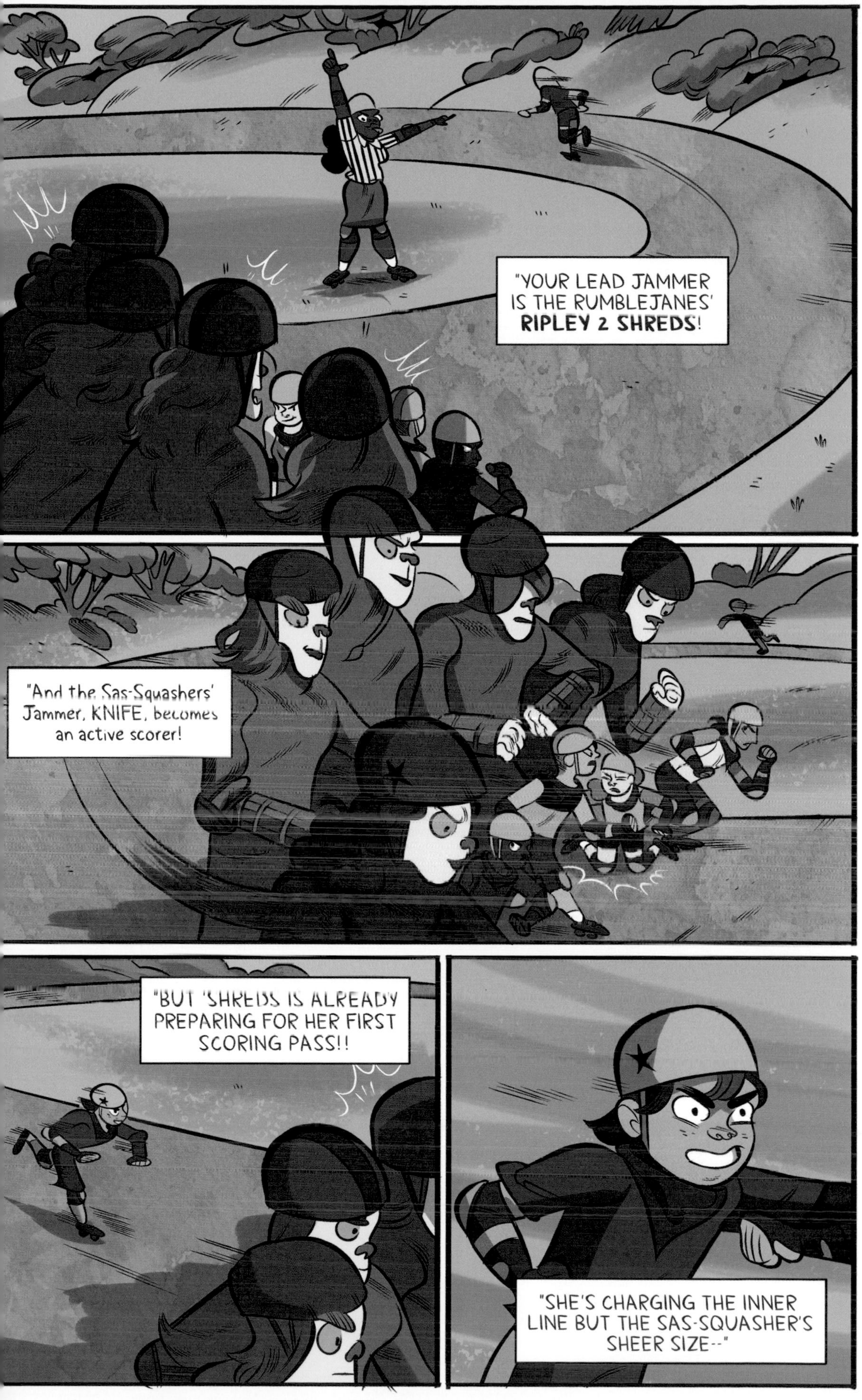
"YOUR LEAD JAMMER
IS THE RUMBLEJANES'
RIPLEY 2 SHREDS!
"And the Sas-Squashers'
Jammer, KNIFE, becomes
an active scorer!
"BUT 'SHREDS IS ALREADY
PREPARING FOR HER FIRST
SCORING PASS!!
"SHE'S CHARGING THE INNER
LINE BUT THE SAS-SQUASHER'S
SHEER SIZE--"

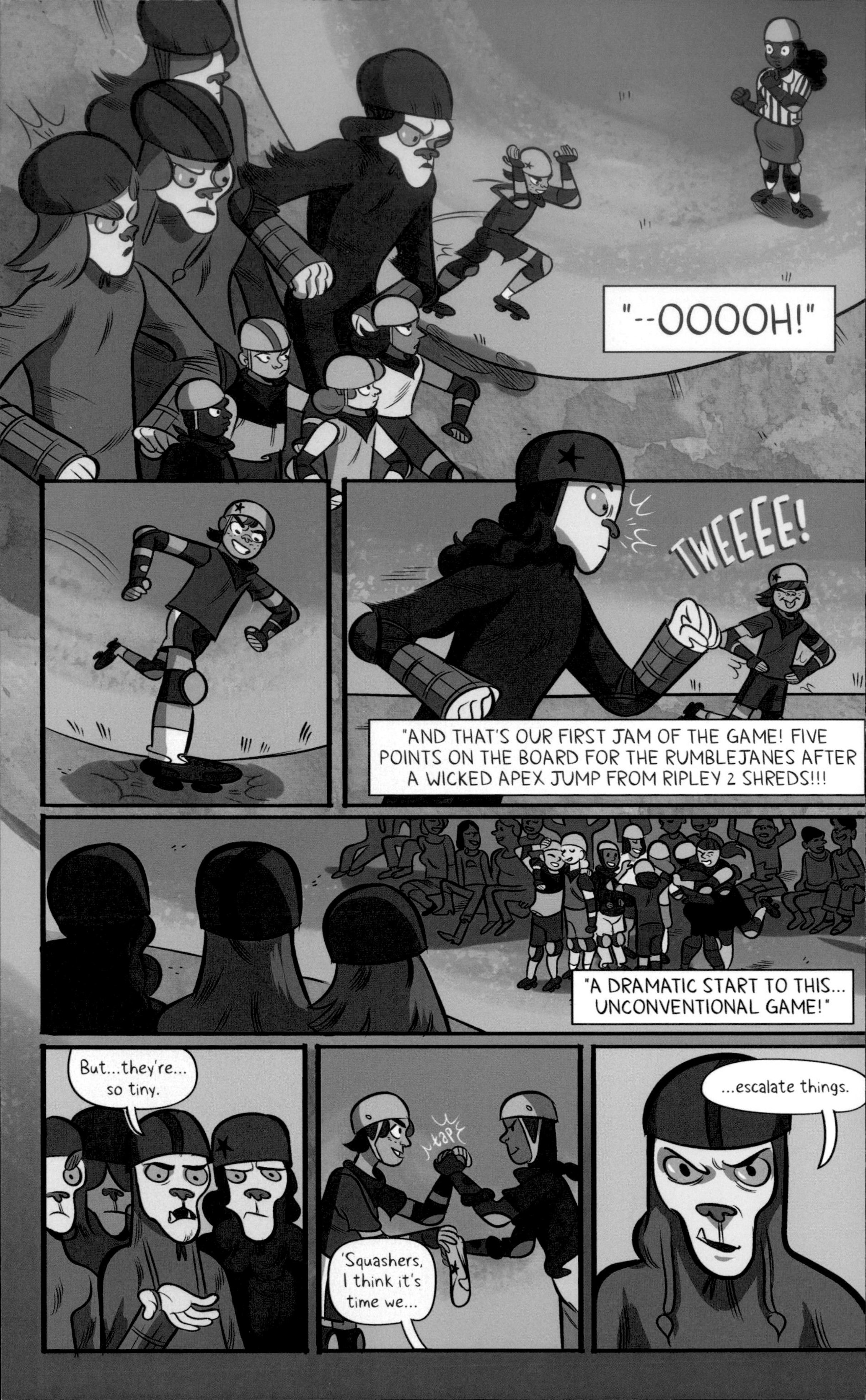
"--OOOOH!"
TWEEEE!
"AND THAT'S OUR FIRST JAM OF THE GAME! FIVE POINTS ON THE BOARD FOR THE RUMBLEJANES AFTER A WICKED APEX JUMP FROM RIPLEY 2 SHREDS!!!
"A DRAMATIC START TO THIS... UNCONVENTIONAL GAME!"
But...they're... so tiny.
TAP
'Squashers, I think it's time we...
...escalate things.

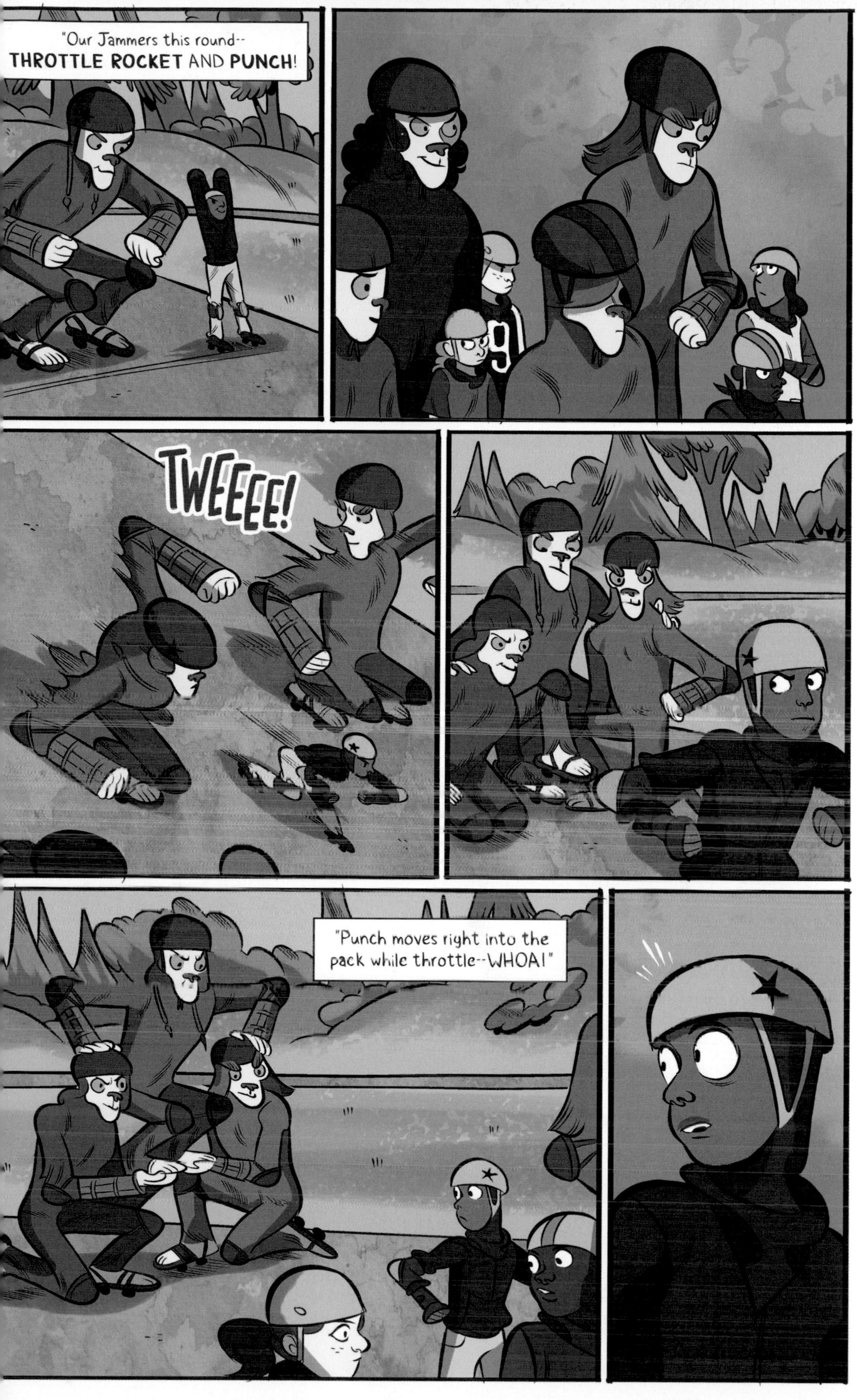
"Our Jammers this round--
THROTTLE ROCKET AND PUNCH!
TWEEEE!
"Punch moves right into the pack while throttle--WHOA!"

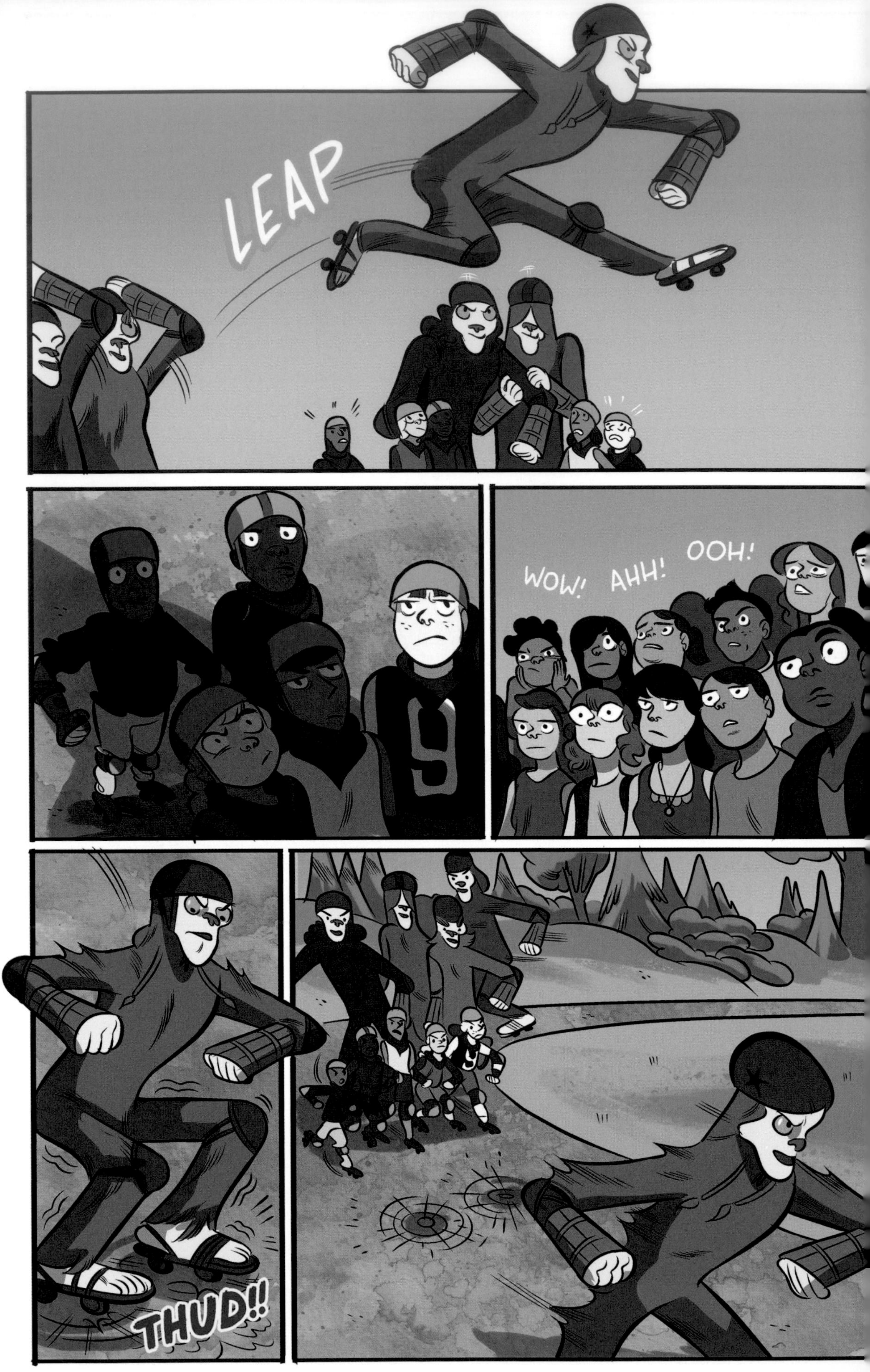
LEAP
WOW! AHH! OOH!
THUD!!

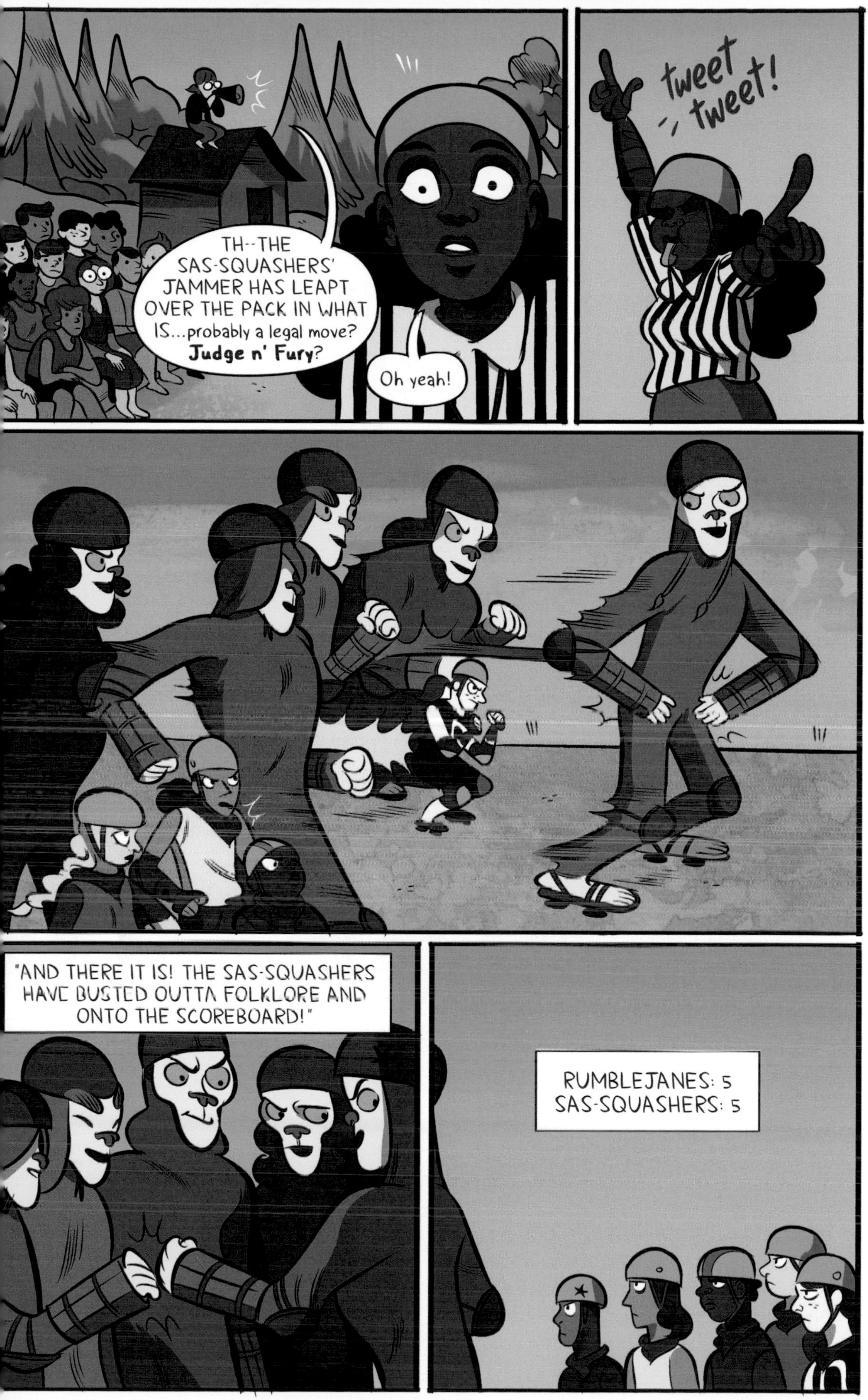
TH--THE SAS-SQUASHERS' JAMMER HAS LEAPT OVER THE PACK IN WHAT IS...probably a legal move? **Judge n' Fury**?
Oh yeah!
tweet tweet!
"AND THERE IT IS! THE SAS-SQUASHERS HAVE BUSTED OUTTA FOLKLORE AND ONTO THE SCOREBOARD!"
RUMBLEJANES: 5
SAS-SQUASHERS: 5

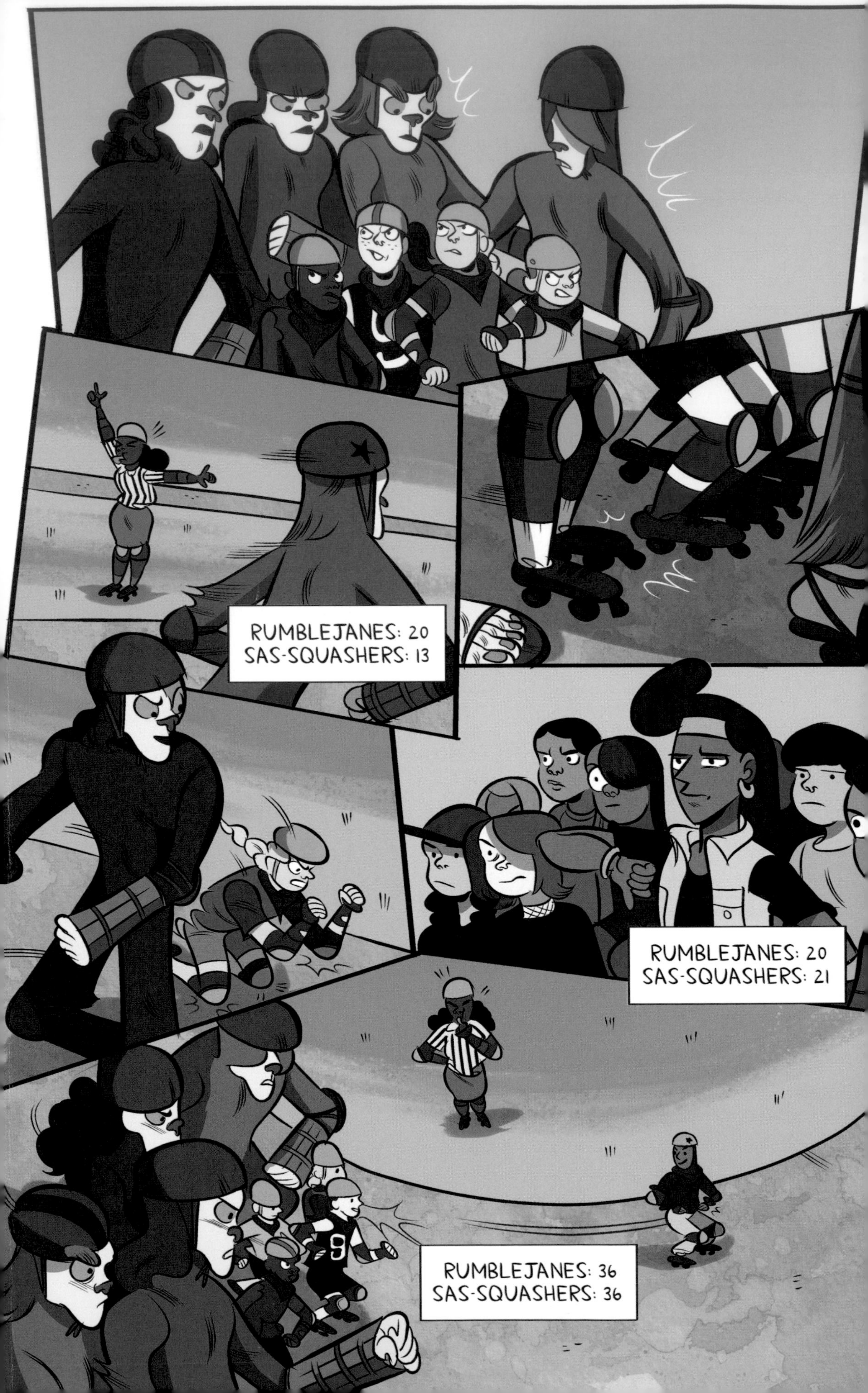
RUMBLEJANES: 20
SAS-SQUASHERS: 13
RUMBLEJANES: 20
SAS-SQUASHERS: 21
RUMBLEJANES: 36
SAS-SQUASHERS: 36

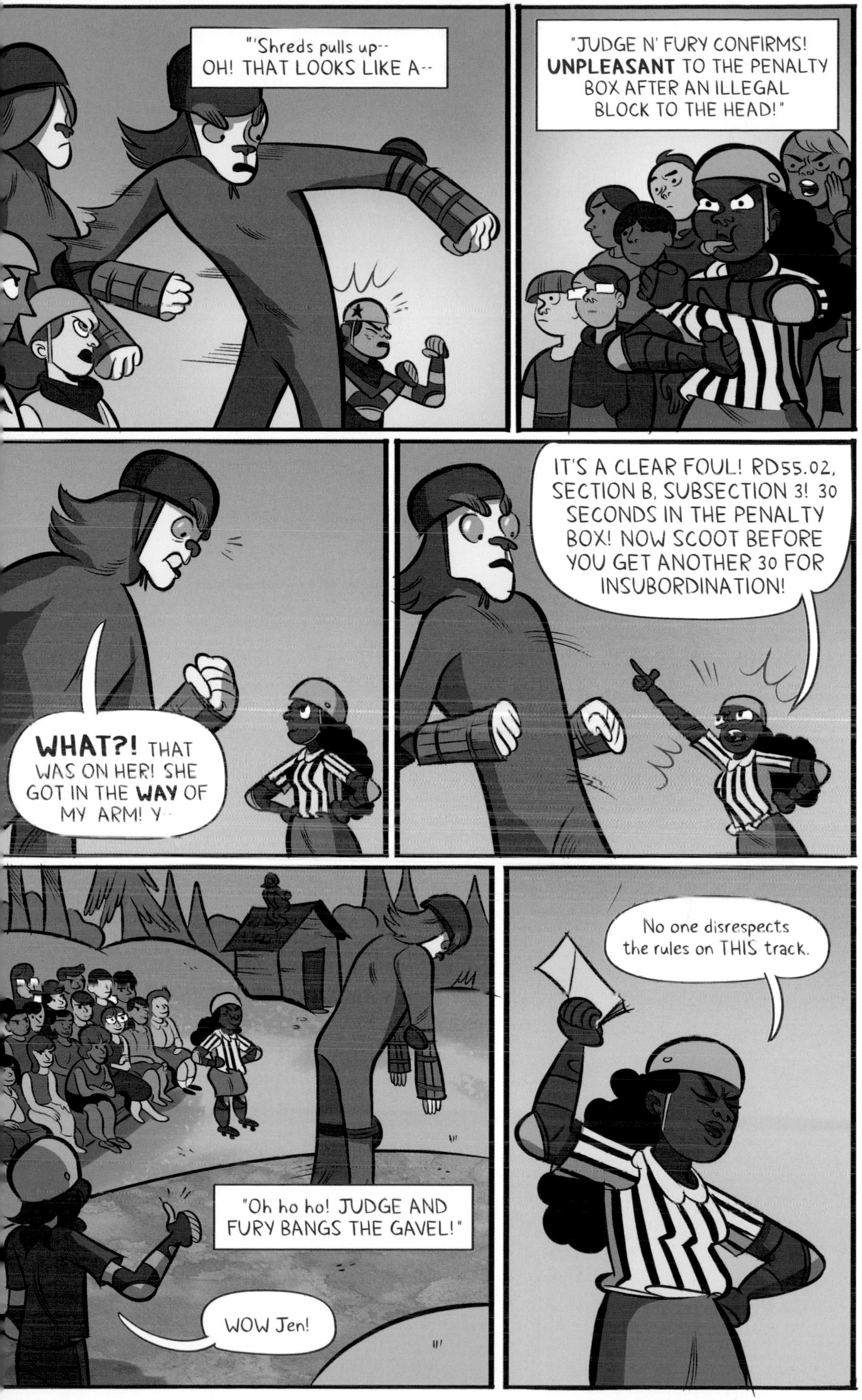
"'Shreds pulls up--
OH! THAT LOOKS LIKE A--
"JUDGE N' FURY CONFIRMS! UNPLEASANT TO THE PENALTY BOX AFTER AN ILLEGAL BLOCK TO THE HEAD!"
WHAT?! THAT WAS ON HER! SHE GOT IN THE WAY OF MY ARM! Y--
IT'S A CLEAR FOUL! RD55.02, SECTION B, SUBSECTION 3! 30 SECONDS IN THE PENALTY BOX! NOW SCOOT BEFORE YOU GET ANOTHER 30 FOR INSUBORDINATION!
"Oh ho ho! JUDGE AND FURY BANGS THE GAVEL!"
WOW Jen!
No one disrespects the rules on THIS track.

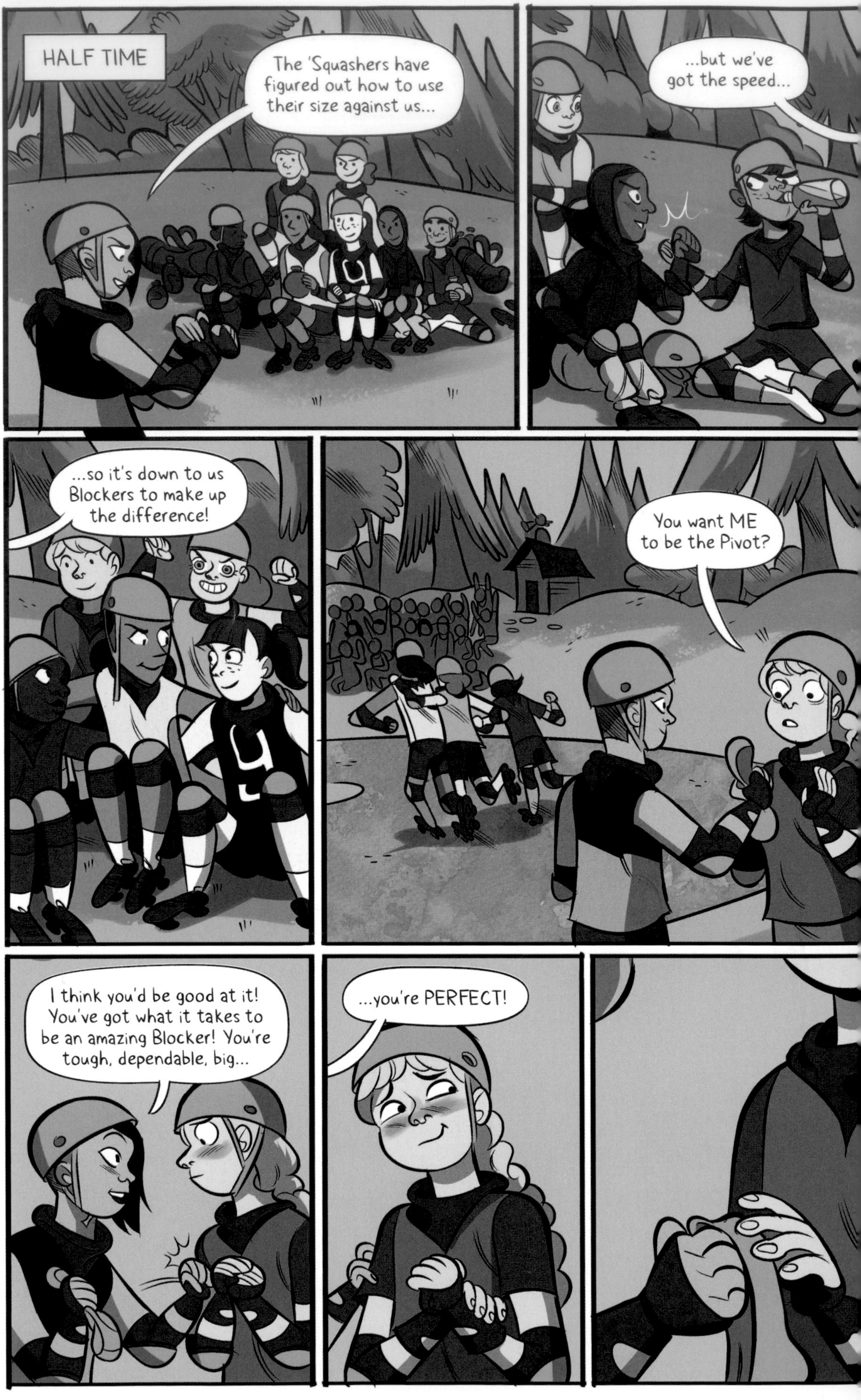
HALF TIME
The 'Squashers have figured out how to use their size against us...
...but we've got the speed...
...so it's down to us Blockers to make up the difference!
You want ME to be the Pivot?
I think you'd be good at it! You've got what it takes to be an amazing Blocker! You're tough, dependable, big...
...you're PERFECT!

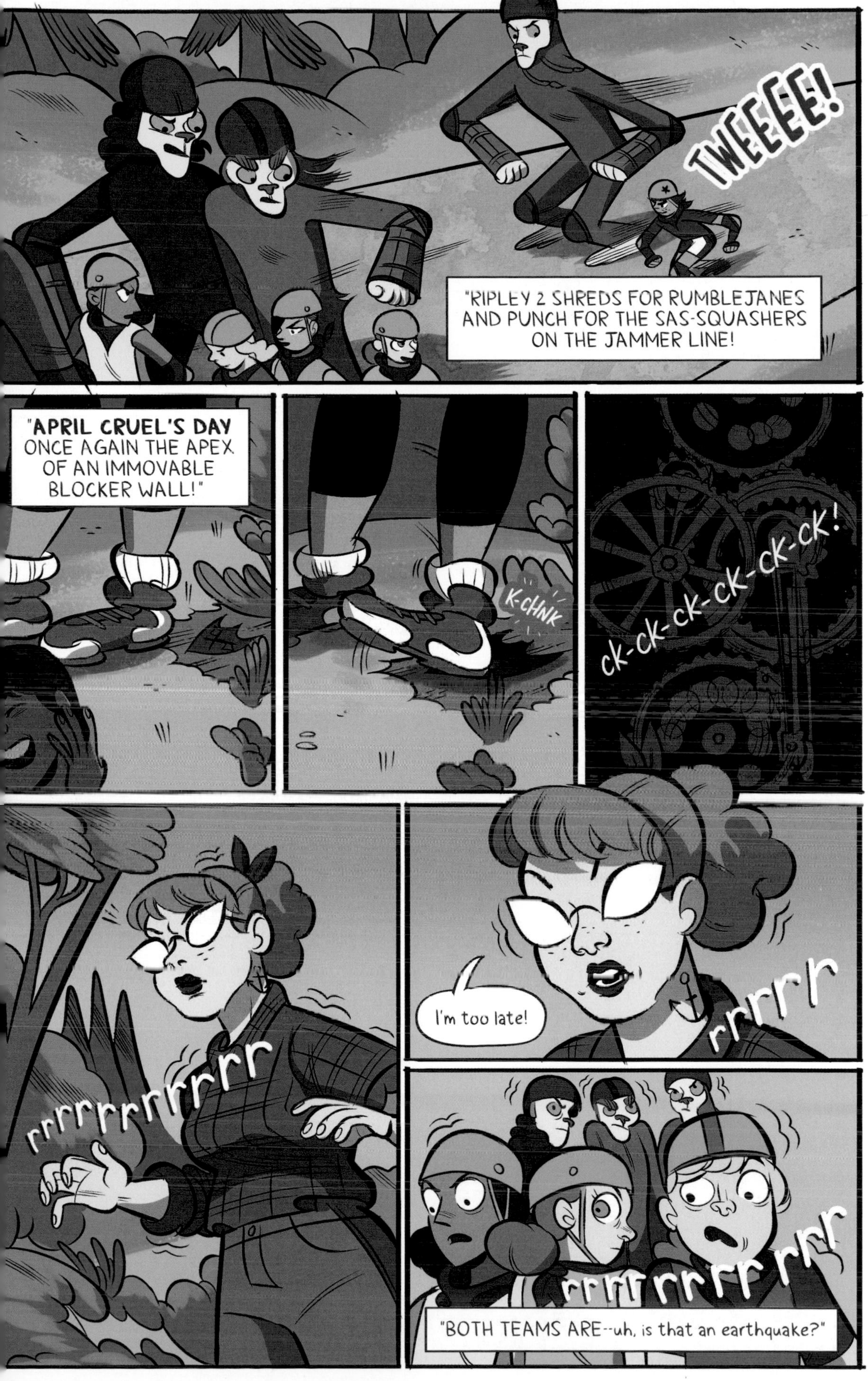
TWEEEE!
"RIPLEY 2 SHREDS FOR RUMBLEJANES AND PUNCH FOR THE SAS-SQUASHERS ON THE JAMMER LINE!
"APRIL CRUEL'S DAY ONCE AGAIN THE APEX OF AN IMMOVABLE BLOCKER WALL!"
K-CHNK
ck-ck-ck-ck-ck-ck-ck!
rrrrrrrrrrrr
I'm too late!
rrrrr
rrrrrrrrrrrr
"BOTH TEAMS ARE--uh, is that an earthquake?"

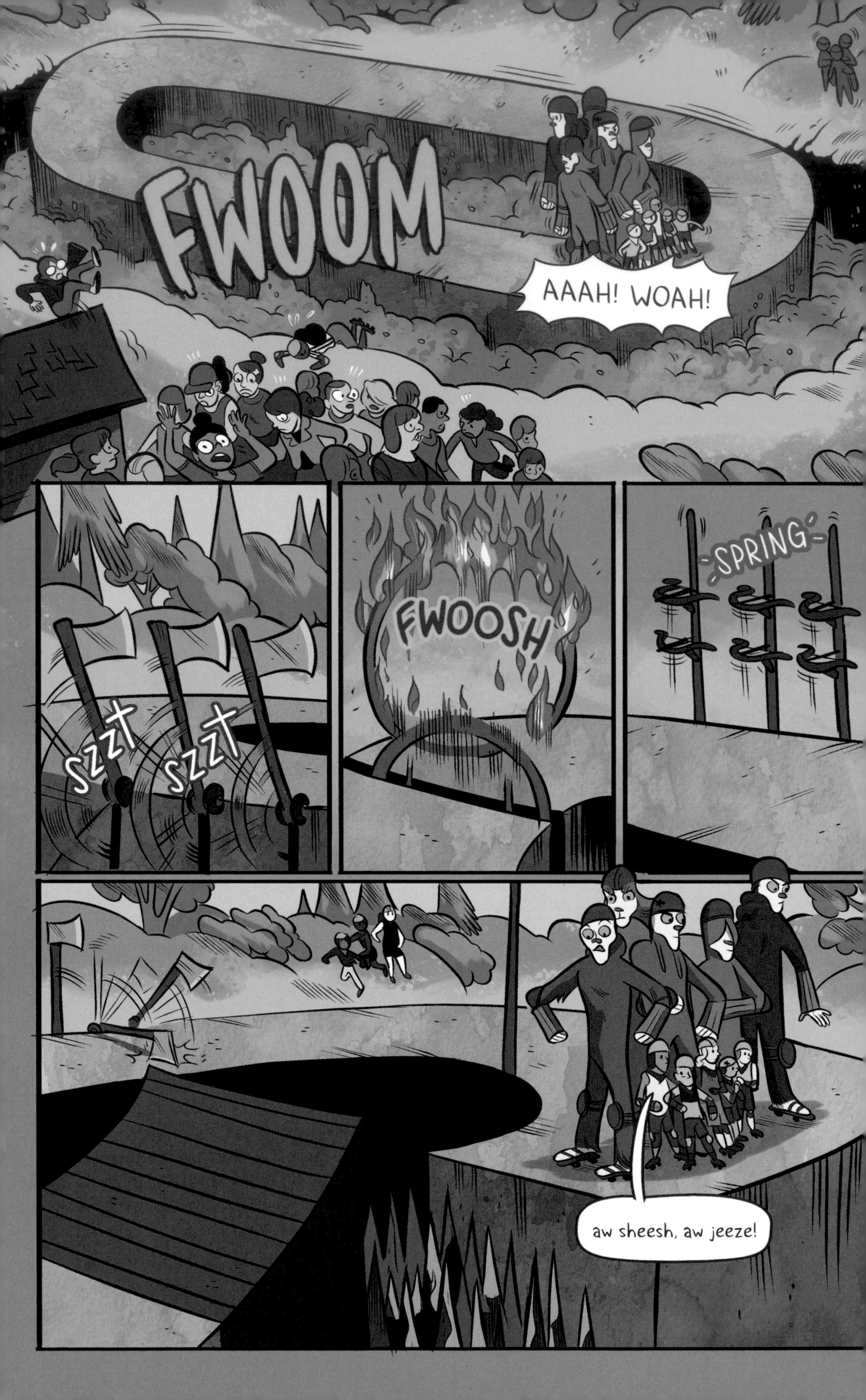
FWOOM
AAAH! WOAH!
SZZT
SZZT
FWOOSH
-SPRING-
aw sheesh, aw jeeze!

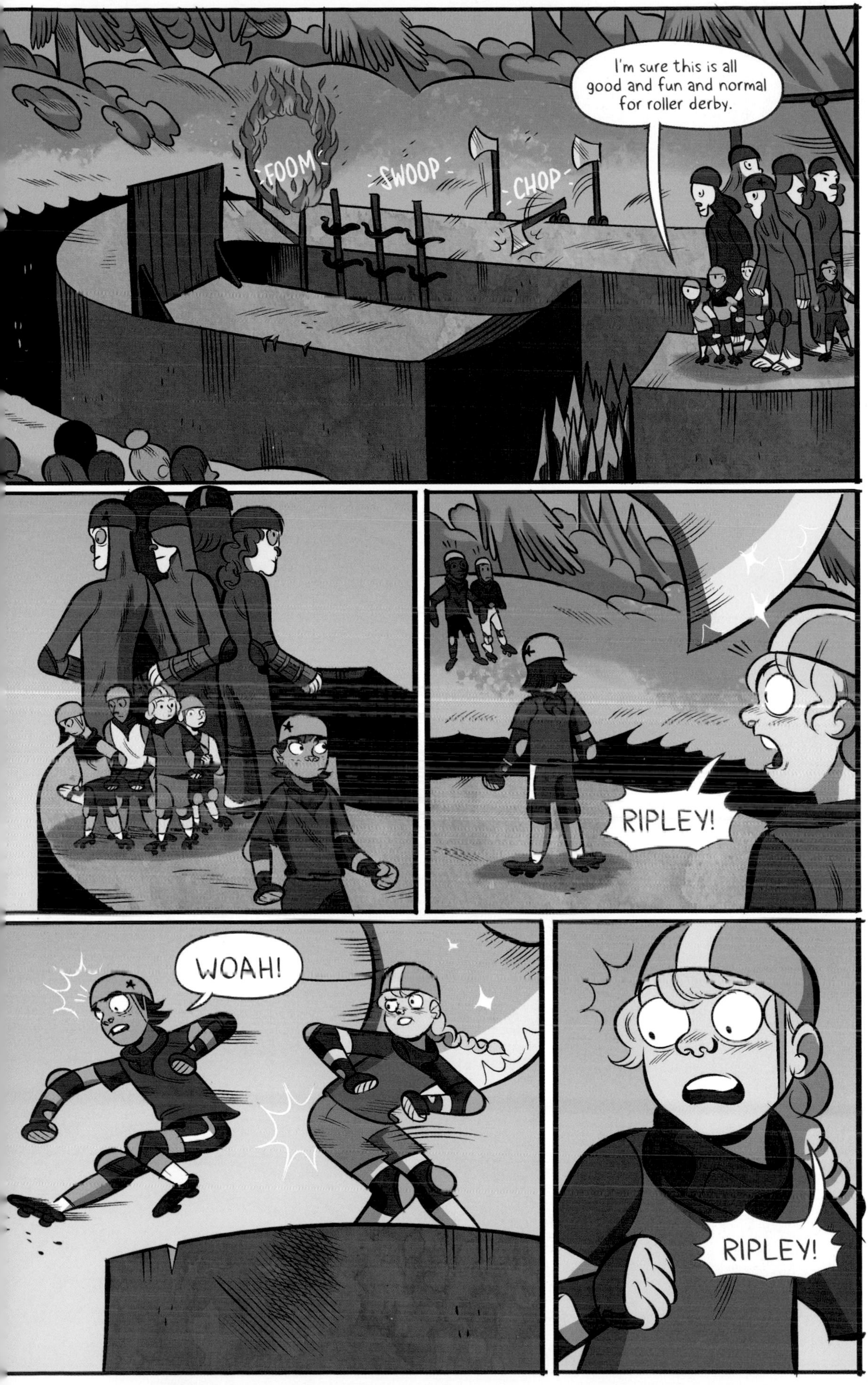
FOOM
SWOOP
CHOP
I'm sure this is all good and fun and normal for roller derby.
RIPLEY!
WOAH!
RIPLEY!

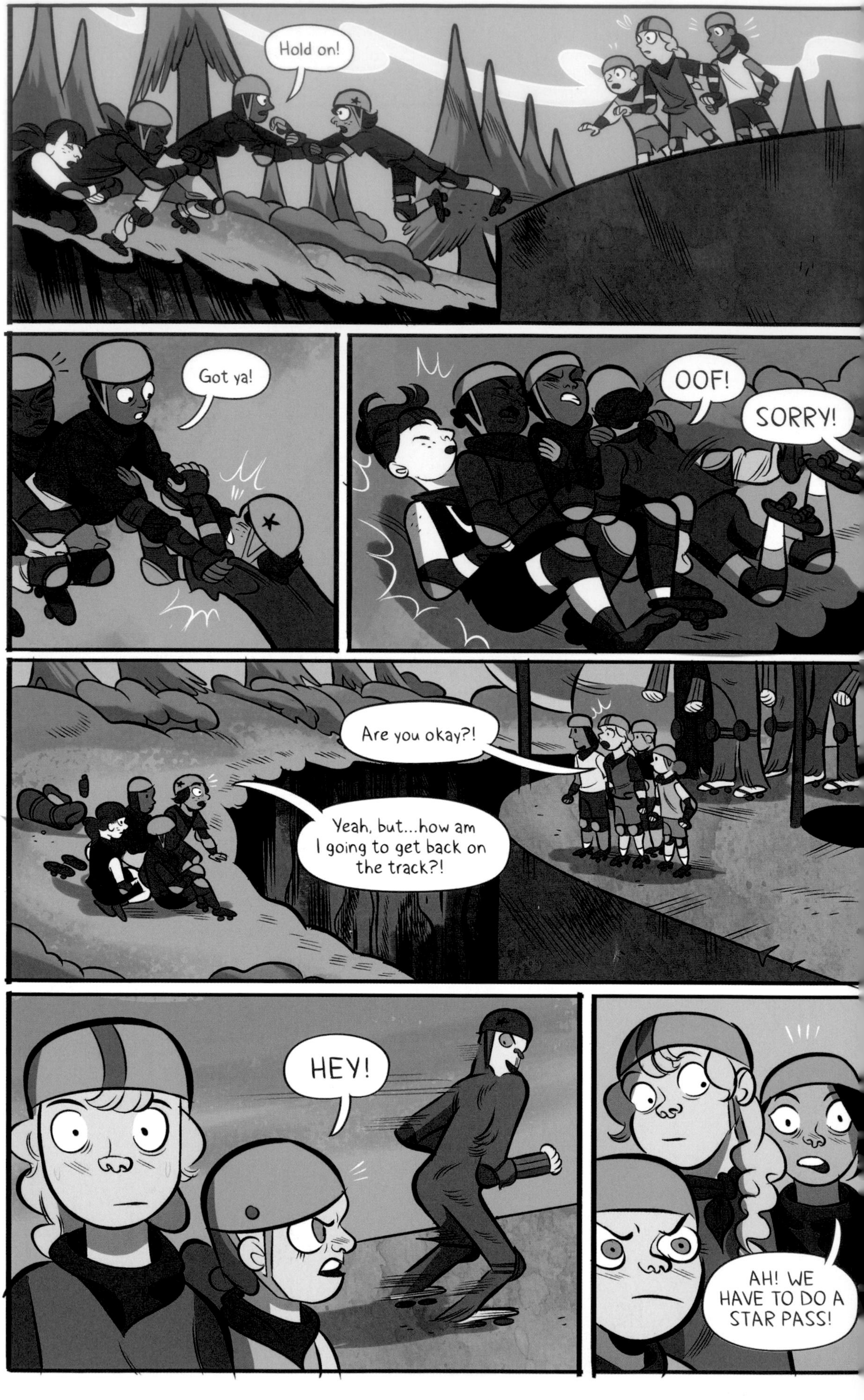
Hold on!
Got ya!
OOF!
SORRY!
Are you okay?!
Yeah, but...how am I going to get back on the track?!
HEY!
AH! WE HAVE TO DO A STAR PASS!

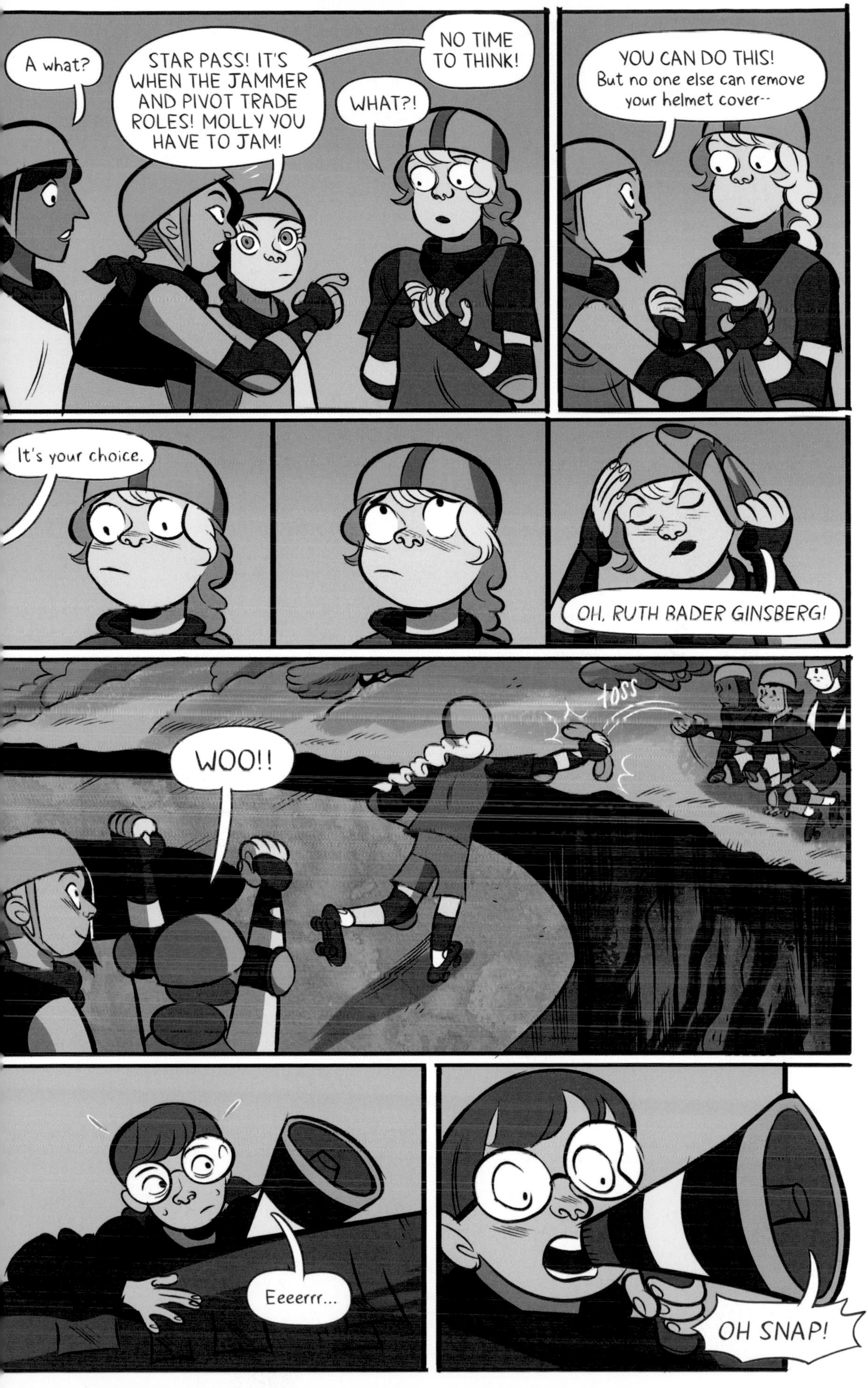
A what?
STAR PASS! IT'S WHEN THE JAMMER AND PIVOT TRADE ROLES! MOLLY YOU HAVE TO JAM!
NO TIME TO THINK!
WHAT?!
YOU CAN DO THIS!
But no one else can remove your helmet cover--
It's your choice.
OH, RUTH BADER GINSBERG!
toss
WOO!!
Eeeerrr...
OH SNAP!

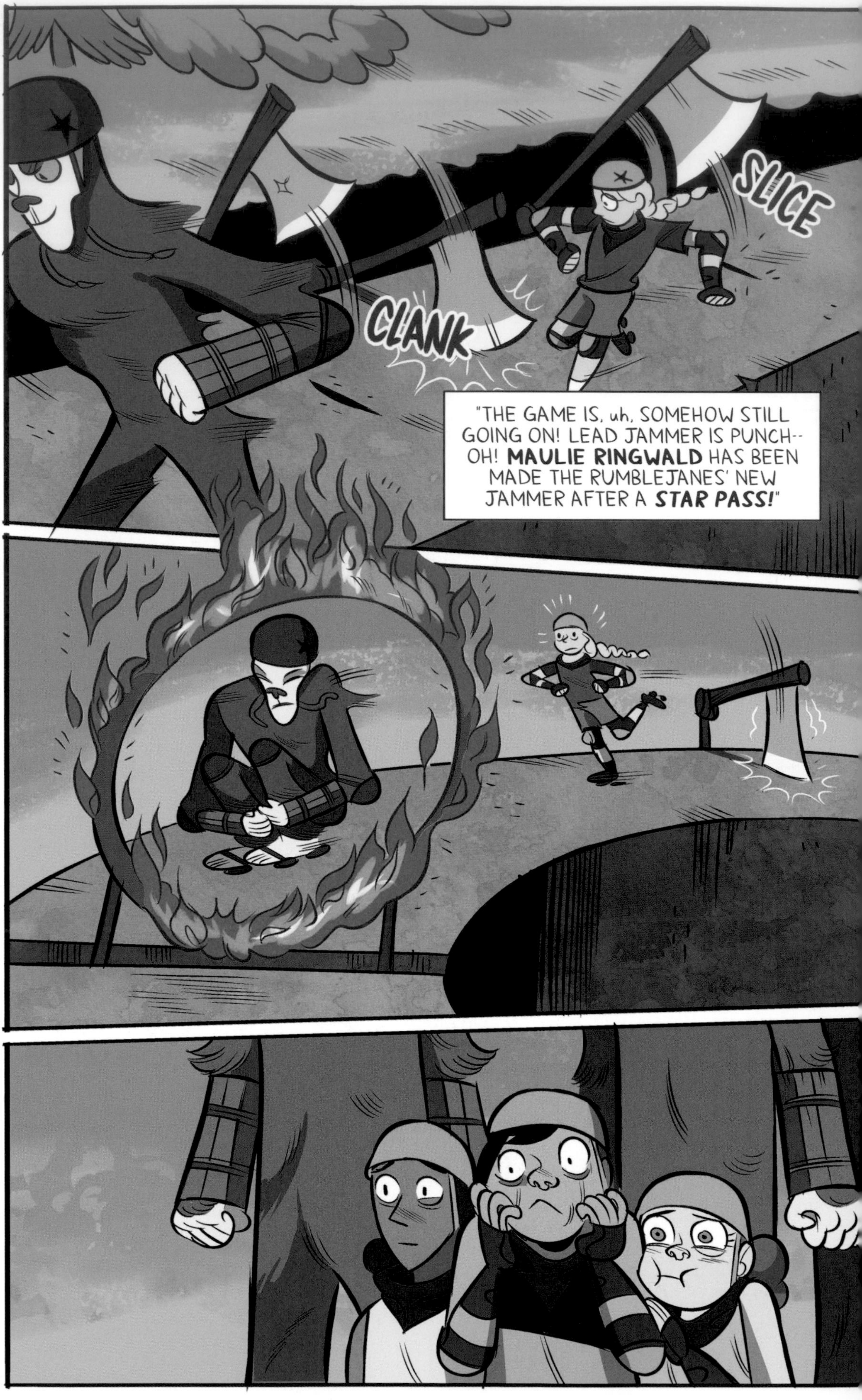
SLICE
CLANK
"THE GAME IS, uh, SOMEHOW STILL GOING ON! LEAD JAMMER IS PUNCH-- OH! **MAULIE RINGWALD** HAS BEEN MADE THE RUMBLEJANES' NEW JAMMER AFTER A **STAR PASS!**"

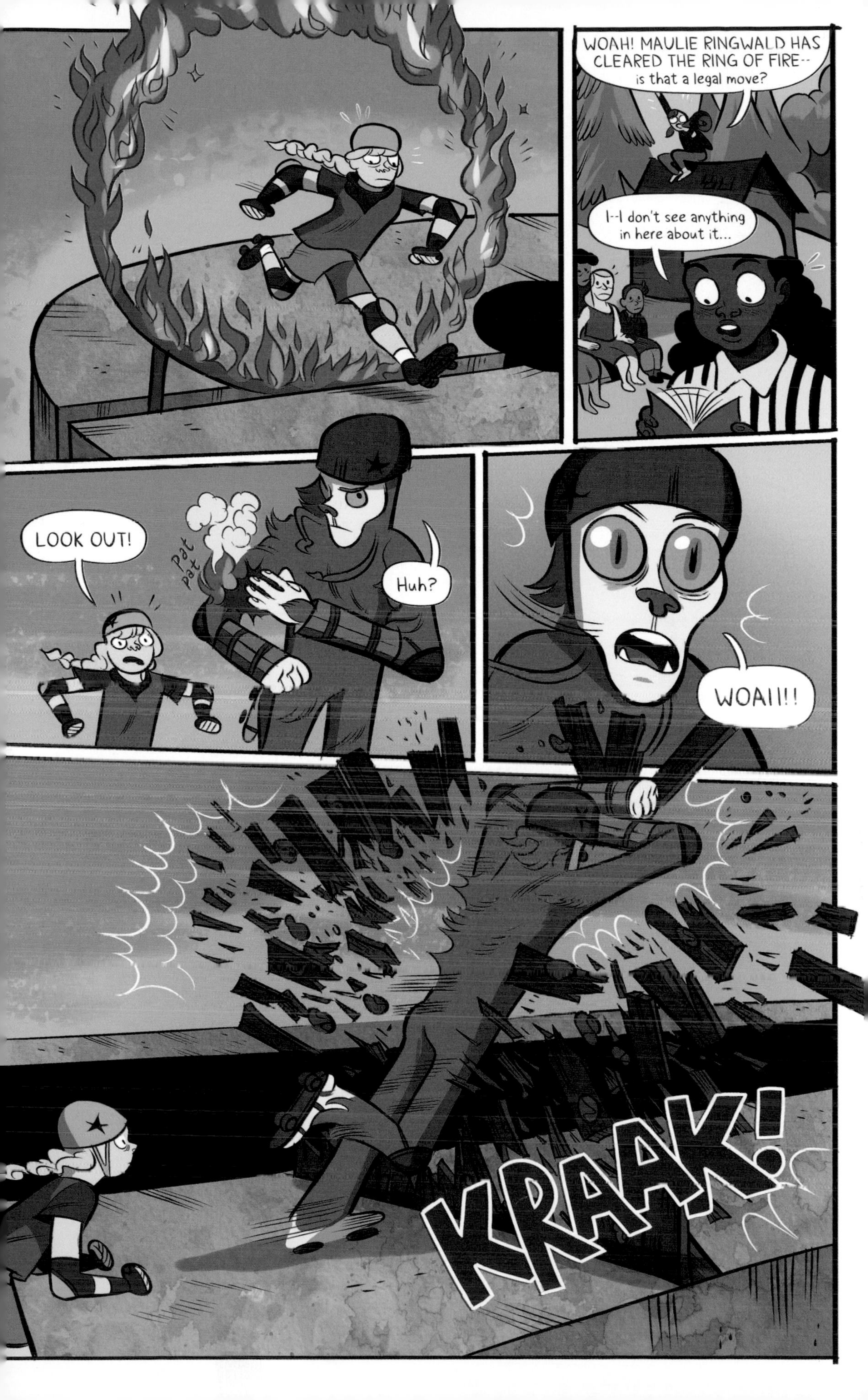
WOAH! MAULIE RINGWALD HAS CLEARED THE RING OF FIRE-- is that a legal move?
I--I don't see anything in here about it...
LOOK OUT!
pat pat
Huh?
WOAH!!
KRAAK!

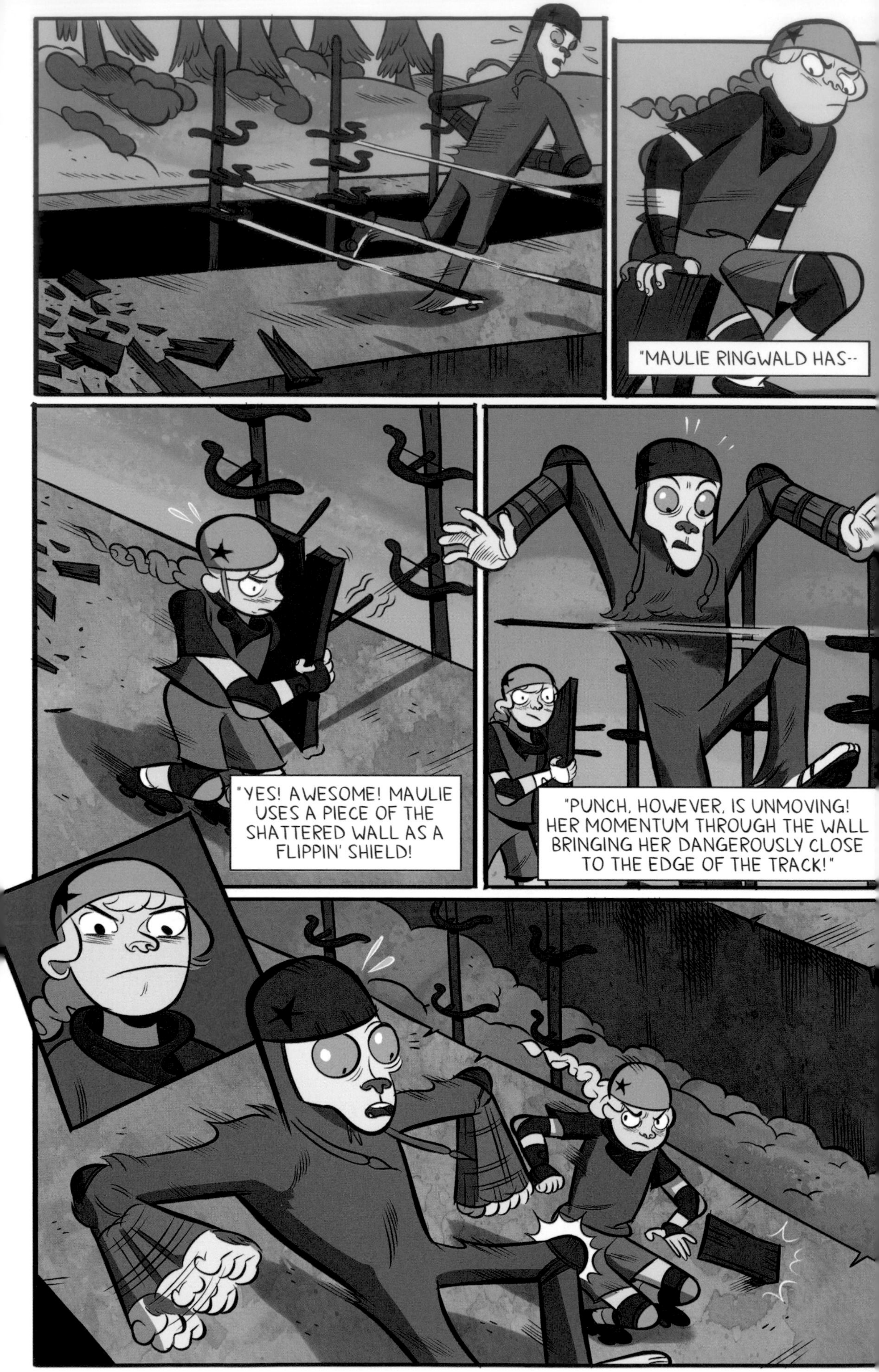
"MAULIE RINGWALD HAS--
"YES! AWESOME! MAULIE USES A PIECE OF THE SHATTERED WALL AS A FLIPPIN' SHIELD!
"PUNCH, HOWEVER, IS UNMOVING! HER MOMENTUM THROUGH THE WALL BRINGING HER DANGEROUSLY CLOSE TO THE EDGE OF THE TRACK!"

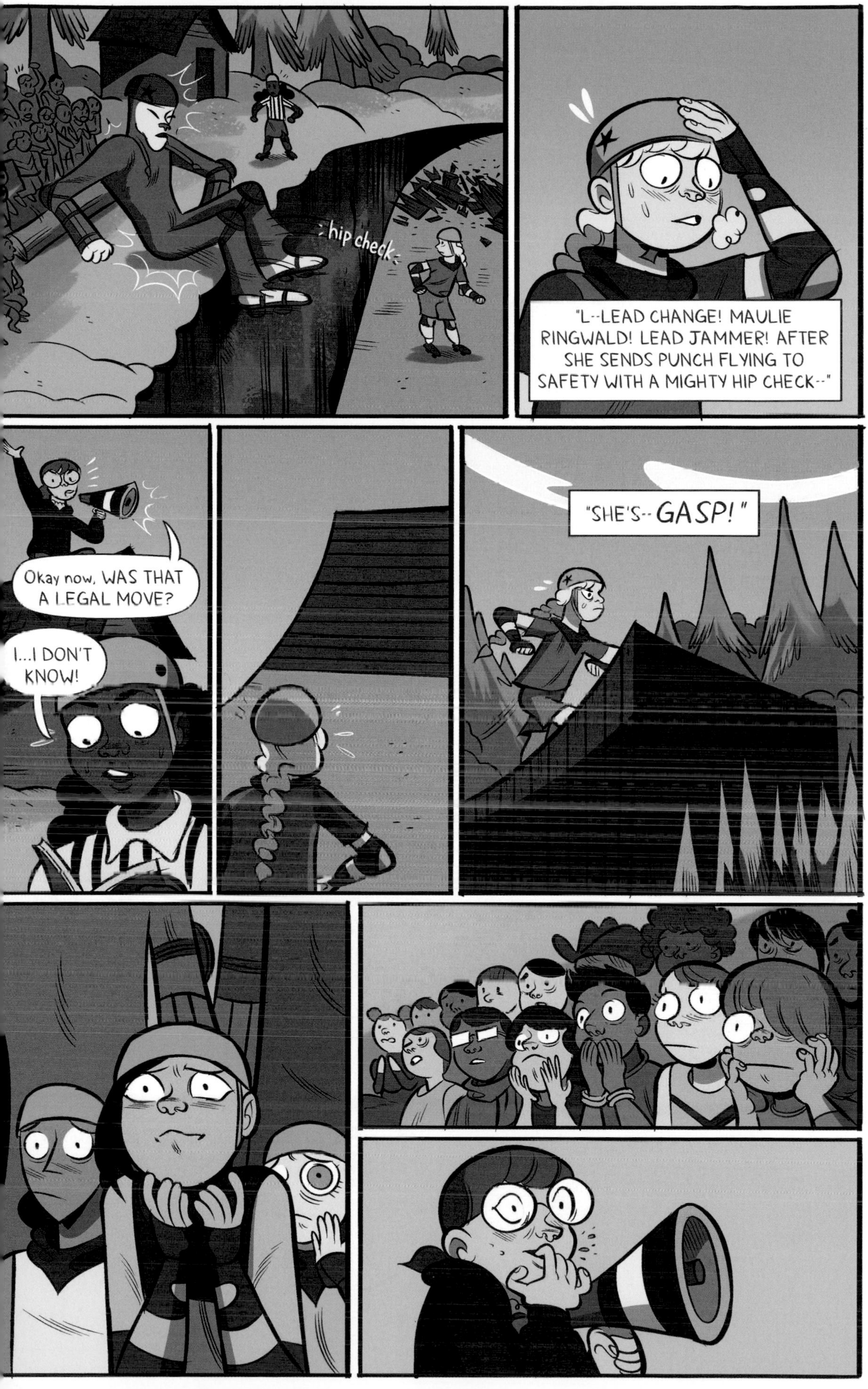
hip check
"L--LEAD CHANGE! MAULIE RINGWALD! LEAD JAMMER! AFTER SHE SENDS PUNCH FLYING TO SAFETY WITH A MIGHTY HIP CHECK--"
Okay now, WAS THAT A LEGAL MOVE?
I...I DON'T KNOW!
"SHE'S--GASP!"

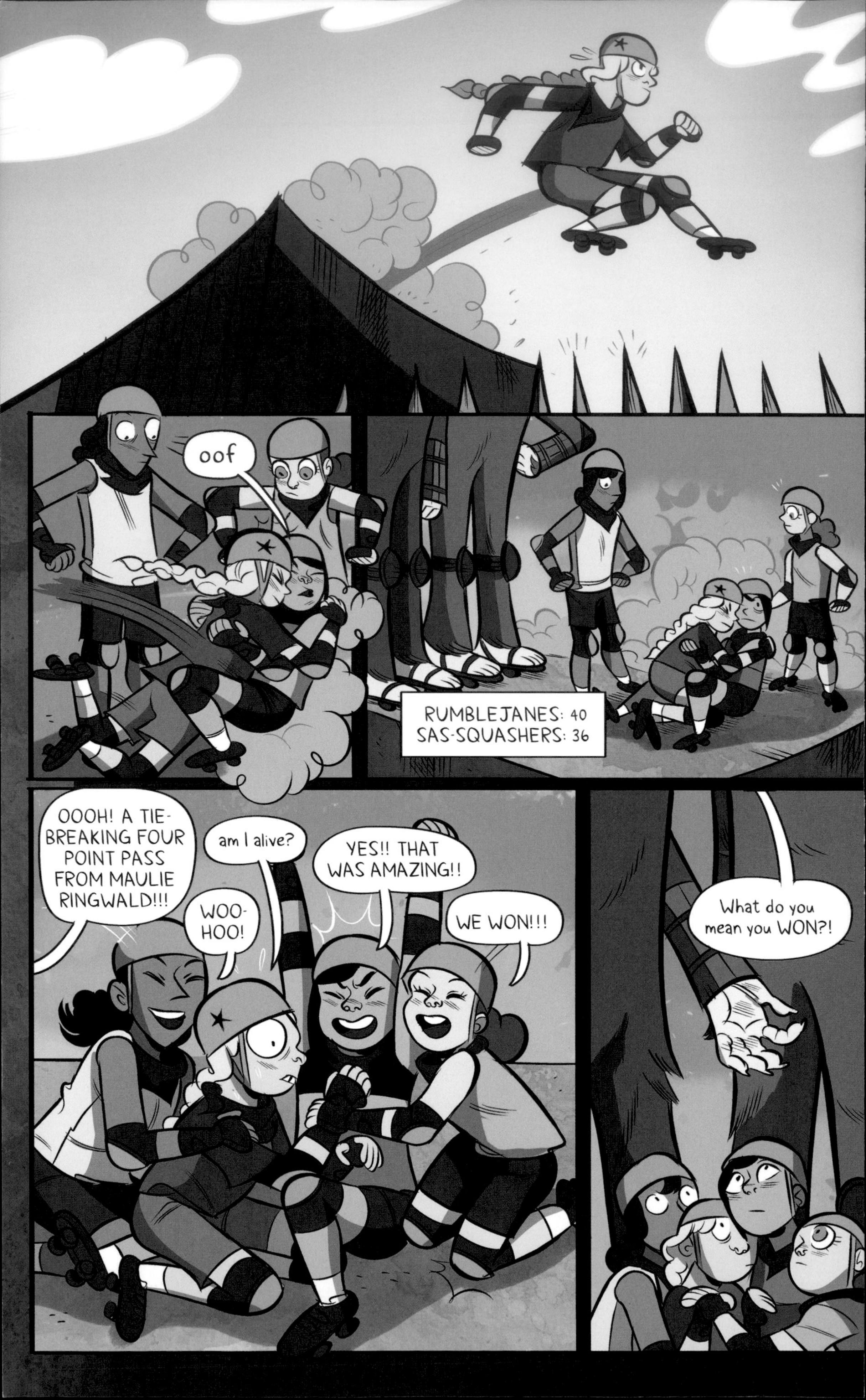

oof
RUMBLEJANES: 40
SAS-SQUASHERS: 36
OOOH! A TIE-BREAKING FOUR POINT PASS FROM MAULIE RINGWALD!!!
WOO-HOO!
am I alive?
YES!! THAT WAS AMAZING!!
WE WON!!!
What do you mean you WON?!

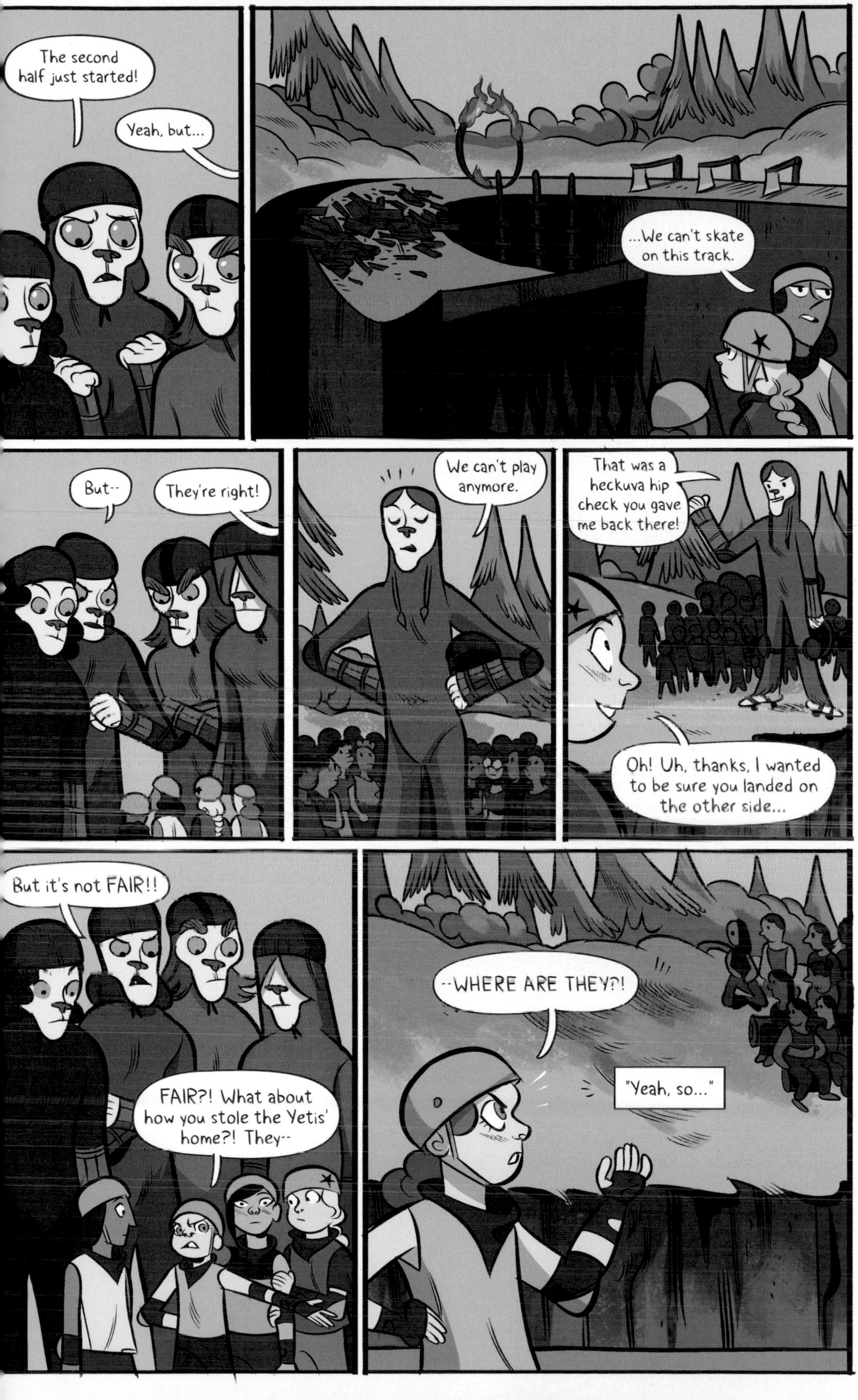
The second half just started!
Yeah, but...
...We can't skate on this track.
But--
They're right!
We can't play anymore.
That was a heckuva hip check you gave me back there!
Oh! Uh, thanks, I wanted to be sure you landed on the other side...
But it's not FAIR!!
FAIR?! What about how you stole the Yetis' home?! They--
--WHERE ARE THEY?!
"Yeah, so..."

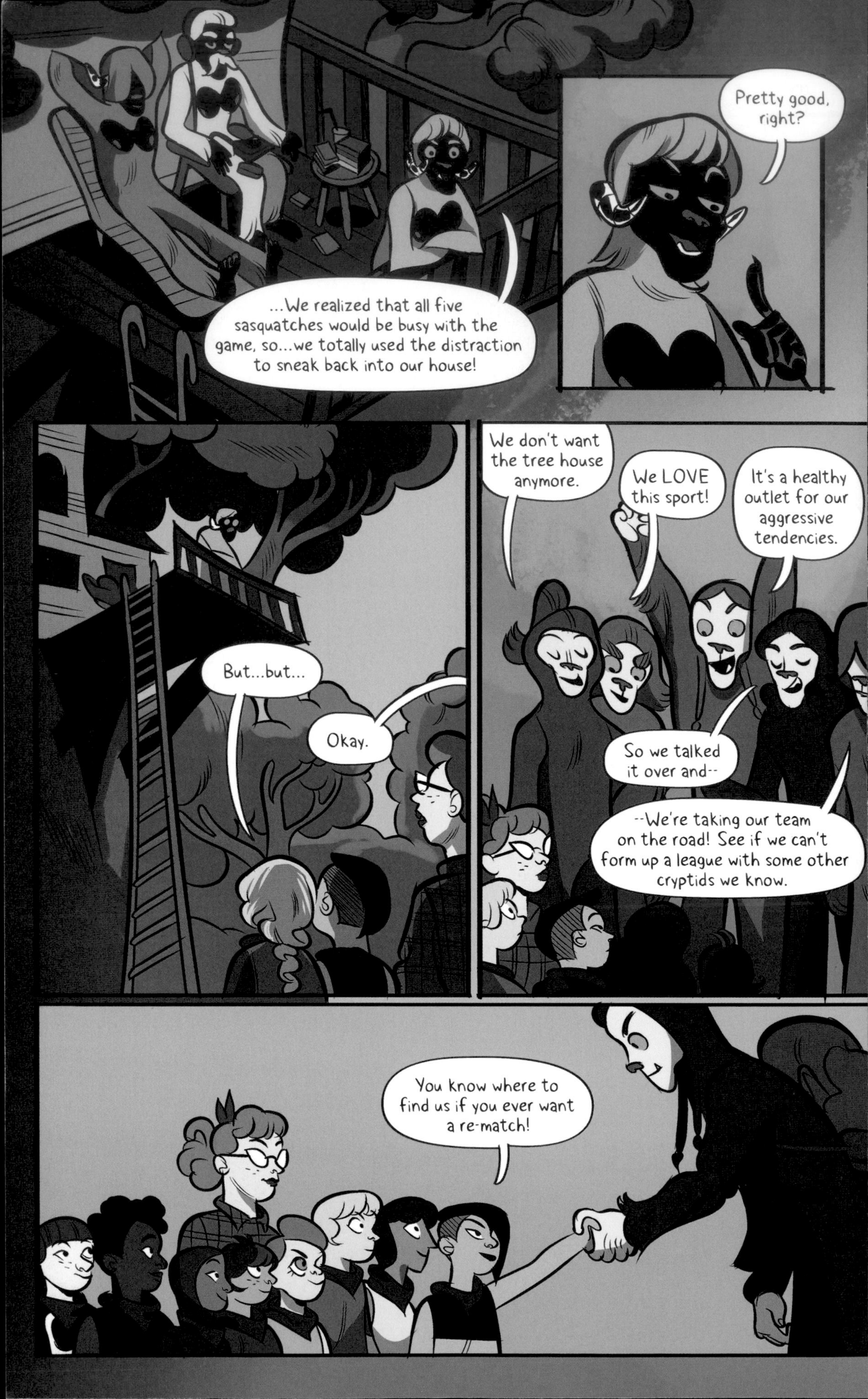
...We realized that all five sasquatches would be busy with the game, so...we totally used the distraction to sneak back into our house!
Pretty good, right?
But...but...
Okay.
We don't want the tree house anymore.
We LOVE this sport!
It's a healthy outlet for our aggressive tendencies.
So we talked it over and--
--We're taking our team on the road! See if we can't form up a league with some other cryptids we know.
You know where to find us if you ever want a re-match!

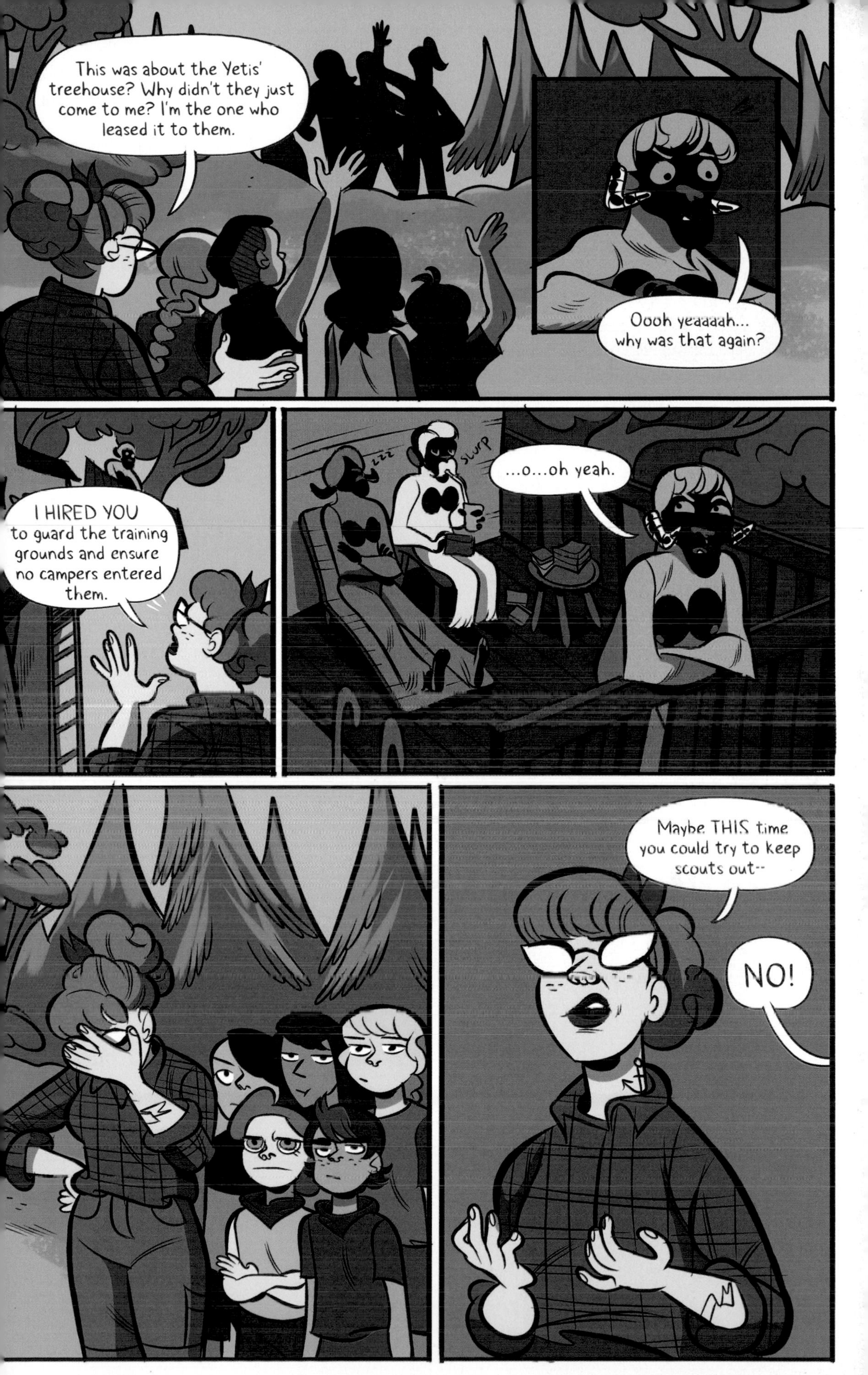
This was about the Yetis' treehouse? Why didn't they just come to me? I'm the one who leased it to them.
Oooh yeaaaah... why was that again?
I HIRED YOU to guard the training grounds and ensure no campers entered them.
zzz
slurp
...o...oh yeah.
Maybe THIS time you could try to keep scouts out--
NO!

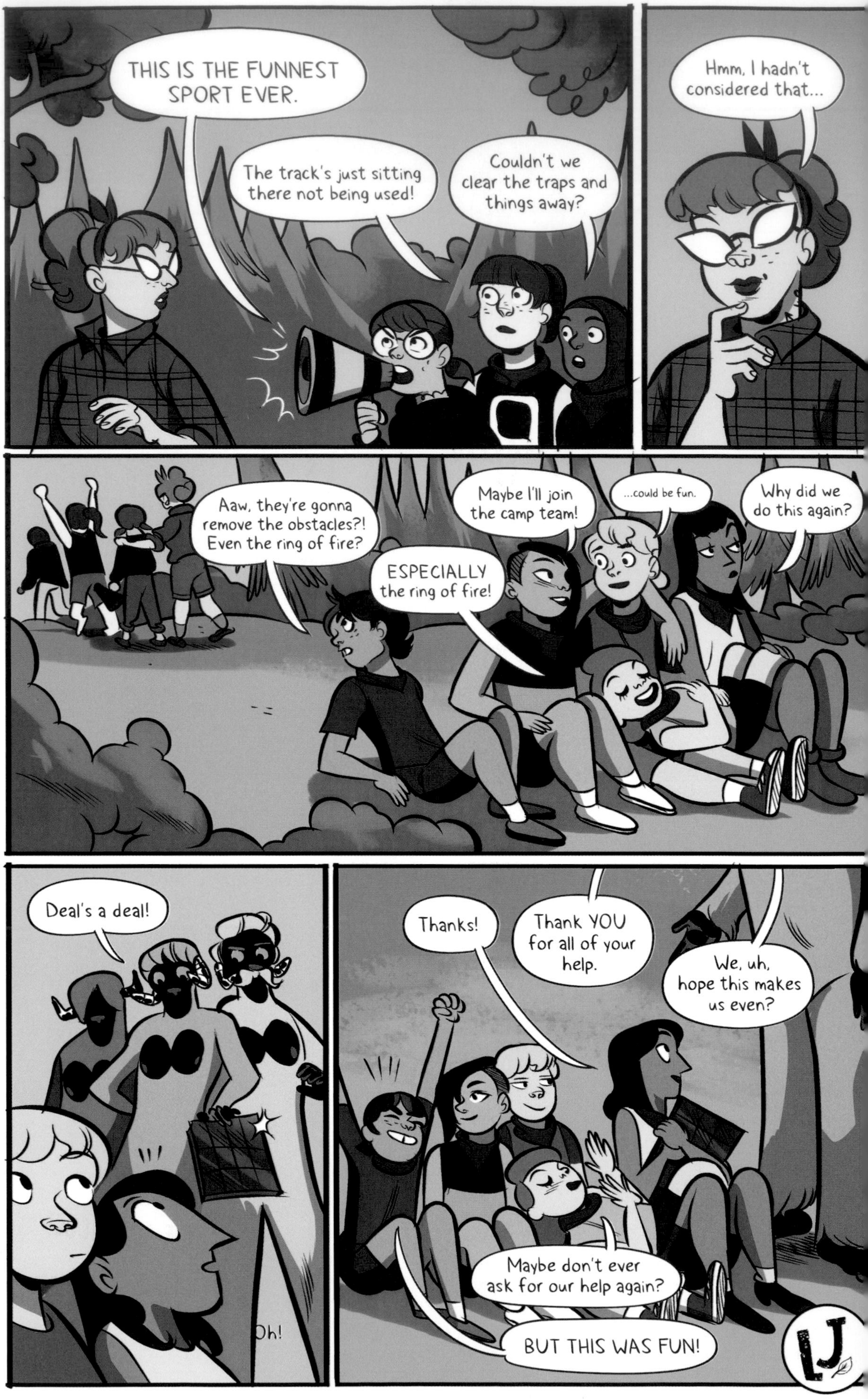
THIS IS THE FUNNEST SPORT EVER.
The track's just sitting there not being used!
Couldn't we clear the traps and things away?
Hmm, I hadn't considered that...
Aaw, they're gonna remove the obstacles?! Even the ring of fire?
ESPECIALLY the ring of fire!
Maybe I'll join the camp team!
...could be fun.
Why did we do this again?
Deal's a deal!
Oh!
Thanks!
Thank YOU for all of your help.
We, uh, hope this makes us even?
Maybe don't ever ask for our help again?
BUT THIS WAS FUN!

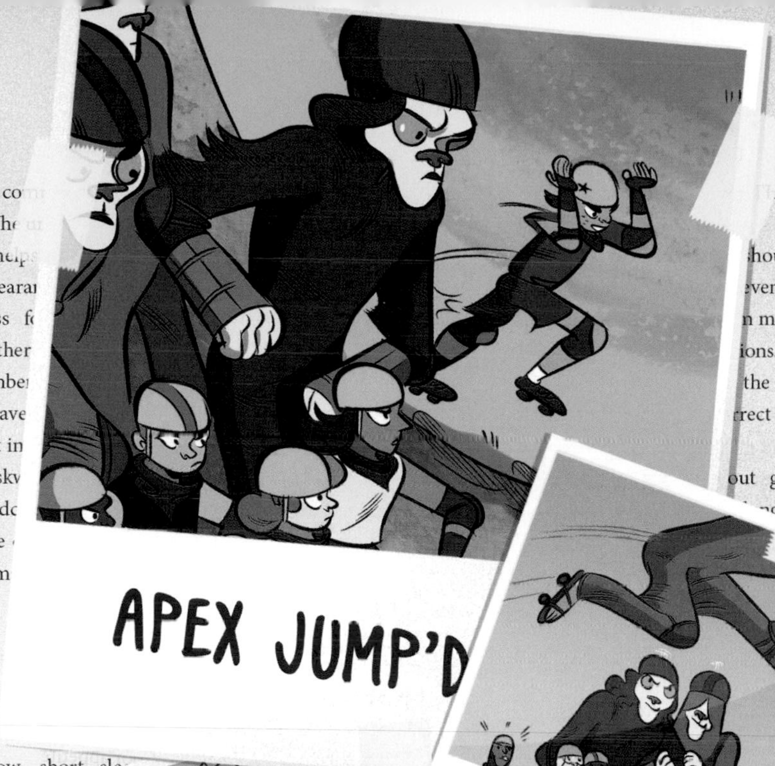
APEX JUMP'D

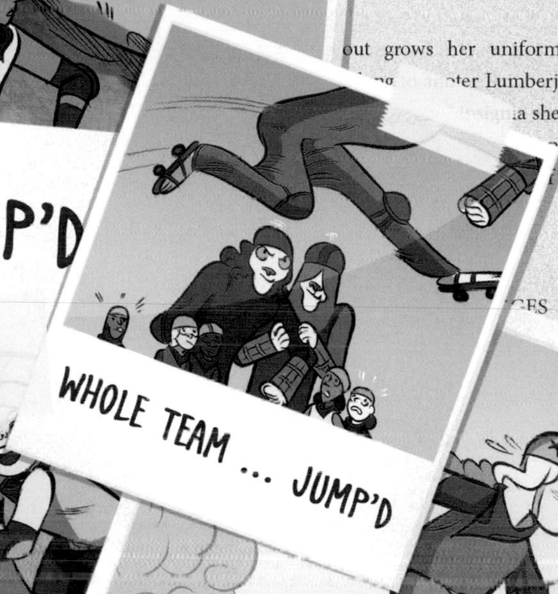
WHOLE TEAM ... JUMP'D

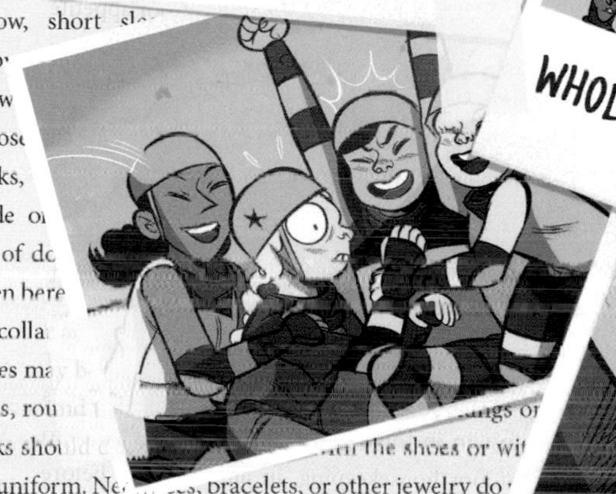

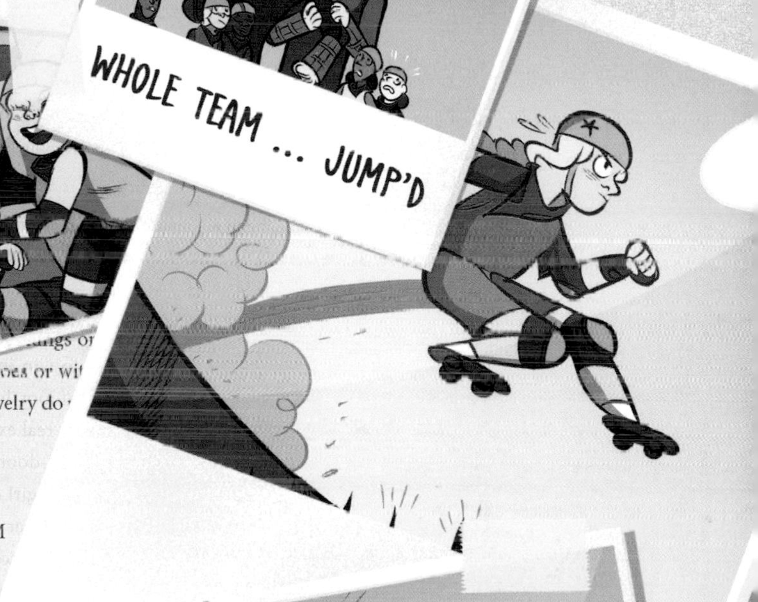

will co

The u
It help
appeara
dress f
Further
Lumbe
to have
part in
Thiskv
Hardc
have
them

HE UNIFORM

should be worn at camp
events when Lumberjanes
n may also be worn at other
ions. It should be worn as a
the uniform dress with
rrect shoes, and stocking or

out grows her uniform or
ter Lumberjane.
a she has
her
her

The
yellow, short sl
emb
the w
choos
slacks,
made o
out of do
green here
the colla
Shoes ma
heels, rou ings or
socks shou th the shoes or wi
the uniform. Ne bracelets, or other jewelry do
belong with a Lumberjane uniform.

HOW TO WEAR THE UNIFORM

To look well in a uniform demands first of
uniform be kept in good condition—clean
pressed. See that the skirt is the right length for your own height and build, that the belt is adjusted to your waist, that your shoes and stockings are in keeping with the uniform, that you watch your posture and carry yourself with dignity and grace. If the beret is removed indoors, be sure that your hair is neat and kept in place with an insonspicuous clip or ribbon. When you wear a Lumberjane uniform you are identified as a member of this organization and you should be doubly careful to conduct yourself in a way that will show everyone that courtesy and thoughtfullness are part of being a Lumberjane. People are likely to judge a whole nation by the selfishness of a few individuals, to criticize a whole family because of the misconduct of one member, and to feel unkindly toward and organization because of the

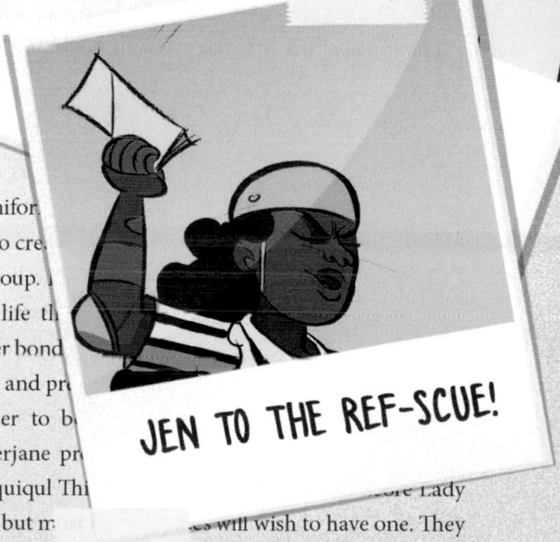
JEN TO THE REF-SCUE!

The unifor
helps to cre
in a group.
active life th
another bond
future, and pr
in order to b
Lumberjane pr
Penniquiqul Thi ore Lady
Types, but m will wish to have one. They
can either bu uniform, or make it themselves from
materials available at the trading post.

COVER GALLERY

Lumberjanes "Out-of-Doors" Program Field

MIGHT AS WHEEL BADGE

"Sometimes, you just got to roll with it""

Sometimes, although the shortest distance between point A and point B is a straight line, the most fun distance will have a lot more twists and turns! Getting where you're going isn't just about making good time, or beating the rush. It's also about finding your way and spending time with the people you love.

Having fun when you venture out into the world can come down to the type of vehicle you're using-- be it plane, train, or automobile-- but it also comes down to your attitude. Sticking to a schedule and being punctual is a key skill to take with you into adulthood, but being flexible and staying open-minded can be just as important. These two skills balance one another out, and help you to have fun along the way, whether your journey is playing out the way you'd hoped, or everything has gone haywire from the moment you put rubber to road!

Sometimes, you can even learn to make changing your plans part of the game of your trip-- yes, you have seen the side streets, the back streets, the hills and dales of your town before, and from many, many angles, but have you seen them from your bicycle?

Roller skates? In a go-cart? You'd be amazed how much just having control of your vehicle can change your outlook on a journey, and even more so by how many exciting details you miss when you're in a car, going straight from home to school! Learning to find your way in the world is about so much more than learning to navigate and making your way directly anywhere-- it's also about learning to be familiar with the things that make up your surroundings, with the natural laws of the world! You might not understand it all, but to know in your bones how things work, whether that's the subway system or gravity, will nurture in you an innate sense that you belong in this world, that it is your world, and that you are safe, even when you venture far afield, or when things don't go the way you planned, or when you try new modes of transportation, go along new paths, or make your way with new friends. So leave fear at the door, but always pack your sense of adventure, and slather on a layer of sunscreen!

Issue Thirty-Three
KAT LEYH

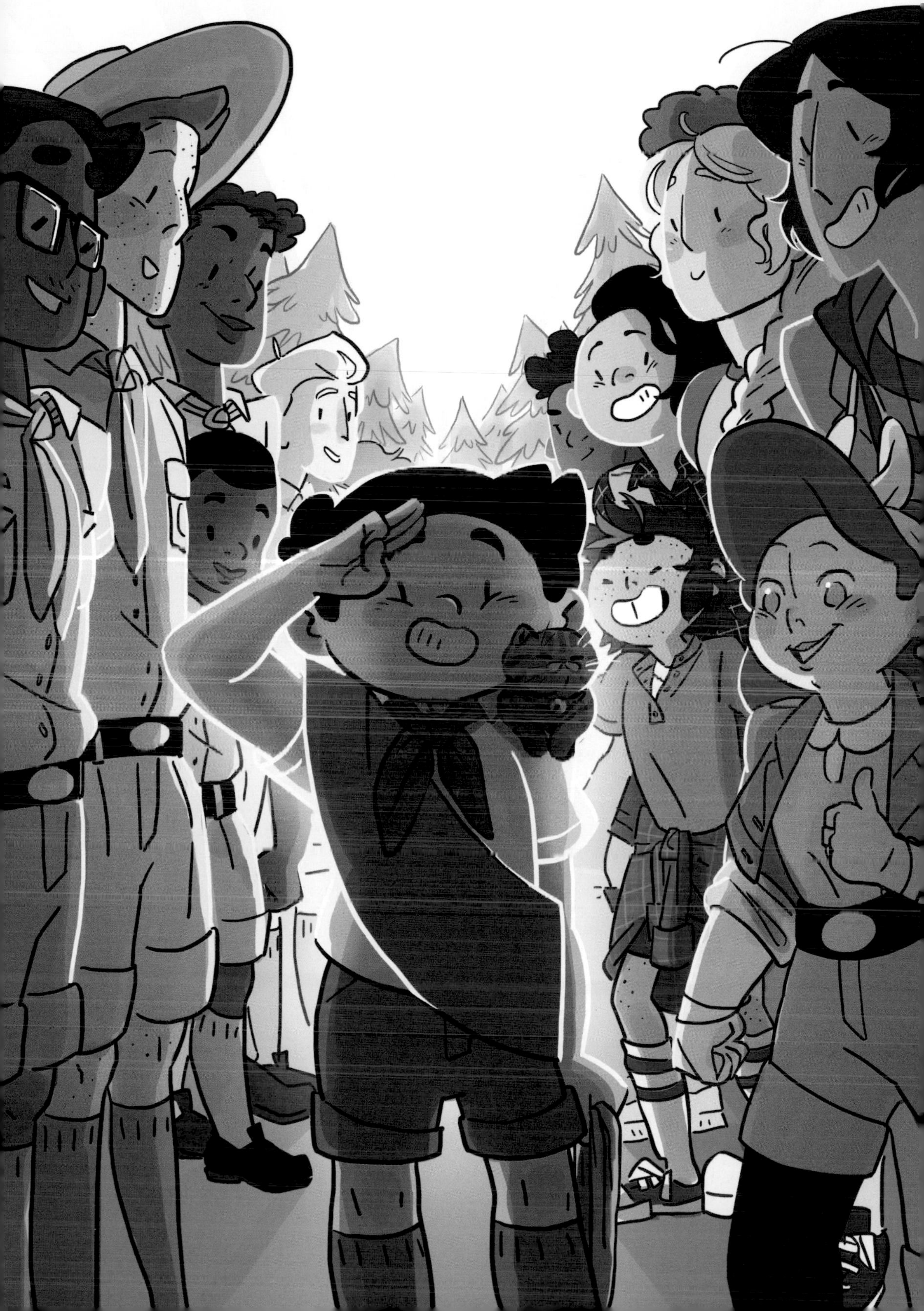

Issue Thirty-Three Variant
ALEXANDRA GLENN-COLLINS

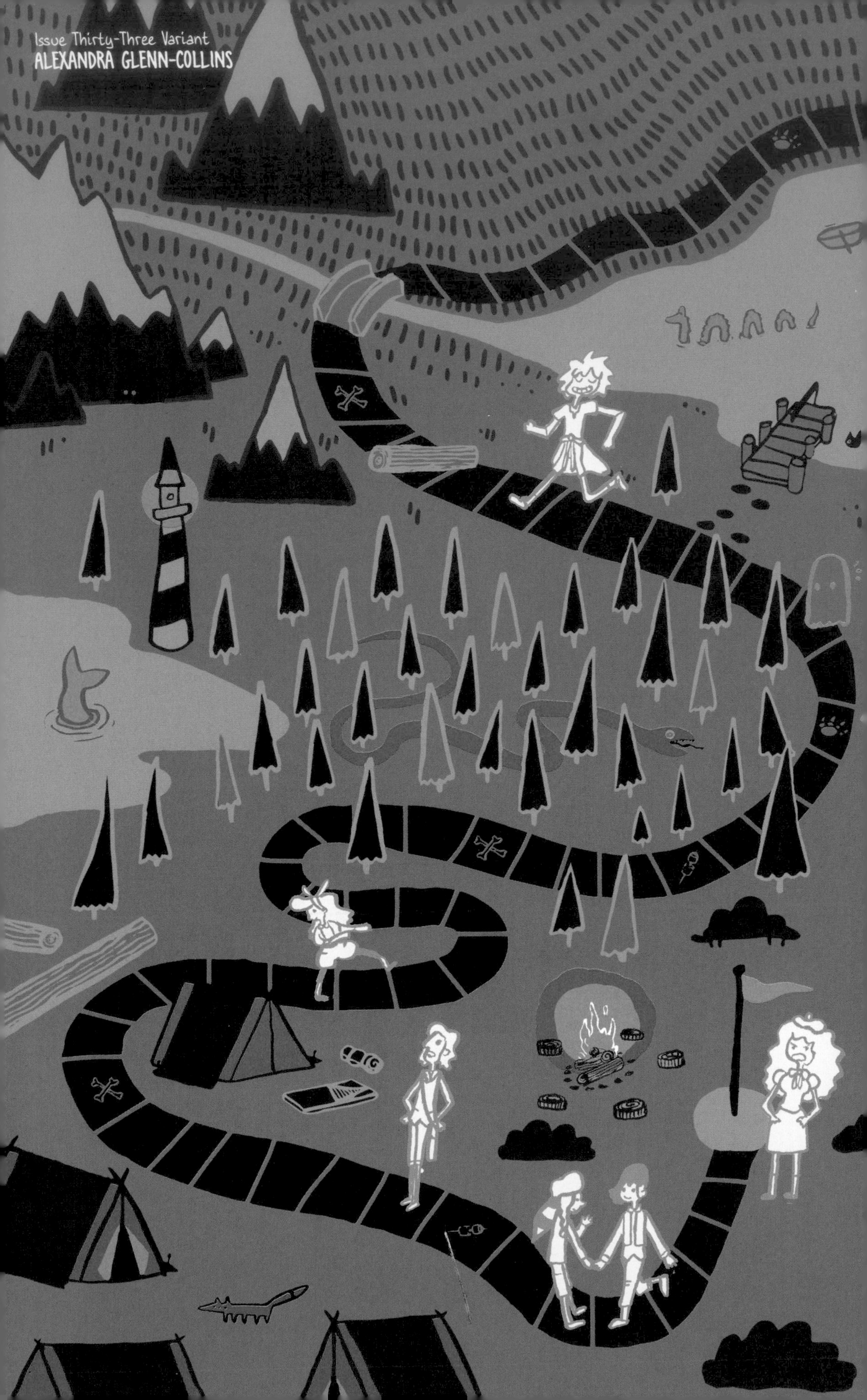

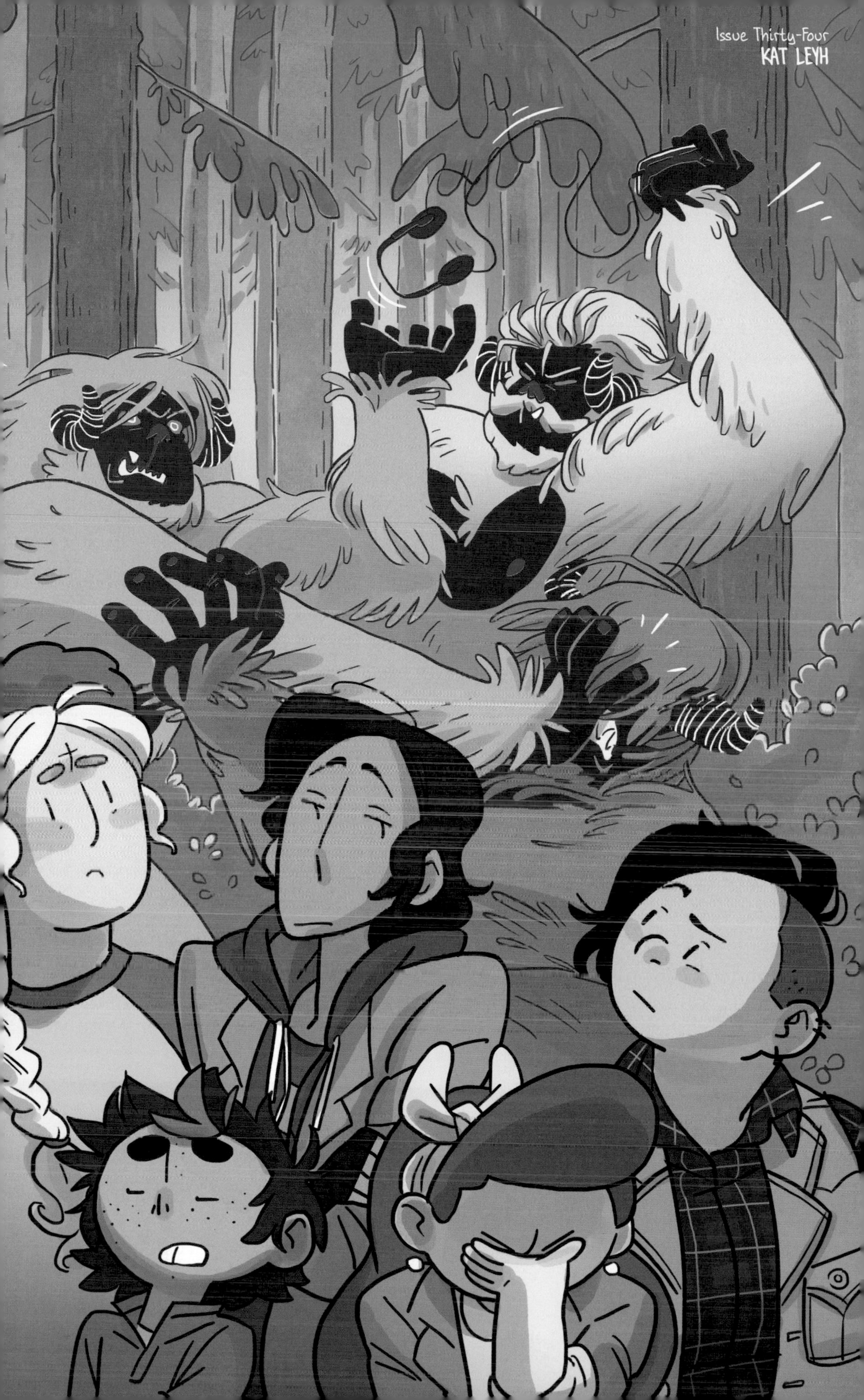
Issue Thirty-Four
KAT LEYH

Issue Thirty-Four Variant
JENN LIU

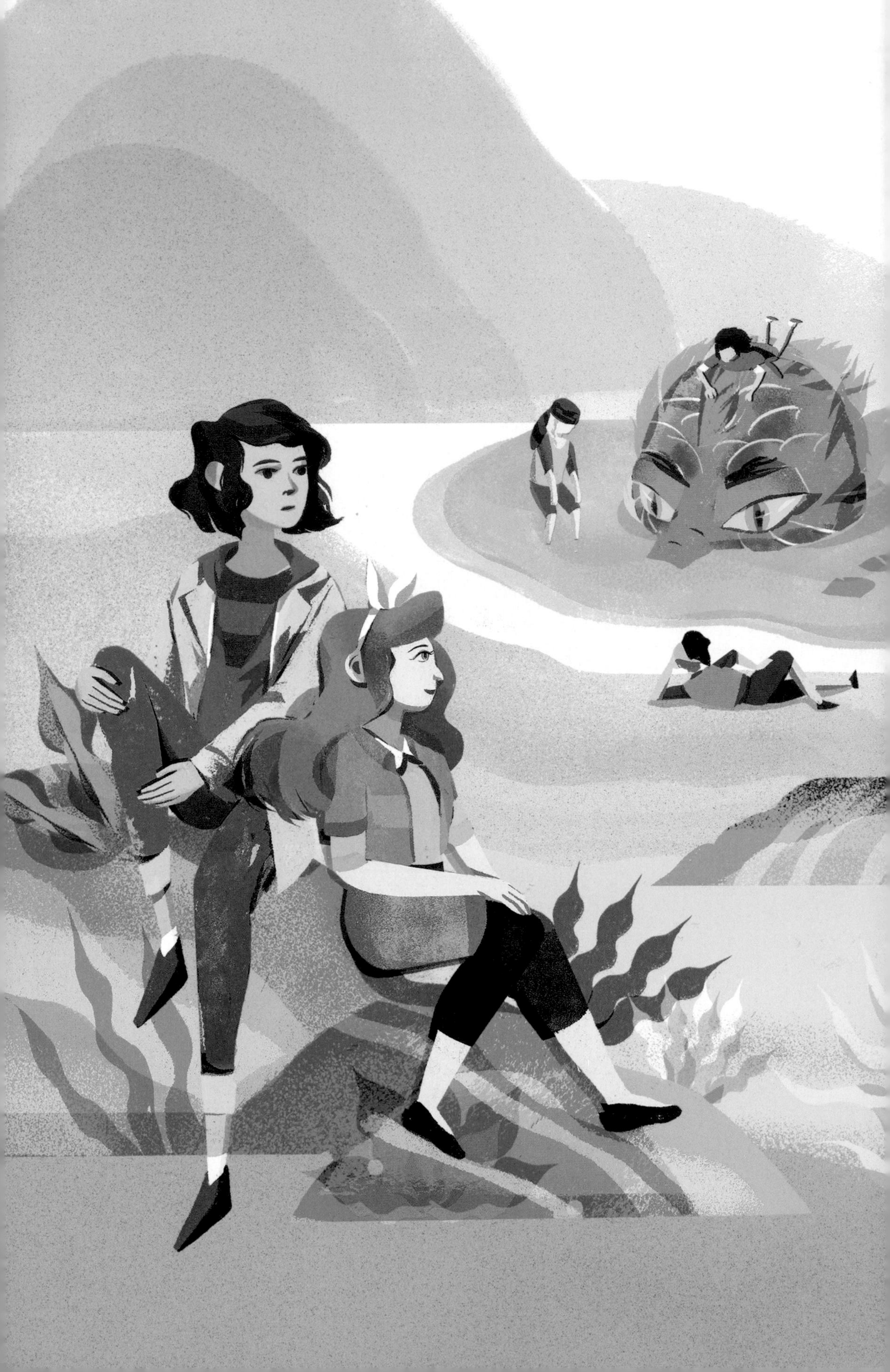

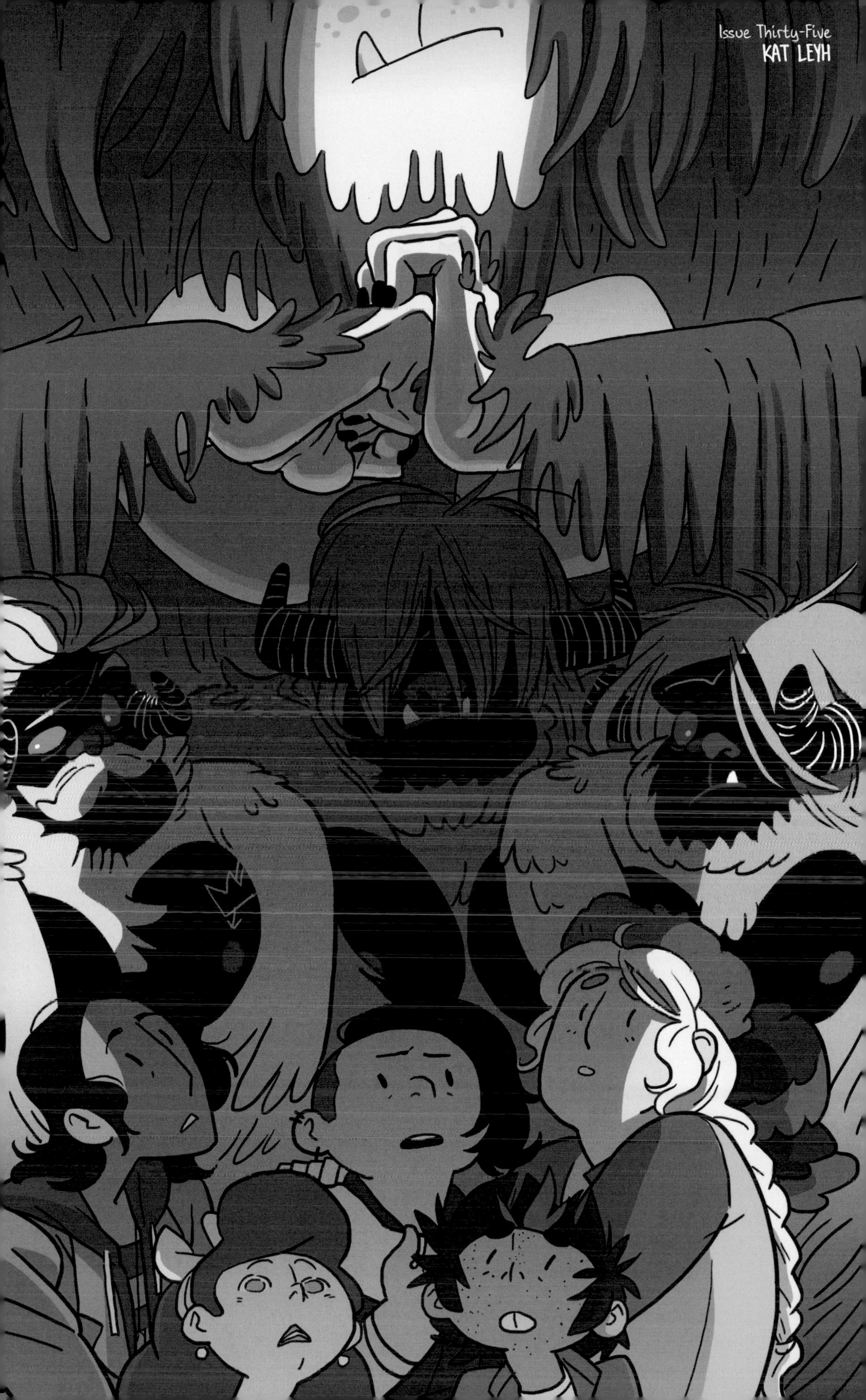
Issue Thirty-Five
KAT LEYH

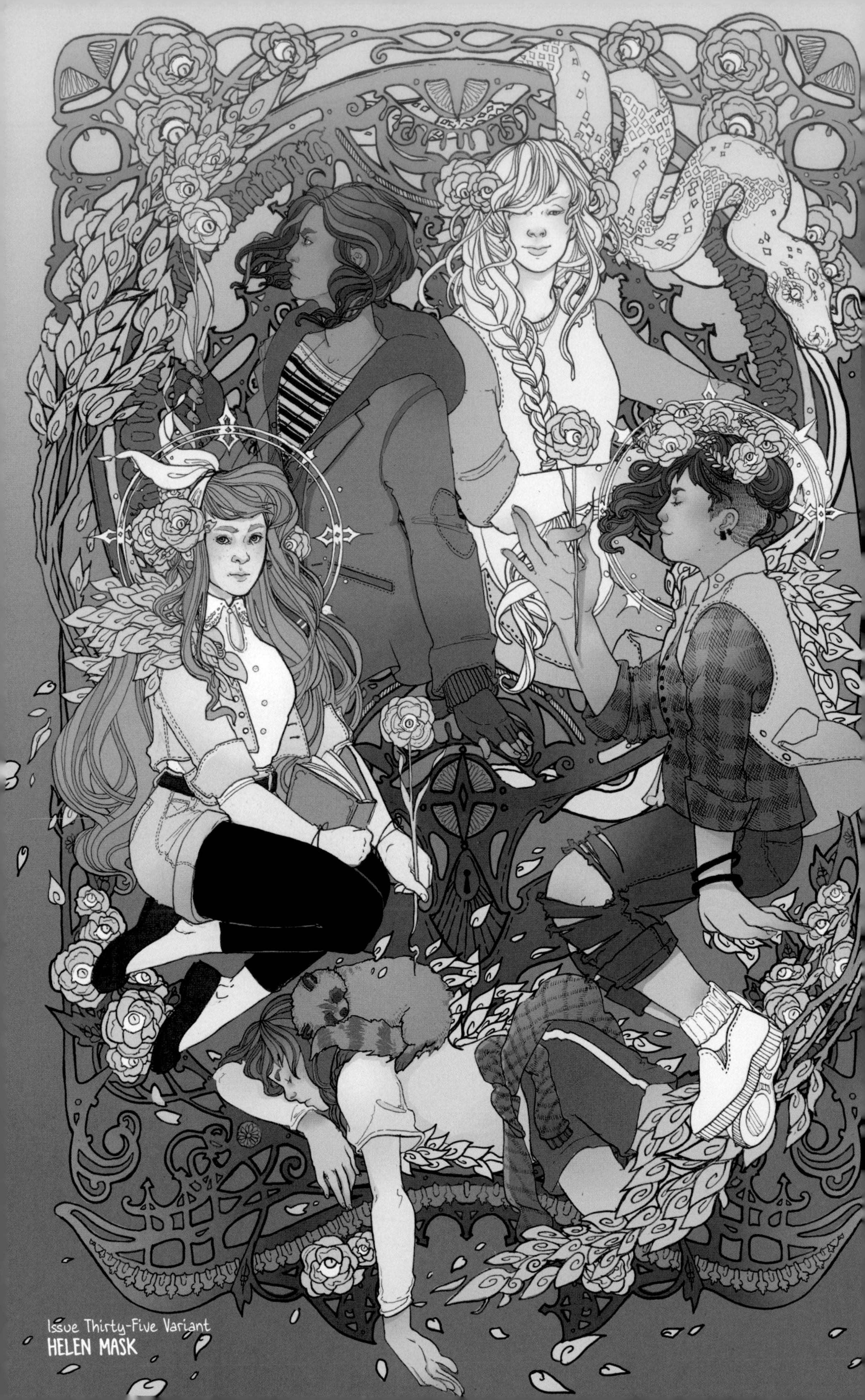

Issue Thirty-Five Variant
HELEN MASK

Issue Thirty-Six
KAT LEYH

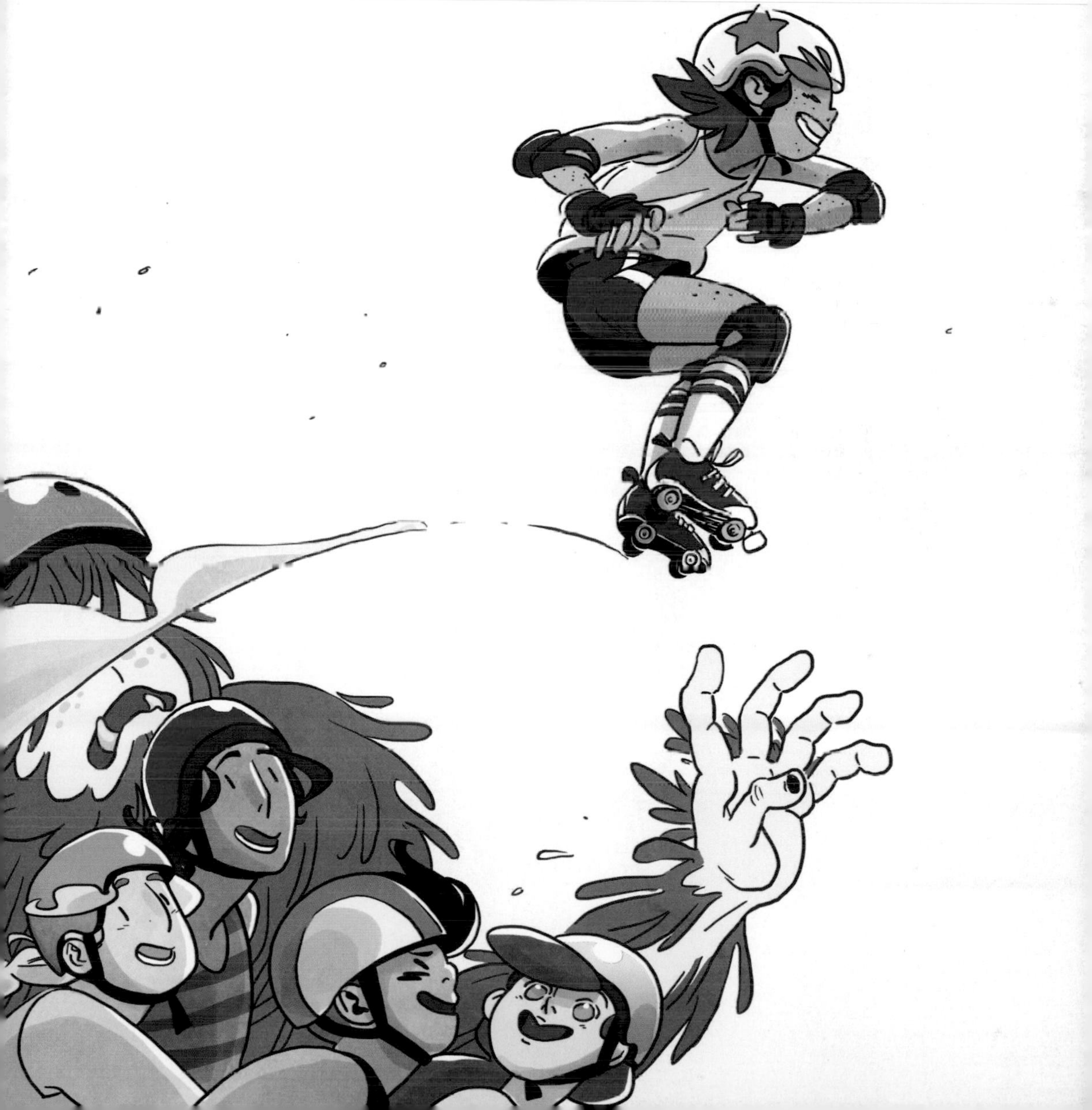

Issue Thirty-Six Variant
SLIMM FABERT

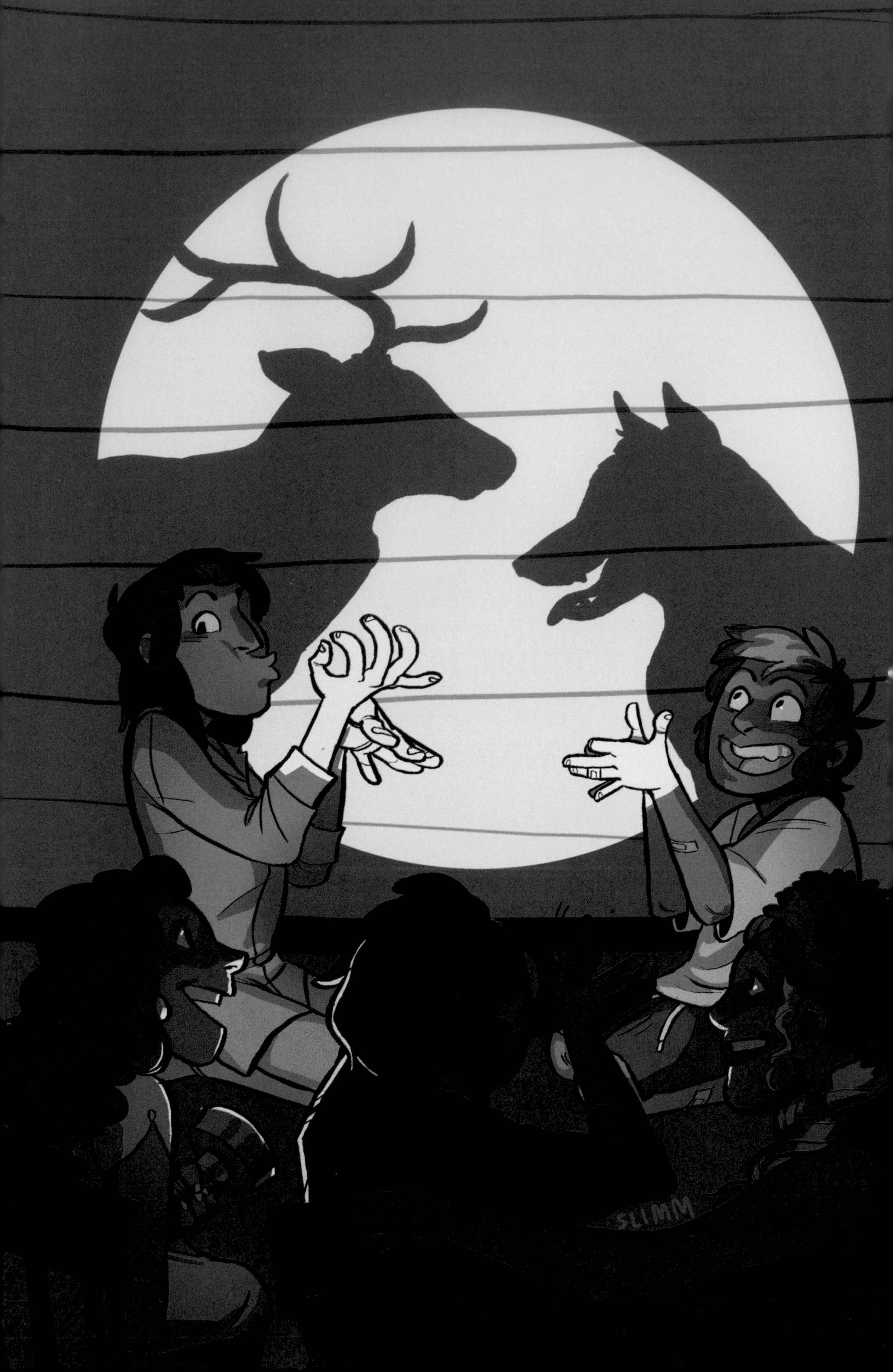
SLIMM